BEHEMOTH

MICHAEL COLE

SEVERED PRESS
HOBART TASMANIA

BEHEMOTH

Don't go into the water…
You may never come out.

"THERE'S SOMETHING IN THE WATER!"

CHAPTER 1

Dressed in fine dark trousers, polished dress shoes, and an Army suit jacket decorated with precious medals earned during his military career, Colonel Salkil clenched his teeth as he felt himself being jolted in his seat while the Army Transport Helicopter entered the gigantic, circular body of storm clouds that formed what weather officials had named Tropical Storm Landon. While trying not to fall over in his seat, he couldn't help but watch the sky through the window on the opposite side of the helicopter. When it had taken off from Airbase Whiteman in Florida, the sky was crystal clear of clouds, with the exception of a cirrus that rested in the high atmosphere. Now it was black as a night with no moon, with the only illumination coming from the lights generated by the helicopter, and the brief but massive flashes of lightning that would bring the whole horizon into view for a split second. The wind hissed like a frightened, wild creature as it pushed against the helicopter. That particular noise didn't bother Colonel Salkil as much as the obnoxious mechanical rattle of the engine and the endless rotation of the blades, which sounded as if somebody was batting on a tarp like a drum for hours on end. It was as if the aircraft had traveled into a black, noisy abyss, cut off from the light of the sun, and with no sign of where it was heading.

Normally, the Colonel didn't mind stormy weather. As a child, he had always been fascinated by the vast groupings of clouds and how electrical particles in the sky could form together to create large bolts of lightning. Through his adult life and military career, whenever he had soldiers ranked below him who would complain about working in the rain, he would tell them that rain was only water and wind was only moving air. However, flying over the Atlantic Ocean in the middle of a tropical storm brought a contradiction to his reasoning. He was in a position where the right amount of rain and wind could be as deadly as the weapons his soldiers carried.

In his mind, he vented his frustration about the terrible timing of the weather to himself. Of course the government agency wouldn't suspend the trip until the storm had passed; it was of great importance on their agenda that Salkil arrived at the Atlantic Warren Laboratory to examine the results of the funding that had been given to the Chief Doctor, Isaac Wallack, for his military research. Salkil didn't even know what was going on in this ocean lab facility. He had never met Dr. Wallack and until he was about to board the chopper for the trip, he had not been informed that this military laboratory was located in the Atlantic Ocean, a few miles away from a collection of islands known as Mako's Ridge. His only knowledge of the expensive, isolated project was the fact that it was registered *TOP SECRET* by the agency who hired him. Questions lined up in his mind one by one, like dominoes waiting to fall. First of all, what was going on that was so important that even *he* couldn't know about it when assigned with the mission? Also, why was this project located in the middle of the Atlantic Ocean, so far away from any land? He took a deep breath and attempted to relax in the uncomfortable leather seat of the aircraft, which continued to bounce up and down due to the turbulence. He could hear the pilots talking to each other in the cockpit, and by the grumbling tones of their voices, they were just as unhappy as he was about the timing of this trip.

"*Yeah, that's the signal of the Warren's beacon,*" he heard one of the pilots say. "*It's about time, 'cause I'm sick of flying through this shitstorm.*"

"*I hear ya,*" Salkil heard the second pilot say. "*Now, if this stupid radar will quit fizzing up, I might be able to point out the--oh, wait! There it is. Yeah, it's three miles south.*"

"*Damn! We almost passed the damn thing!*"

"*Yeah, almost. Just turn right and we should be good. Hey, go check on the Colonel will ya?*"

With this, Salkil heard the mechanical thuds from the copilot's boots against the metal floor of the chopper. He heard him walk through a small, four-foot hallway between the cockpit and the cabin. The copilot, a rather short man dressed in a dark uniform with a blue vest, stood at the hallway entrance and stuck his head into the cabin to make eye contact with Salkil while pressing his hands against the walls of the hallway to keep his balance.

"Colonel Salkil, sir?" His voice was suddenly sounding professional and disciplined, compared to the casual talk he was having with the fellow pilot in the cockpit. The Colonel looked up at the young pilot.

"Yes?" Salkil asked, even though he already knew what he was about to be told.

"Sir, we are approaching the location," he said. "We should be there in approximately three or four minutes." Colonel Salkil nodded his head with a neutral expression on his face. He wasn't happy to be arriving at this place; he'd rather be home with his wife and two daughters right now instead of checking up on some doctor's progress in the middle of the Atlantic Ocean. On the other hand, he was somewhat relieved to now be arriving, mostly due to the fact that he couldn't take much more of the jerky ride. His stomach felt like a shaken can of soda, giving him the knowledge that he definitely would not be able to hold down any meal. Thirdly, he had to take a leak.

"Okay," he responded in a dull tone of voice. The copilot turned around and walked back to the cockpit, struggling to keep his balance as the helicopter jerked up and down. The Colonel felt the chopper turn to the right as it adjusted its direction to reach the desired destination. Again, despite the roaring of the storm, hissing of the wind, and the annoying rattle of the engine, he could hear the two pilots exchanging words with one another.

"*There it is,*" one of them said. "*Reduce speed and lower our altitude by three hundred feet. Maintain a steady course.*"

"*That's the landing platform over there. See those green lights?*"

"*Yes, I see them. I've flown before, sir.*"

Colonel Salkil felt a sudden jerk in the helicopter, causing him to bounce in his seat more violently than when they first struck turbulence. His seatbelt was already buckled, and it pulled against his lap as the shaking of the chopper attempted to throw him off the seat. He felt his ears pop as the pilots lowered the altitude. He didn't care for the idea of being closer to the raging body of water that was the Atlantic. He couldn't see it yet, but he could imagine what it probably looked like; circular clouds overhead, torrential rain pouring down, and a dense fog attempting to form, but being destroyed by the intense winds, creating ghost-like figures of "flying clouds". He could hear the pilots repeating procedural phrases from the cockpit as they lowered the aircraft closer to the landing platform. The turbulence decreased and the annoying rotation of the propellers began to slow down. He felt the chopper decrease more of its altitude and its speed slowed down immensely. In a few seconds, the Colonel felt no momentum carrying the helicopter forward. It now hovered over the platform like an enormous humming bird over a garden. Finally it slowly descended downward directly toward bright green lights on the square-shaped platform. After a few moments, the Colonel felt a brief thud as the chopper connected with the cement of the platform; the two pilots landed the bird harder than what they were supposed to.

"We're here, sir!" called one of the pilots back through the small hallway. "There are some of Wallack's men near the door, waiting to greet you, sir." Colonel Salkil took a quick, deep breath and moved to the door, which was on the opposite side of the cabin. Normally, helicopter pilots were polite enough to open the door for him in recognition of his rank. These pilots were probably too sissy to step out into the rain. He quickly pulled on a blue raincoat to keep his formal uniform dry and turned the door handle towards the right. The chopper door slid open, and the Colonel finally took a long awaited step out of the chopper. The intense winds immediately grabbed hold of his raincoat, tugging away at it. The rain came down on his face, causing him to pull the coat's hood over his already soaked head. Ocean water slammed into all four sides of the platform, splashing up over the rims onto the flat cement surface. A few yards ahead of Salkil was a small building that resembled a black metallic garage, which in reality was an elevator unit that led to the interior of the underwater laboratory. In front of the unit were six or eight armed guards, each holding M-16 automatic rifles, and in front of these men stood a short, skinny man wearing a long, red raincoat. The hood had been pulled over his head, which made the top half of his face difficult for Salkil to see.

"Hello, Colonel Richard Salkil," the man said, extending out his hand in a manner of greeting. "I am Doctor Isaac Wallack, the man in charge of the operations going on in this underwater facility." Salkil briefly shook the doctor's hand. "It's an honor to have you here, sir."

"Well, I must say that it's not an honor for me to be here," the Colonel said in a strict tone. "The agency told me that some pretty high tech stuff was going on here, but honestly I would much rather be home with my family than be shipped out here in the middle of nowhere. So, Dr. Wallack, I'm warning you that whatever I'm about to see right now better blow my mind or your ass will end up in a grinder."

"Yes, sir," Dr. Wallack responded. Salkil could see a small smile forming on his host's face. "Well let's get you out of this rain, shall we?" The two men jogged at a speed just short of a sprint towards the elevator unit. One of the armed guards hit a button on a small control panel on the side of the small building, causing a steel door to slide open horizontally. Salkil and Wallack stepped inside. The door slid shut, and the lights inside the elevator lit up, reflecting off the silvery walls in the unit.

"The first thing I want to know is why you guys are stationed out here in the middle of the ocean," Salkil said. The elevator began to descend into the interior of the station. Wallack removed the raincoat and folded it up, exposing his expensive grey trousers, white dress shirt and grey tie, along with his shaven head and rectangular shaped glasses.

"Well, let's just say it's a proper environment for our projects," Wallack answered with another grin on his face. "I guess you can say we prefer to be isolated."

"If you want to be isolated so badly, why the hell don't you set up a base of operations on one of the islands of Mako's Ridge? One of those islands doesn't have any people on it, though I can't remember which one it is." The elevator came to a stop and the metal door slide open again. Both men stepped out, walking into a massive room that appeared to be more of an aquarium than anything else. Just a few yards from the elevator entrance was a metal railing that lined the edge of a large rectangular-shaped pool. Salkil took a longer look at the room, realizing that there were at least five pools, each one surrounded by six or seven people in white coats. In almost every section of the room were numerous guards, armed with deadly automatic weapons, who kept watch over the facility. Dr. Wallack led him to the nearest pool.

"You didn't answer my question," Salkil continued. "Why not set--"

"--Up base on Mako's Ridge," Wallack finished the sentence for the Colonel. "I'm not avoiding your question, sir. You asked why we didn't set up a base of operations on the unpopulated island, which for your information is known as Mako's Edge."

"Yes," Salkil said, waiting for Wallack to explain. They walked to the railing and looked down into the pool, seeing nothing but a deep tank of sea water.

"Well, the truth is, Colonel, is that we actually attempted to put up a facility in that location. However, the geography caused a problem for our major specimen. It liked it too much."

Salkil looked at him with confusion. "What the hell do you mean 'specimen'?" he said, his voice getting a bit louder.

Dr. Wallack pointed his finger down towards the pool. "Here's an example," he said. "Don't you see it?"

Salkil looked back at the water. "See what?" Suddenly his eyes grasped what Wallack was referring to. An object, shaped like a right triangle, cut through the water in circles as it followed the perimeter of the pool. It seemed to be a dorsal fin, only instead of it being the usual murky grey in color, it was a deep red. "I see it. It's a shark." He wasn't impressed with what he was seeing. "Okay, so I understand you have sharks in this facility. Is this a way of telling me our military funding has gone to you housing fat-ass fish?!" His temper was starting to heat up.

"I'm sorry?" Dr. Wallack questioned. "Do you find something wrong with *Isurus Palinuridae*?"

The Colonel stood silent for a few seconds, attempting to

understand what the doctor just told him. "What the hell is that?" he questioned. "I mean, *Isurus*-- that's some sort of shark. A Mako shark I think."

Dr. Wallack chuckled for a moment. "Well you know more than I would have ever expected you to," he said. "Take a closer look at *Isurus Palinuridae*." Salkil decided to be patient with the doctor. He looked at the shark, which had come up closer to the surface, exposing most of its back. Watching the animal, he noticed something he thought was quite strange: the exterior of the creature seemed hard and spiny, as if it was a crustacean in the form of a ten-foot shark. Continuing to watch the shark, he noticed a small metal plate on its head, with a green bulb in the center that blinked green.

"Okay," Salkil said, "you've got my attention, somewhat. What the hell is that thing, exactly?"

"In simple terms, Colonel, that is a hybrid specimen. A genetic combination of *Isurus,* which as you pointed out, is the Mako Shark, and *Palinuridae*, which is the spiny lobster." The Colonel stood speechless for several moments as he attempted to grasp the reality that such a bizarre creation was directly in front of him. Dr. Wallack chuckled again. "I'm sure you've noticed that metal object on the creature's head. That is something most people thought they'd only see in movies; simply put, it is basically a mind control device. So, if you haven't figured it out by yourself by now, this means we can control these creatures by remote control. Send them into enemy territory with a bomb strapped to them, and BOOM! No more enemy ship. The shell would provide protection against incoming firepower, allowing the shark to move into the desired location, unharmed." Salkil took a deep breath as he allowed Wallack's words to sink into his mind. He looked up from the pool, staring across the room at the other pools.

"Are all of the hybrids in this particular room the same?" he asked.

"Yes," Dr. Wallack answered. "Every hybrid in this chamber is *Isurus Palinuridae.*" Salkil kept his eyes on the massive room. At the far end of the room, he noticed an entranceway to another large chamber, causing him to realize that there was more to be seen. His temper was now replaced with curiosity.

"Just… how?"

"Well the explanation is easy. The procedure is what's difficult," Wallack said. "To put it simply, we spliced the DNA of these creatures. But we needed only certain parts of the spiny lobster, I.E. the shell. So we had to splice the genetic code for the shell into the DNA of the Mako Shark. A process that took ages to complete."

Suddenly a loud beeping noise echoed across the facility, signaling that an intercom message was about to be broadcast. *"Surgical Procedure for implantation about to go underway for Project 241,"* squawked a dull mechanical voice.

Colonel Salkil finally looked back at Dr. Wallack.

"Well, I'd be lying if I said you didn't have my attention. However, I'm willing to bet that these aren't the only hybrids you've got. You've been splicing other forms of DNA, haven't you, Doctor?"

Wallack crossed his arms. "Nothing that we don't have control over, sir," he answered.

"What is Project 241? Is it just another hybrid like these things in here?" the colonel questioned. Wallack paused for a second as he took off his glasses to wipe them clean with his dress shirt.

"It's another hybrid, yes," said the scientist, looking down at the glasses in his hand. "However, it's different from the hybrids in here."

"What's so different? What's this one called?" Salkil asked. Dr. Wallack put his glasses back on.

"Architeuthis Brachyura," he said.

****

The water remained calm and undisturbed. Above the surface, the smaller captors kept watch on it, but this reality meant nothing. For hours on end, it waited. Time meant nothing. It rested patiently on a smooth, alien surface, allowing its several tons to keep it beneath the surface of the water. It did what it did best; wait. To the naked eye, it would seem as if it was asleep, or even dead. But time meant nothing to it. Patience was a gift it possessed greater than anything that may have ever lived. And during its long wait, it learned. It came to learn that it wasn't free. It learned that this so-called home was not a home. Instinct flooded its ability to think. This instinct knew that this was not its habitat. Instinct told the creature that it was trapped. Instinct informed the creature that it could escape. It knew its strength, it knew its surroundings, and it knew it wasn't free. It was the master of its own world. It was hungry. It was trapped. It was ready.

****

"Good God, man, what the hell are you thinking?!" Colonel Salkil said in a livid tone. "You've got something that big, and you're saying you're in control?" Dr. Wallack held up his hands in manner of surrender.

"Calm down, Colonel," he said. "This thing is the next step in true biological warfare!" Salkil chuckled sarcastically, waving his hand in the air to halt the doctor from speaking further.

"Uhh, no! These things, here, are the next step in biological warfare," the Colonel pointed at the sharks. "What you have just described to me, the creature in the next chamber, might as well be five more steps! Too far ahead! What the hell are you thinking, doctor?"

"Like I said, I assure you that *Architeuthis Brachyura* is a successful project in our experiments and we are very proud of it," Wallack defended. "As you heard on the intercom, the creature is about to have its implant. It'll be under our control."

"Look," the Colonel continued, "I'm no scientist, but something that big is not going to be controlled easily. I'm telling you, doctor, I'm going to recommend to Washington to pull the plug on this one. If that thing goes out of control, we'll have a catastrophe on our hands. I don't mind the plan with these sharks, but *Architeuthis*-- whatever the damn thing is called, is too far."

Wallack crossed his arms, and his facial expression showed that he wasn't happy with what the Colonel was saying. "Understand, sir," he began, "the military wanted a killing machine; that's exactly what I have created for them. Just wait until they hear what you have to say when you return and tell them what you saw here tonight!"

The conversation came to a sudden stop as the entire facility began to shake violently as if an earthquake had begun to tear through the area. A sudden loud banging noise could be heard from the next holding chamber. Every one of the armed guards rushed toward the entrance of that chamber as members of the science personnel began to go into a panic. As soon as the men had rushed into the room, the sound of gunfire joined the horrifying racket of grinding metal and the screams of people who were trapped in the chamber. The facility continued to shake like an aircraft in heavy turbulence. Red emergency lights flashed overhead in every room throughout the laboratory, and an emergency siren began to sound. Each of the shark hybrids splashed viciously in the water, adding to the immense chaos that had suddenly swept through the laboratory. Dr. Wallack's radio buzzed with static, with crazed voices screaming into the microphones of their own radios. He unclipped his from his belt and held it up to his mouth.

"This is Chief Doctor Wallack! What the fuck is going on?!" he shouted into the radio while watching the far end of the chamber. "I repeat, what is going on?! Somebody answer me!"

"Dr. Wallack!" shouted a crazed staff member though the radio frequency. *"Sir, number 241 is escaping! It's escaping!"* Within seconds, his white dress shirt was drenched in sweat, as if he had just stepped into the rain outside.

"What do you mean, it's escaping? I mean, how? What the hell is it doing?"

"It's chewing through the wall! There's water leaking in! It's breaking through the fucking wall! Oh my God! People are dead! There's blood everywhere! We can't get out!" Suddenly another beeping noise echoed across the facility as the intercom activated to deliver a message.

"Attention all personnel. Breach in lower level experimentation chambers. Everyone in those chambers must evacuate immediately. Flooding is reported to be increasing. Severe casualties. All personnel must make their way for the top levels of the facility."

"Let's get the hell out of here!" Colonel Salkil yelled. "Come on!" Wallack didn't bother to waste time. He ran behind the Colonel towards the elevator. They quickly opened the door and rushed their way in as several staff members rushed into the stairways and other elevators, fighting and knocking each other down in order to get away. As the door closed, they briefly witnessed the far wall bulging inward, as water was filling the second holding chamber. Through the doorway, ocean water began flooding into the first chamber, sweeping personnel off their feet. As the water approached, the elevator door shut, and the unit began to move upward to safety.

****

Its claws and beak tore open the hard object that blocked its path from the rest of the world. The smaller creatures running about in the prison didn't matter to it. It embraced the familiar feeling of ocean water as it invaded the prison in the form of a deadly tsunami. The creature didn't waste time to leave. It had no conscience, it had no real intelligence, but it just had a strong instinct. In a number of hours it wouldn't even remember this place. Its gift and its curse was its ability to forget. But it didn't matter now. All that mattered was that it was free. Instinct immediately kicked in; it needed to find a proper habitat. A place where it could lie and wait. A place where it could blend in without being seen. A place where it could kill, and keep killing.

CHAPTER 2

The sun's rays stretched endlessly over the now calm Atlantic Ocean. The sky was clear of the huge storm clouds that reached out for hundreds of miles, replacing them with gentle cirrus clouds. The endless body of water that roared in sheer mindless power during the previous night was now a calm, blue surface, seemingly smooth as glass, reflecting the beautiful light of the sun. The reflective water stretched out endlessly into the horizon, rippling every few minutes after a gust of wind would sweep the area.

In the center of this fascinating location rested a small grouping of islands that rested a few hundred miles southeast of Cuba, known as Mako's Ridge. These islands rested a few miles apart from each other, forming a crooked shape that resembled a serrated-edge knife. On the north-east end of Mako's Ridge was the island known as Mako's Edge, which was known for its jagged formation of rocks that surrounded the island, making it nearly impossible for any ship to dock. In addition to the rocks that made up the exterior of the island, several razor-sharp rocks also extended out from the beach, making it dangerous for any ship to come within one-hundred and fifty feet from the shore of Mako's Edge.

Almost one whole diagonal mile southwest of Mako's Edge was the largest of the islands, known as Mako's Center. Unlike its neighboring island to the northeast, Mako's Center was very approachable. The water gently brushed up to its shores in small, rippling waves. On the east side of the island was a large white-tan beach, which attracted many tourists during the last century. Near these beaches, beautiful tall trees known as *Roystonea regia* and Cuban royal palms, formed giant patches of canopy. Each of these trees stood around fifteen to twenty meters tall, holding about fifteen four-meter long leaves near the top. Also near these beaches were ports, most notably East Port, where fishermen worked hard to bring in their catch and sell it for profit. During the early morning of each day, fishing boats would scatter around the island like an army of ants, until early afternoon when they would come back into port. Throughout the island were several coves that would cut inland, making good locations to do some sport fishing for Atlantic salmon.

****

The summer morning sun gave a wonderful view of Razortooth Cove as Rick Napier stepped out onto his front porch, dressed in simple blue jeans, brown steel-toe boots, and a white t-shirt. With thin black hair, a clean-shaven face, and a fine muscular build, he stood proud as he breathed in the warm July morning air. He had just finished some maintenance work on his front porch a few days prior, so the light brown wood looked especially new when it was seen against his tan colored house. He leaned against a pillar that supported the hardwood cover overhead as he looked across his green front yard at his fishing yacht, *The Catcher*, which rested calmly at the dock. Although he was very good with the occupation, fishing was not Napier's main line of work. For the past five years, during the school year, he had been teaching basic Marine Biology and Oceanography courses at Mako's Senior High School… that is, until the School Board members cut the budget and removed a few programs from the curriculum. And his subjects were among the first to go. Oceanography was a career he became fascinated with while he attended several special science events during his high school years when he lived in Florida, ultimately leading him to earn his Master's degree at the age of twenty-seven from Florida State University. However, a job as an oceanographer was very hard to come by, as no institutes had a budget to commence research projects. The few positions that became available required the applicant to have a Ph.D, which Napier was only halfway to getting. So for the next three years, he fished alongside his father until finally a job offer came to him from the high school of Mako's Center. He was never a true islander, but the locals living on the island usually assumed he was, as Napier had always lived by the sea, and knew more about it than any of the other fisherman.

"Hurry up, will ya," he spoke aloud to himself as he waited for Wayne Michaels, his friend and partner, to arrive. Michaels had a natural habit of being late, and sometimes that bad habit would get on the bad side of people. The gift of patience was something Napier lacked to an extent, which led to him having to get a grip on his temper while working with rebellious students at Mako's High School. Teaching wasn't his forte. He waited and eyed the cove in which he lived. Razortooth Cove was marked by two high peaks of land that were partly separated by an inlet of water that grew narrower the further inland it went, creating a tooth-like shape. Napier's dock rested at the point of this cove, where he would fish from the shoreline on some evenings.

The creaking of the front door caught his attention, causing him to turn sharply around. Stepping out onto the new porch was Jane, his seventeen-year-old daughter. Unlike many girls her age, she didn't sleep in until noon during the lovely summer vacations. She was usually up by eight o'clock and dressed within the next ten or fifteen minutes. Her hair was of a red tinge, just like her mother, who passed away back when she was five years old. She also had a few other features that her mother had, which included a few freckles that were hard to see because of her tanned face. Also, like her mother, she enjoyed wearing denim jackets over her shirts when it wasn't too hot. Along with this article of clothing, she wore a purple t-shirt and an old pair of slightly worn blue jeans. She looked at her father and gave a wonderful morning smile.

"Good morning, Daddy!" she said. Napier smiled back at her, full of fatherly love in his heart.

"Good morning, Jane," he said. "What do you plan on doing today?"

"I was thinking of going out with Amanda, but I haven't been able to get ahold of her cell phone. She's probably still sleeping," she answered, looking out into the front yard. Seeing that her father wasn't already on his boat, she figured that he was waiting on Wayne. "I'm guessing Wayne is holding you up yet again." Napier nodded his head with a small grin on his face.

"You know, he's a good buddy and partner. He works hard and is very reliable on the job; but holy shit, can't he ever show up without being fifteen minutes late?! It drives me nuts," he vented. This wasn't the only time he complained to Jane about his friend. She figured it happened at least once a week.

"Perhaps you could suspend him or something," she suggested, shrugging her shoulders.

"That probably wouldn't be such a bad idea if I had somebody to replace him with. Rolling up a net is no easy business when the winch needs replacing," Napier said. "Besides, I view myself as his fishing partner, not his boss. These days, fishing is an entrepreneurship rather than an employment. I swear, Wayne would be lost when it came to the business aspect of this job if I wasn't around." Jane chuckled as she listened to her father let off his frustration.

"Yes, I know the next part," she said. "If Wayne had gone to school, learned some things about business, and actually learned how to sell things and balance a checkbook." Napier's grin grew a bit bigger. Jane reminded him so much of his late wife, Katherine, whom he tragically lost to a car accident during his years in college.

"You know me all too well," he said. Finally, the sound of a truck engine rattled as Wayne's truck finally pulled into the driveway. Stones and cement crunched beneath the old tires as Wayne drove the black Ford vehicle steadily through the driveway, which hooked around the side of the house. Much of the paint had fallen off the truck, exposing large areas of rust and wear. The truck was older than Jane. Wayne parked it next to Napier's much nicer looking white Chevrolet, and stepped out. He was a scrawny looking man in his mid forties, although he looked sixty. He was dressed in his usual attire: old, torn jeans that were nearly green from all of the seaweed and slime he had to deal with from fishing. His red t-shirt and fishing cap weren't in much better condition. It was obvious to Napier that these particular clothes were washed only once in a while.

"Hi, guys," he said, walking up to the porch.

"Hi, Wayne," Napier said. "You ready to get going?"

"I'm ready whenever you are," Wayne said. Napier opened his mouth to say the next thing that came to his mind, which would have been something like "well that would mean you were ready fifteen minutes ago, dumbass." However, he stopped himself and simply stepped down the porch steps to walk towards the boat. Jane stayed where she was, leaning against the pillar, watching her father go off to work.

"Have fun, Dad!" she called out after him, waving her hand. He turned around to wave back at her.

"See, ya, kiddo," he said.

"I think I'm going to head into town for a few things. Probably meet up with Amanda," she said. Napier felt his stomach tighten. His daughter had her driver's license, but she had no car of her own at the moment, meaning she would be taking the Chevy.

"Okay! But you be careful with that truck, you hear!"

"Yeah, yeah, Dad," she joked. "I know it's like another one of your children. You'd be crushed if anything ever happened to it."

"Yeah, but at least that child tends to do whatever its daddy wants it to," he joked back. He turned back around and continued walking to his boat. Wayne caught up alongside him, walking at a matched pace. The stench of his fishing clothes ran up Napier's nostrils, bringing the disgusting scent of rotting fish scales, and bits of decaying bait.

"Which buoy are we gonna go after first?" Wayne asked. Napier stepped onto the deck ahead of him, walking up to *The Catcher*. The vessel was about a decade old, but it operated as well as any brand new boat would. It was by far one of the largest fishing boats within the island community, stretching to nearly sixty feet from stern to bow. The white paint had been chipped off at certain points, mainly at the bow where the tip of the vessel cut through the water. The main deck on the stern stretched twenty feet across. At the front of the deck was a wall and ladder which led to the second level, which elevated seven feet, where a second smaller deck was located, surrounding the vessel's cabin. However, the vessel was in desperate need of repairs. At the port side of the vessel, at the corner of the main deck was a large winch, which was used for hauling in large trawl nets full of fish.

Due to a massive crack at the base of the device, it was in dire need of replacement, which had come at an incredibly inconvenient time due to Napier's employment situation. He grabbed the steel railing and pulled himself onto the deck of the fishing boat.

"Well, the first one will definitely be the one just up by the Razortooth Cove entrance," he said. The entrance of the cove was a common place for him to place his buoys because he knew nobody else would occupy that spot. He normally had three different nets and buoys, each one marked with a different color. The net at the cove was marked with a red buoy, while the other two nets were marked with a black buoy and a brown buoy. Each of them had Napier's initials on them, which kept him from confusing them with other's. "I think we'll go over to the one at the east coast after that." Wayne pulled himself onto the boat's deck as Napier went into the cabin. He stuck the boat's key into the slot and turned it. The engine rumbled and water boiled up from the propellers in the back as they began to rotate.

"Hey, did you hear the news?" Wayne called from the deck. Napier stuck his head out from the cabin to pay better attention.

"What news?"

"You know Old Hooper?" he said. "Remember how he has that crazy net up over by Mako's Edge?"

"Yes, I know," Napier said. He already thought poorly of Old Hooper. He was a grumpy elderly fisherman in his fifties, who despised almost any person who he couldn't make a profit from. He greatly despised other fishermen, possibly because of the competition that had begun to spread around the island due to the heavy loss of jobs. What most of the fisherman found to be controversial was the fact that Old Hooper had a buoy along the south side of Mako's Edge.

"Well, you know of that underwater cave that's over there?" Wayne inquired.

"Uh-huh."

"I guess Old Hooper's taking some scientists over there tomorrow. Go figure, right? Anything for an extra dollar." Napier shook his head. Ever since he first met the old, grumpy fisherman at the main port nearly a decade ago, he almost always tried to avoid him.

"That old toad can do whatever he wants," Napier replied. "I just hope he doesn't expect any of us to risk our necks to go out there and fish him out if he ends up wrecking his boat on those rocks surrounding that place." Wayne nodded his head in agreement.

"And you may find this interesting," Wayne continued. "Steven Hogan has pulled something just as stupid." Napier's eyes widened slightly, as this news interested him.

"Are you telling me he's also setting up a buoy over by that hellhole?" he asked. Wayne nodded his head.

"I guess he's having a bit of bad luck with his normal fishing grounds," Wayne answered. "I think he's getting desperate." Steven Hogan wasn't a best friend of Napier's, but he respected the man enough because of his decent personality.

"Great," he said in a stern voice. "I'll have to knock some sense into that man. I understand he's down on his luck, but if he gets himself in a bind over there, then others are going to have to risk the same thing happening to them just to help him." He looked at his watch, seeing that the time was going on eight-thirty. "Alright, let's get going. Did you untie the line?"

"Yes, sir, I have," Wayne said. Napier climbed the ladder and stepped into the cabin. Once in there, he pushed the throttle forward. The engine of the boat roared and the propellers spun with intense power, pushing *The Catcher* forward.

****

The creature glided through the ocean, filling jelly-like sacks along the side of its oval shaped body with saltwater, then expelling it to gather more speed. For hours, it had traveled, searching for a familiar scent. Instinct served in the place of memory and intelligence. Instinct was all it needed. It barely had any memory of where it had just escaped from. The fact that it had just been a long-time captive made no difference in its life now. All that mattered to it now was to find a habitat, suitable for its needs. It needed to blend in. It needed to be able to hide. Not because of fear, but because of the element of surprise. A hiding place would allow it to wait and hunt for food to attempt to fulfill its insatiable appetite. Its instincts would always be calling for it to kill.

The ocean water was much calmer than it was hours ago, making it much easier to swim. As its sacks flooded with water, they would pick up certain scents that the water carried with it. It sensed natural rock and soil. Not from above, but from its level within the water. The creature squeezed more water from its jelly-like sacks, accelerating its speed in the water. Its eyes opened, giving it a goggle-like vision underneath the waves. It was a nearsighted creature, causing it to rely mostly on its sense of smell. The desired scent grew, signaling to the brain that it was nearing a possible hiding ground. It continued on its straight path towards the scent. The ocean floor was now becoming shallow as the creature's eyes examined several rock formations that stuck upwards from the sea floor like stone knives. With the water becoming more shallow, the creature expanded its numerous tentacles, stretching a few dozen meters from its main body. Each of these limbs were armed with suction cups that contained spiked claws that pointed out directly from the middle of each cup, allowing for impalement of any prey. The creature reached with these deadly tentacles, using them to grab some of the spiked rock formations and pull itself forward. As it neared the structure of land, the water became cloudier due to the increase of dirt and waste particles surrounding it.

Its eyes scanned the location, unaffected by the dirt and salt in the water. The underwater world appeared to be of a bluish-green color, with black bits of rock and dirt floating lifelessly in random directions. The ground was covered by a layer of rocks, with dirt and sand creating a slippery surface. However, sharp rocks posed no threat to the creature; its thick shell would provide plenty of protection for its body. With gentle squirts of water from its sacks helping to push it along the sea bottom, it searched for the perfect habitat. It moved through the turbid water, crawling past more of the jagged rocks that guarded the structure of land it approached. Finally, it came to a black, rock-hard wall. It had reached the main island formation. This area appeared to be a good habitat, but instinct continued to warn the creature to keep searching the area.

It turned left and crawled along the black wall with its tentacles. Its side brushed against the rocky barrier, breaking off bits of debris as it explored.

As it traveled along the island wall, its goggle-shaped eyes followed some of the floating debris in the water, moving into a dark location. The wall seemed to have an enormous, circular gap within it. The creature reached out with one of its long tentacles, examining the edge of this gap. Tiny pieces of rock broke off the edge, floating into a tunnel that appeared to be carrying some of the water into the interior of the island. The creature glided up to the edge of this dark tunnel and slowly slithered inside. Its desire to find a home was now replaced with a feeling of satisfaction. This rocky tunnel provided the perfect camouflage and shelter. However, there was no happiness to be felt; it had no emotion. It couldn't feel happiness, pity, glory, or fear. All it felt was instinct, hunger, and a lust for satisfaction. It allowed the weight of its thick, heavy shell to sink its body to the bottom of this tunnel. In a few hours, the memory of this search for a home would disappear as if it had never happened.

It would now wait until instinct demanded it to feed. However, it would not end up waiting long. Swimming through the rough and wild ocean in search of a hiding place required an enormous amount of energy. It wouldn't be long for it to leave its new home in search of food. With the overwhelming drive for hunger would also come the irresistible urge to slaughter. However, until it could find a suitable prey to feast upon, it would have to scavenge. But in good time, it would find something to unleash its carnivorous wrath.

****

The sun was now almost in the exact middle of the sky as the time neared one o'clock P.M. *The Catcher*, anchored along the east side of Mako's Center, bobbed with each wave that brushed towards the island. On the deck at the stern end of the vessel stood Napier and Wayne, who were in the process of passing out a fresh netting line. Both their outfits were soaking wet, mostly from sweat rather than the seawater that came aboard with the tuna, mackerel, and other commercial fish that were caught in the drift net. Napier unfolded the net while Wayne passed it out into the water. In a holding tank nearby was a pile of the day's catch, which was composed of large tuna, mackerel, cod, and some Atlantic salmon that managed to travel that far south. Fishing work was always hard labor, and it usually took some time to bring in a net, pick the fish from it, and spring out a fresh net in its place. Usually Napier would use the winch to reel the net in, but because the device had broken down, the two fishermen were forced to do the hard labor themselves. Even down near Mako's Ridge, drift nets were slightly controversial due to dolphins and other creatures being caught in the nets. In many places around the world it was even illegal, but a political battle between the Mayor of Mako's Center and the Environmental Protective Agency resulted in an exemption for the island chain. Napier was always respectful of the marine life, and preferred a midwater trawl, which was a fishing tactic in which he would lower a large cone-shaped net, called a trawl, either connected to the winch or clamped to large bolts at the edge of the stern. After arriving at a fishing area, with the net in the water he would drive the vessel in a large pass, scooping up several catches in the process. However, he faced another problem: the bolts on the stern had become severely rusted and needed to be replaced. Unfortunately, bolts for a vessel his size were both expensive and hard to come by, leaving him solely with the option of drift netting. When he first started living on the island, he made a personal study of where dolphins and whales would normally be seen, for the sole purpose of keeping them out of harm's way. This was a quality that his daughter always admired about him; he wouldn't allow himself to benefit at an unnecessary expense.

The two men continued unfolding the net, which had another twenty feet to go. Wayne puffed quietly on a cigarette that dangled from his lips as he passed the net out into the water. Napier, a nonsmoker, hated the smell of burning tobacco, but even on his boat he never saw himself fit to tell Wayne to not smoke.

"Almost done," Wayne said. His voice sounded muffled with the cigarette in his mouth. A light summer breeze passed by, pushing the thin, dark cigarette smoke in Napier's direction. He exhaled sharply through his nose to rid himself of the nasty smell. He glanced over at the holding tank. Though it seemed to contain a large number of fish, it was actually about a quarter of the amount that they normally brought in at this location.

"I'm just wondering what was up with today's catch," he said. "Usually we bring in much more than that." Wayne shrugged his shoulders as continued stringing out the net.

"I don't know, man," Wayne replied. He didn't sound too concerned about it. "Sometimes you just have an off day, you know? Bad luck." Although Wayne wasn't the smartest of all people he knew, he did know his fishing very well. He was probably right. Though, it didn't happen very often that catches would suddenly decrease in numbers. Mako's Center was highly known for its fishing because it was literally a breeding ground for commercial fish, which was the main reason why drift netting wasn't as controversial in this location compared to the rest of the world.

"Yeah, I wouldn't be surprised," Napier said. "It's just that we've had some bad luck with most of our nets today."

"I didn't think the Razortooth Cove net was too bad," Wayne said.

"Oh, no," Napier said, trying to correct himself. "I meant the brown buoy net on the southeast side. That one usually contains the most of our catch, and yet it wasn't even half full today." The southeast net, marked by a brown buoy, had been set up in a path where cod and tuna frequently migrate back and forth. It had never failed Napier in creating a decent catch.

"Well, I will agree that that seemed a bit weird," Wayne said. "But, like I said, sometimes you just have an off day. It's nothing to worry about. Now if the amount of catch remains like this for days, or weeks on end, then I'd say it's time to worry." While Napier knew what Wayne said was true, he was already starting to worry. He had bills to pay, a daughter to provide for and hopefully put through college, and he was behind on his finances already. Finally, he handed Wayne the last fold of the net, which had a buoy line attached to it. Wayne flung it out into the water and tossed the buoy in along with it, watching the floating black ball splash on the water's surface. He stretched his arms out to the sides, quietly groaning as his tense muscles began to relax. Unfortunately, with the catch being a bit smaller than the norm, they both knew that the day's earnings wouldn't be as high.

"Alright," Napier said. "Done with the hard part! Now let's bring this stuff into port. Mr. Gary will purchase these as he usually does."

"Sounds good," Wayne said. He tossed his cigarette butt onto the deck and smothered it with his boot, blowing one last cloud of smoke from his mouth. He then reached into his pocket and pulled out his worn, partly crushed Marlboro pack. He lifted the white cardboard hood and shook the pack a bit, causing one of the light orange cigarette butts to come out a bit from the rest. He then lifted the pack to his mouth as if it was a candy bar, and bit down on the filter, pulling the rest of the cigarette from the pack. He stuffed the pack back into his pocket and pulled out a lighter. He flipped the metal wheel, igniting a spark that turned into a small flame as it connected with the flammable gas. The white tip of the cigarette glowed a bright orange as he held the flame to it, blowing a fresh puff of smoke from his mouth. Napier splashed a bucket of water into the first rectangular holding tank to keep the fish moist, and pulled a large plastic cover over it, protecting the catch from the scorching rays of the sun. There were two tanks that rested in a square-shaped hole that was made for the sole purpose of containing them, but only one of them had fish due to the lack of catch.

Wayne bent down to collect the old net that had been brought in earlier, folding it up carefully so it would not become entangled within itself. As he worked, he glanced up at the buoy, watching it bob with the ocean current. Watching the water, a sudden bright sparkle of light within the water caught his attention. He stood up straight, staring out hard into the water as he tried to get another glimpse of what he just saw. He'd lived on the water almost all of his life, and he knew what the reflection of light from water itself looked like compared to an object in the water.

"Hey, Rick," he called out. Napier was just about to step into the cabin as he heard Wayne call his first name. He walked around the cabin onto the stern of *The Catcher*, seeing his partner standing at the railing.

"What do you need?" he asked. Wayne glanced back at him for a moment, then looked back out into the water.

"I think there's something out there," Wayne said. Napier tried to follow Wayne's eyes, attempting to see what he might have been looking at. All he could see was a black buoy, a thin grey line that was the top of the net, and a blue ocean sea.

"Give me a minute," Wayne said. Napier crossed his arms and waited. As usual, he had to get control of his lack of patience. He stood and watched the boring sight of Wayne looking out into the water like some ten year old who never saw an ocean before. Suddenly, his facial expression lit up from the concentrated state it was in. "There it is!" he exclaimed, pointing his finger directly in front of him. "About forty feet away, I'd say. Something's floating out there."

"Alright," Napier said. "Just keep your eye on whatever it is, and I'll swing the boat around so you can fish it out." He walked to the cabin and started the engine. The boat roared and water splashed as the propellers turned. The *Catcher* turned left and slowly moved forward. Wayne grabbed a hooked pole that lay along the stern and held it over the rail.

"Okay, stop there!" he called out to Napier. The boat came to a stop and Wayne reached into the water with the pole. Napier stepped out of the cabin and walked back around to the stern.

"What is it?" He asked. Wayne grunted as he hooked the object and pulled it towards the boat.

"Looks like a piece of metal," he answered. He grunted louder as he brought it closer. "A big ass piece of metal." The object was now alongside of *The Catcher*, scraping against the paint. Wayne and Napier ducked under the rail and reached down for the object. They both got a decent hold along the edge of the object and pulled it up, gently flipping it over the rail and laying it down on the deck. It was definitely a chunk of steel, almost circular in shape, nearly five feet across, and weighing nearly one-hundred pounds. Seaweed and kelp leaves pressed flat against the dark surface. Some parts of the edge were thick, but other parts appeared chipped and pointed, making the two fishermen realize how lucky they were to have not sliced their hands open while bringing it aboard. The center portion of the piece of metal was heavily dented, as if something had rammed headlong into it numerous times. Napier and Wayne looked at each other in confusion.

"Where the hell did this come from?" Napier asked himself. Wayne was thinking the same question.

"It looks like it came off of something," he said. "Like it was part of a ship or something like that." Napier bent down, brushing off some of the seaweed and tossing it overboard.

"It does look like it could be part of something like that," Napier agreed. He ran his hand over the surface and examined the edges. Some parts of the edges, mostly the ones near the right side of the chunk, appeared to be slightly rigid, but almost flat, as if it had been cut. Other parts, especially near the top of the object, appeared much more jagged, bent and flaked, as it had been ripped from the main body of wherever it came from.

"What could do something like this?" Wayne asked.

"I'm not sure," Napier said, equally as confused. "I honestly have no idea." He continued examining the object, pulling a large kelp leaf from the bottom edge. "Wait a minute!" As he removed the leaf, his eyes beheld an engraving in the chunk of metal: *Warren.*

"What does that say?" Wayne asked.

"*Warren*," Napier answered. "That's all that's here at least. I don't know what that means."

"Well, it's definitely a name," Wayne said.

"Yeah, but a name of what?" Napier said. "A ship; a scrap piece from some Navy base; I have no clue." He stood up and stuck his wet hands in his pockets. "Well, when we get into port I'll have Mr. Gary call in Chief Bondy. Maybe he'll have an idea what it might be from."

"You think so?"

"I don't know. But I'm not keeping this thing. I don't have the space, nor the use for a big ass, heavy chunk of metal. It's shitty enough that the thing ended up scraping off some of the paint on my boat." Wayne began to laugh.

"Like your boat hasn't been losing its paint in the last decade anyway," he joked.

"Oh, be quiet," Napier bantered back. "Alright, let's move

back into port. And we're gonna make this quick, too. I wanna go home; I'm hungry." He strolled back into the cabin as Wayne stayed on deck. The engine rumbled again and the water kicked from the back of the vessel as it pushed ahead, turning back around on a path to port.

****

A few fishing vessels were docking in at East Port, unloading their catch onto pickup trucks that shipped the fish to the companies that would distribute them. East Bay was located in a cove that was shaped like a semi-circle, with the docking center in the middle. This was a preferable port compared to the one on the north end of the island, which was located in a much narrower cove, resulting in overcrowding of ships in tight spots. In East Bay, it was much easier to simply bring the ship in, unload, and leave. That was one of the main reasons that Napier would bring the *Catcher* to this area, also because his main buyer, Mr. Gary, had a market near the cove. The two had reached an agreement for the purchase of Napier's fish as long as the catch was made accessible at East Bay, something that Napier had no problem with.

The *Catcher* throttled towards the curved bay, aiming straight for a dark brown dock that extended twenty feet from the shore. Behind that dock were two large pickup trucks with tarps in the beds to keep any dirt from catching on the fish, and in front of those trucks stood a man dressed in black khaki pants with a clean red t-shirt. Wayne stood at the bow rail as the *Catcher* closed the distance.

"There's Mr. Gary," he said. Napier could see him through the windshield of the boat's cabin. He pulled the throttle back a bit to slow the boat down as the dock neared. Just as the *Catcher* came to a stop, another fishing vessel entered the cove. Along the side of the bow read the name *Thunderhead* in large orange letters. The vessel originally had a blue painted bottom, but the chipping and wear over the years had revealed the old, cracked wood that made up the exoskeleton.

"Oh great, we had to arrive just at the same time as Old

Hooper," Napier grumbled aloud to himself. As the *Catcher* pulled alongside the wooden dock, Wayne grabbed a holding line from a pile of miscellaneous items near the tip of the bow. The vessel came to a complete stop and Wayne hopped over the rail onto the dock and tied the line to a thick, metal pole. Napier shut the motor off and stepped out of the cabin, seeing the *Thunderhead* cut through the waters of the port, pulling up next to a nearby dock that rested about twenty-five feet away. Wayne hopped back onto the vessel, getting onto one side of the first holding tank as Napier got on the other. The tank had to be lifted from the square-shaped hole in the middle of the stern. The two fishermen grabbed hold of handles on each end, and at the same time they pushed up with their legs. The heavy metal tank lifted from its secure hold, and the two men stepped to the side to avoid stepping in the empty hole. Once they were clear of it, they carried the large container to the side of the stern, lifting it over the rail, lowering it onto the wood surface of the dock. Mr. Gary, a six-foot tall man in his thirties who wore circular glasses over his eyes, walked up the dock.

"Hello, gentlemen," he said in a very deep voice.

"Hello, Mr. Gary," Napier said. Each day was like a set schedule; they went to each netting location, brought in their catch, sprung out fresh nets, drove the boat into East Bay, greeted Mr. Gary, gave him the recorded number of catch, took their check, and went home.

"How has the day been treating you guys so far?" Mr. Gary asked. Napier bit his lip, not wanting to admit that the day's catch wasn't quite as good as it normally was.

"Hate to say it," he began, "but one of our nets was short today. We'll be receiving a smaller check today, unfortunately." He pulled a folded sheet of yellow paper from his back pocket, which revealed the day's catch numbers, and handed it to his buyer.

"I did notice that you guys were able to get your holding tank out by yourselves," Gary said. Usually the load he received from Napier was so large that he brought assistants to help unload the vessel and load the catch into large trucks.

"Yeah, our east net was short. It only had about a fourth of what we normally catch. And hell, that's the one that we get most of our fish from," Napier said. "The one set near the cove I live in did as well as it normally does, but that net is only a third of the size of our other ones."

"Is there anything in that other tank?" Gary asked.

"No," Napier said, shaking his head. "Like I said, it'll be a small paycheck today." Wayne walked to the back rail of the boat, whistling to his partner. Napier turned to face him and realized he was standing by the mysterious chunk of metal that they had found. "Oh, yeah!" he exclaimed. "Hey, Mr. Gary, would it be too much trouble for you to get a hold of Chief Bondy? We found a big chunk of metal near our eastern net, and we don't know what it's from." Mr. Gary looked over the vessel's railing at the shiny chunk of metal that rested on the deck.

"Oh, wow," he said. "Sure, that won't be any problem. I'll have my guys bring it into the shop along with the rest of the stuff.

"I appreciate that, sir," Napier said, politely. Suddenly, the peace was disturbed as the yelling of an old, unhappy man permeated the air. The three men looked towards the other dock, seeing Old Hooper, a man with an unshaven face, worn clothing worse than Wayne's, and a beer gut that nearly prevented his shirt from staying tucked in. The fisherman was walking down the shoreline towards the *Catcher*, appearing to be holding what looked like a folded net. On his face was a fiery expression that showed no intention of making a friendly conversation.

"Hey!" he called out. "Rick Napier! Get over here! I need to ask you something!" Napier knew of the short fuse that Hooper carried around with him, so the easiest choice of action was simply to see whatever it was he wanted. It wasn't that he was following orders; rather he was just trying to prevent a conflict. He quickly walked down the dock onto the warm white-tan sand that made up the shore. Wayne and Gary followed him to help prevent any possible trouble.

"What may I do for you, Hooper?" Napier said, trying to keep a polite tone of voice.

"I want to know if you had anything to do with this, asshole," Hooper snarled. He threw his net onto the sandy ground, partly unfolding it. Napier looked down at it, noticing massive rips and tears in the strings. The entire net was destroyed. He reached down and unfolded the rest of it. It was as if somebody had taken a massive pair of scissors to it. There was hardly a square foot of the net that was usable. On some portions of the shredded net were pieces of fish that looked as if they had been put through a grinder, creating a horrible stench. Napier stood up and looked Hooper in the eye.

"I certainly had nothing to do with this," he said. "Where did you set this net?"

"Who gives a shit?!" Hooper snapped. "I just want to figure out who shredded my net and cost me most of my day's earnings!" His breath carried the foul smell of whiskey, and his teeth were stained yellow.

"Was that the net you had by Mako's Edge?" Mr. Gary asked. Hooper felt his temper boil. He hated when another person would cut into his business.

"Who cares if it was, hotshot?!" he growled. "You mean to tell me that you were the one who fucked my net up?" Gary rolled his eyes and shook his head.

"No, Hooper," he said. "I was at my store all day. However, you know it's a bad idea to be having a net out in that location anyway. You're lucky that it was only the net that got damaged."

"Hey! That's none of your concern. It doesn't make a difference to me that you morons are too scared to earn a few extra dollars!" He kicked up a bit of sand over the net as he vented his anger. Finally he took a deep, angry breath, and stuck his hands in his vest pockets. "Just stay the hell away from my shit!" He turned and walked back toward the *Thunderhead*, leaving the devastated net behind. Napier rolled his eyes as he thought of how ridiculous Hooper was. Wayne began to chuckle, finding Hooper's behavior rather amusing.

"What an unbelievable jerk," Napier said.

"Oh well," Gary said. "Things like this come to pass. That moron deserves a no-profit day anyway."

"Yeah, I'd say so," Napier said. He turned his attention to the *Catcher*. "Well, I'm in the mood to go home and eat. Let's get this stuff unloaded. Maybe we'll have better luck Monday."

"Oh, I'm sure you will," Gary said. "And I'll get that weird metal shard to the Chief and see if he'll do anything with it.

"Appreciate it, sir," Napier said as the three men walked back to the *Catcher*.

CHAPTER 3

The sun glowed dark orange as it slowly descended down into the horizon. A few isolated thunderhead clouds drifted in the atmosphere, glowing in a carroty color as the dying rays of the sun covered them like a never-ending sheet. The water surrounding the black, rocky shore of Mako's Edge reflected the almost-horizontal rays of light. The rocks that peaked over the surface had shadows that stretched for several feet, providing extra darkness to the world below. With the exception of water splashing on the rocks, there was almost no noise. Seagulls flew around this area often to hunt around the nesting grounds near the rocky island, but tonight they sensed a presence that they didn't find welcome. Fish would normally feed near the top edge of the water where insects would land on the rocks, but as the late evening sun sank into the horizon, no sudden splashes from feeding activity could be seen.

A new presence moved into the deserted area floating on the surface of the water, its curved bottom submerged, allowing for buoyancy. The sound of a humming motor disturbed the peaceful silence and the calmness of the water was replaced by the splashing that resulted from the movement of a bow slicing the surface and the spinning of a razor sharp propeller. Watching the horizon from his small, enclosed cabin stood a man in his thirties, dressed in an army-colored vest, grey pants, and a worn fishing cap. An unlit cigarette dangled from his lips as his hand scrambled in his right vest pocket for his lighter. Pushing aside the worthless wrappers and pieces of paper, he gripped the metal object and pulled it from the pocket. Carved on the side of the lighter were the man's initials, S.H.; Steve Hogan.

"Are we almost there?" called a voice from the stern of the vessel. Hogan glanced back at his first mate; a scrawny gentleman who went by the name of Burke.

"Yes, we're close," Hogan answered. He throttled the boat slowly to avoid crashing it on any of the rocks. When traveling along this island, a path had to be carefully memorized. Not all of the rocks were exposed over the surface; some of them would be just under, creating hidden death traps. Watching the water, Hogan couldn't help but notice the silence and lifelessness of the area. The sky was empty of birds that normally patrolled the sky, and the south end of the island lacked the chirping of south island insects that took refuge throughout Mako's Ridge. What Hogan found even more strange was the strange rippling in the water, despite the fact that there was no wind. The water began to glow with a mixture of dark orange and pink lights as the sun continued to set. Hogan knew that he better hurry up and find his buoy before darkness would destroy his vision. The net had been set earlier in the day, giving it just enough time to do sufficient catching. Under normal circumstances, he would wait until the next morning to bring the net in, but he had to catch a plane flight to visit his sister who lived in Florida. The vessel curved around the island, narrowly dodging a few rocks.

"I see it," Burke called out, pointing off the portside. Hogan took his eyes off the throttle for a moment and saw the yellow buoy floating peacefully near a rock that pointed towards the sky like a large spear. He steadily turned the steering wheel to the left, making sure he was very careful not to veer too hard and end up smashing on a rock. Finally, he was alongside the buoy, and Burke flipped a switch on the outside of the cabin, creating a cranking noise as the boat dropped its anchor into the water.

****

Gravity pulled down hard, allowing for the creature to rest comfortably without any unnecessary floating. The tunnel was pitch black, impossible to see through. But it didn't matter. It had little use for its eyes in its new habitat. Though it was certainly new, the creature had no memory of finding it. For all it knew, it had been there its whole life. In the bottom of this deep, dark tunnel, it rested… and waited. While it appeared lifeless, it was wide awake. There was no need for sleep; its small brain worked on a twenty-four hour cycle. Rather, it waited patiently as it rested on the sea bottom. Boredom didn't exist to it. All there was in the world was the need to wait, slaughter, and devour.

Sound traveled faster and further in water than in air. A mysterious hum echoed into its eardrums. Nerves on its shell detected a nearby presence, one that was not there moments before. The hum came to a stop, being replaced by a rattling noise alien to it. Its tentacles extended from the main body as blood pumped through the veins, energizing the enormous muscles. Inside the main body were large oil sacks, in which the creature would produce organic oil. Tube-like veins pumped oil into these sacks, helping to give it some buoyancy. The sacks that were lined along its sides swelled with water as the creature pointed its body towards the entrance. The sacks gently released water as it clutched the rocks on the sea floor, pulling it along towards the presence.

The rattling came to a stop, but it was only a few dozen meters from where the creature was positioned. It continued to creep along the sea bottom through the forest of rocks. The dying rays of the sun provided a little light, but even without it, the creature would always find what it was looking for. Crawling a little further, it finally came across something. It was an object, smaller but very different from the rocks. It rested on the bottom, next to a few larger rocks. A tentacle slithered like an enormous python towards the object, slowly wrapping around the thin body. It was a heavy object, though the creature would have no trouble dragging it back to its hideout. However, it had no interest in this particular object alone. Attached to it was a long extension that reached up like a large, solid string. Its nerves lit up like Christmas trees, continuing to sense the presence of something; something that was in its range of sight. As its eyes followed the strange extension of the object, its eardrums absorbed the echoes of nearby prey. Directly above the creature was another body in the water, all the way up at the surface. The echoes continued, originating from this vulnerable presence.

****

"Holy mother of God," Hogan snapped as the two men reeled in the net. The strings that made up the drifting trap had been shredded, as if a lawnmower had run over it. Bloody pieces of fish hung from bits of the remains, creating a horrible stench that made Burke's stomach churn.

"What the hell is that smell?" he asked, plugging his nose. It didn't do him any good; as he breathed in through his mouth, he tasted the horrible texture in the air, causing him to put his hand to his mouth and cough.

"What I want to know is what the fuck happened to my net!" Hogan snapped. He turned and kicked the wall of the cabin, leaving a small brown mark where his boot had connected with the wood.

"I have no clue what did this," Burke said. "Hey, didn't that guy, Old Hooper, have a similar issue today?" Hogan shrugged his shoulders.

"I don't talk to that jerk," Hogan answered. "Why would I? He's an angry guy who has nothing to do in his life except find a benefit for himself and make everyone else's day miserable. I don't care, anyway. This is my net that got destroyed, and I want to know why." He inhaled a deep, horrible-smelling breath, relaxing himself. There was nothing else to do. Only the top half of the sun was peaking over the horizon, meaning they had very limited time to get clear of the rocks. "Alright, haul up the anchor, please. Let's get moving." He opened the door to his cabin and walked in. Burke walked to the control panel, clicking a switch to bring the anchor in. The chain rattled and the mechanical hauling unit cranked loudly as the heavy anchor pulled upward. Suddenly, the cranking noise turned into a sharp, screeching noise as the hauling unit struggled to bring the anchor up. Hearing the commotion from his cabin, Hogan poked his head out to see what was happening.

"What's going on?" he called out. Burke stared at the chain and the round, metal unit, and glanced at Hogan with a very puzzled expression on his face.

"I don't know. I think it's caught on something." Burke

replied. He flipped the switch off and reversed it, allowing it to lower back into the water. He stopped it again, and then flipped the switch the opposite direction. The metal gears tightened and screeched as the anchor failed to pull up. Hogan stepped out from his cabin and walked to the starboard side, where the anchor hung from the boat.

"We better figure out what's wrong pretty quick or we're gonna be spending the night out here!" Hogan snapped.

"Hey, dude," Burke argued. "Don't look at me! I was the one who agreed to come out here as a favor to you."

"No," Hogan yelled. "You came out here because I employ you. Now I want you to help me figure out what the hell is wrong with this thing."

"Well, I'm not the one who got this thing snagged. It was stupid to put a net out here anyway!"

"Hey! Don't argue with me, you got it?! Now shut up and work on this thing!" A massive crushing noise roared from underneath them, creating a massive sound wave that rushed through the water. Both men suddenly stood silent as their hearts became flooded with an unexpected fear. After a few brief seconds of silence, the boat jerked upward, following a gigantic unknown force that generated a crashing noise of splintering wood. Both men collapsed to the deck as the boat bobbed violently before coming to a stop. Hogan and Burke pushed themselves to their hands and knees, looking up at each other in sheer awe and terror.

"What… the hell… was… that?" Burke said, shaking with intense dismay. The sound of screeching metal caught their attention, and both of them slowly turned their heads to the starboard side. The anchor chain was moving, slowly swaying towards the bow. The vessel began to rock left to right like a cradle, kicking up water on both sides. Each sway became more violent, and both of the fishermen felt their stomachs tighten as another horrifying thud crashed from underneath. Metal and wood from under the boat came apart like warm bread, and Hogan's muscles tensed as he could hear the dreadful sound of seawater rushing into the boat from underneath.

"What the hell is going on?!" Burke yelled in a panic. Another bizarre noise hummed underneath them, almost sounding like a gurgling of fluids. The vessel suddenly started tipping towards the left. Burke began to hyperventilate, believing that the boat was about to overturn. The starboard side rail rose higher into the air while the port side edge nearly touched the surface of the sea. As water was just beginning to creep under the rail, the tipping came to a dead stop. It remained in that tilted position for only a single brief second as the vessel was suddenly pulled viciously to the left. Both men screamed for their lives as the bow crashed with intense force into one of the deadly rocks surrounding the island, causing a shock wave that threw both men onto their backs. Seawater poured rapidly into the engine, generating smoke as the mechanics and water did not get along.

Hogan and Burke huddled in the middle of the stern. Burke continued to hyperventilate while Hogan simply knelt in a frozen position. Over the crackling noises from the exploding engine, they both heard a strange splashing from the back of the boat. They slowly looked back, beholding a sight that brought a terror they thought only the devil could offer. Like the numerous heads of a hydra rose three enormous tentacles, slithering over the metal stern railing. The rubbery skin of these monstrous limbs generated a disgusting odor that smelled like rotting flesh. On the bottom of each tentacle were rows of donut shaped suction cups that contracted each time they touched something. As if each one had a mind of its own, they slowly slid over the rail, curling upward like a group of cobras. Helplessness and fright struck together as both men screamed for dear life as the tentacles sprung with a snapping motion, shredding deck as they reached for their prey. Burke, on his hands and knees, desperately attempted a fast crawl towards the cabin. He only got about two steps in when one of the mysterious organisms wrapped around his waist up to his lower back. His eyes bulged as pointed barbs in the middle of each suction cup slowly plunged into his flesh, rupturing his kidneys and bladder. The slimy flexible arm dragged him towards the edge of the stern, his arms flailing wildly as his nerves burned with pain. Hogan sat paralyzed with fear, unable to move as he watched his friend getting pulled across the splintering deck, leaving a thick trail of blood that oozed from his waist. Blood began to bubble out of Burke's mouth as he reached out frenziedly, grabbing the metal bar of the rail. His arms became fully extended as the slithery arm tugged against his waist, tearing the musculature in the lumbar section of his back. His teeth clenched tightly as he felt his pain sensors pulsing through his entire body. The tissue in his arm began to stretch, but he refused to let go. He wheezed as he attempted to breath, but his lungs had become nearly paralyzed from the hyperventilating and screaming. The carnivorous tentacle made another vicious tug downward. Burke's elbows made a loud, popping sound as the joints disconnected. The blood vessels in his arms burst, and the biceps and triceps tore. He watched, horror-struck as the skin just above his elbow joints pulled apart. His mouth opened to make one final scream, but before he could puff the remaining air from his tensed up lungs, water flooded into his mouth as the tentacle took him underneath the surface, leaving his severed forearms hanging at the stern, with the hands still tightly gripping the rail.

Shock had overtaken Hogan, who sat motionless just a few feet from the cabin. There was no train of thought or attempt to flee. The sight of blood dripping from Burke's dangling forearms had destroyed any rational thought. Another powerful thud hit the bow, creating further mayhem as the front of the boat detached from the main body, tipping upward as it slowly started sinking into the water. Hogan's breathing rate started to increase again as he heard a huge splash of water slam into the inside of his vessel, causing it to go down, slightly tilting towards the front. He looked up and managed to take a single breath as the other two tentacles lunged for him. One wrapped around his legs as the other grabbed him by the torso, wrapping underneath his armpits. Almost instantaneously, his arms reached for the sky, his eyes swelled, and his jaw stretched widely as the barbs sank into his chest and legs. The tentacle that had wrapped around his chest, which was rising from the portside, began to pull its prey towards toward the left side of the boat. The other tentacle rose from the stern, coming up under the rail, towards which it also began to pull. Hogan gurgled as each muscle in his torso stretched. His stomach muscle split, spilling the digestive containments into the rest of the body. The intestines unfolded and pulled apart. Several disks along the spine violently herniated, creating several painful bursting sensations along his back. Veins and arteries exploded, causing blood to mix with the other numerous fluids. Hogan made a painful squeal as the skin, containing his now mushy insides, tore open. His kidneys fell out onto the deck, rolling like fist-sized tennis balls over the starboard edge. Intestines and stomach tissue dragged along the bloody deck as his upper body was pulled toward the port edge. Before the shadow of death finally overtook him, he watched as his lower body, containing everything below his abdomen, slid over the back of the boat into the water. The last thing he felt was the slapping of water against the shredded flesh on his back.

Pieces of wood and metal drifted in opposite directions; some toward the island shore, some away from it. What was briefly chaos was once again a dark, gritty peace. And beginning at the edge of the horizon set a blackness, as the sun's rays disappeared into the other side of the earth.

CHAPTER 4

"Oooh, good Lord," Napier moaned, stretching his arms out into the air. His eyes were still feeling heavy, keeping him from getting out of his bed. Lying on his back, he continued dozing in and out. As he roused, he could hear thunder rumbling overhead, along with a light rain that patted on the roof. Luckily, Sundays were his day off, so he wouldn't have to go out on the *Catcher*. He looked to his right at the window on the center top of his wall, seeing the grey storm clouds that hung over the island. Rainy weather always helped him fall asleep, which was probably why he was having a hard time waking up. The brown bed sheets were peeling off the corners of the mattress from Napier's tossing and turning overnight; he was a very uncomfortable sleeper.

The clock clicked to nine a.m. as he finally sat up, yawning quietly. Even as he sat up, he felt very comfortable in his black sweatpants and white t-shirt... almost too comfortable. The idea of sleeping in some more did not bother him. His eyes were still somewhat heavy, and his black hair stood up on end where he slept on it. He swung himself around, sitting up over the edge of the bed. Light thunder continued to roll as he touched his bare feet to the oak wood floor. He stood up straight, bending backwards a few times to help relieve some of the cramps in his back. He walked to his dresser, pulling out a drawer at the top and one at the bottom. The one on the top contained t-shirts while the other one contained jeans. He reached into both, pulling out a comfortable pair of ocean-blue jeans and a black t-shirt. Piling the set of cloths in his hands, he walked out the bedroom door into the living room. The walls of the room were made from a fine red brick, covered by a white layer of plaster. In the center of the front wall was a large window that brought all of Razortooth Cove into view. Napier stood in the middle of the living room, watching the storm clouds still floating overhead, as a steady rain continued to trickle, causing numerous circular ripples in the cove. His attention was then taken by the sight of Jane, who walked into the room from the kitchen, fully dressed in long khaki shorts and a yellow short-sleeve shirt.

"Good morning," she said.

"Hey, kiddo," Napier greeted back. "I'm guessing this weather formed directly over us."

"Yeah," Jane said. "I'm already preparing for the humidity that will probably come along in a couple hours."

"I can see that," her dad said. He took another glance out the window. The rain had stopped and the clouds continued moving south. "Looks like the sun will be peeking out soon."

"Well that's good 'cause I was planning on going out in about a half hour," Jane said. Napier had to sometimes remind himself that Jane was growing up and people her age always loved to be around friends. He and his late wife were always together daily, causing both their parents to be constantly worried of their whereabouts.

"Where are you going this time?" he asked.

"I'm going to be with Amanda again," she said picking up a blue school backpack from beside a couch that sat in front of the window. She usually packed lunches and soda in it whenever she went out with friends.

"You guys have been hanging out a lot lately. What were you two planning on doing today?" Jane shrugged her shoulders.

"Well, Dad, we just play it by ear," she said. "We figure out what to do as we go along. I mean, sometimes we plan stuff ahead, but usually it's spontaneous."

"I see," Napier said. He always trusted his daughter, but something in his gut was telling him that there was something more going on than simply hanging out with her friend. He had no clue what could possibly be going on, but there was something else happening in his daughter's life. "Hey," he said, "Did you want me to take you around on the *Catcher* one of these days? I know how you always liked boat rides." Jane stood by the furniture, thinking for a moment before looking back up at her dad.

"Well, that'd be nice," she said, almost sounding as if she felt awkward. "Well, we'll see. I'll have to figure out when I can get a day to myself." Napier knew that this meant she had no real interest in going. She had the whole summer off, so there should be no trouble getting a day to herself. Of course, what high school age teenager wanted to be with his or her parent?

"Well, only if you want to," he said. He took a deep breath as the remainder of the sleepiness left his eyes. "Well, I'm going to take a shower. Then I'm going to drive into town."

"Where are you going?" Jane asked, trying to sound interested.

"I'm gonna go talk to the chief. I want to see if he found out anything about that weird piece of metal that we hauled out of the water yesterday," he answered. "But first, I'm gonna head into the shower. Were you planning on taking the truck?"

"Oh, no," she said. "I was just gonna go ahead and walk there. It's only like a ten minute walk. If we go into town we can take her car."

"Alright. Well, by the time I get out of the shower you'll probably be gone, so you keep yourself safe, you hear?"

"Will do, Dad," Jane said, cracking a smile. Napier walked through the kitchen into the bathroom. Jane heard the knob in the shower squeak as her dad twisted it to open the flow of water. She knelt down and grabbed her tennis shoes. She placed them on her feet and tightly tied the laces. Finally, she grabbed her backpack and walked out the door.

****

The storm clouds had drifted away towards the south, giving clear passage to the bright yellowish beams of sunlight. The ocean water sparkled; the grass lit a bright greenish color, as did the tropical trees all over the island, and the sandy beaches glowed like shiny gold. Dressed in his blue jeans and black short sleeve shirt, Rick Napier locked the front door of his house, breathing in the surprisingly fine morning air. He thought that the humidity would spike like an angry volcano, but this turned out to be one of the few times it didn't happen. He walked down the porch steps to his white truck, opening up the driver's side door and sat on the comfortable cushioned seat. He grabbed the key from his pocket and jammed it into the slot. He twisted the ignition, creating a light roar in the engine. Napier pushed the transmission into DRIVE, and steered the vehicle through the driveway, hooking around the side of the house into the road, where he turned right and began his short trip to Chief Bondy's office.

The scenery was usually the same on any trip: local children would play near the edge of the road, usually with a soccer ball or a basketball; elderly people enjoyed tending gardens around their homes; maintenance men and carpenters were always putting up luxury houses, giving tourists a place to stay during their summer visits. Napier drove the truck into the town, where business flourished. Countless business stands lined the road as people sold hot dogs, lemonade, beer, and some things that Napier couldn't pronounce if his life depended on it. In the middle of the town was a large supermarket, where most of the islanders did their shopping. He slowly drove past it, being especially careful because the area in front of the market was usually teeming with shoppers heading in and out.

He pulled the truck onto a small blacktop driveway, carefully aiming the truck in-between the yellow lines that made up the parking spaces. In front of the blacktop was a small, brown building with a sign that read in large letters: *Chief of Mako's Center.* Shifting the transmission into PARK, he pulled the key out from the slot and stepped out of the truck. He entered the front door of the building, embracing the sudden chill of the air conditioning. A few feet in front of him was a counter that stood about chest high. He walked up to it and rested his elbows on the flat surface, seeing Chief Bondy sitting at his desk. The entire building was composed of empty desks and chairs.

"Yo! How are you doing, buddy?" Napier called out with a smile. Chief Bondy looked up from the paperwork on his desk, returning with a small, but pleasant smile. His uniform was made up of light grey trousers and a short sleeve shirt that read *Mako's Center Police Department.* He stood up and walked to the counter.

"I'm not doing too bad," he said. "However, I got a lot on my hands today."

"Oh, really?" Napier said. The chief usually didn't have much to do except settle local disputes and keep the people in order, which wasn't hard to do because disputes didn't happen very often. For him to have his hands full meant that this would probably be a memorable day.

"Yeah, I guess a boat went down over near Mako's Edge," he explained. "This is tough shit because I'm so short staffed. I've got a small crew out over there to try and collect as much of it as they can. Deputy Drake should be back here shortly."

"Oh my God," Napier exclaimed. "You said it was near Mako's Edge. Was it Old Hooper's boat?"

"No," Bondy answered. "We're not one-hundred percent sure yet, but we believe that it was Steve Hogan's boat."

"Oh, son-of-a-bitch!" Napier said, almost in an angry tone. "That man had a drift net out there. I was actually gonna meet up with him and give him a bit of hell for being a big enough fool to even think of such a thing. Did… did they find him?"

"Obviously not, or we would know for sure what had happened," Bondy said.

"Oh," Napier said, adding up the logic in his mind. Bondy grabbed his dark windshield jacket and buttoned it up.

"I'm gonna have to go out there," he said. "I'm sorry I can't help you with whatever you came here for."

"Oh, no. Don't worry about it," he said. "You said you were shorthanded; do you want me to go out there with you? I'd like to help in any way I can." Bondy bit his lip as he thought the idea over.

"If you don't mind, then yeah, sure," he said. He pushed a small door open at the center of the counter and the two men walked out the entrance. Chief Bondy only had a few deputies due to the lack of action that happened near Mako's Center, so he was normally pretty open to the idea of having outside help. He held the door open for Napier, who stepped back onto the heated asphalt. Bondy followed him out and shut the door just a few seconds before he beheld the sight of Deputy Drake, who had just pulled into the driveway. Drake was a chubby lawman, but it didn't surprise most because there wasn't much for them to do except drive around the island a few times a day, then go back to the office and eat donuts.

"Hey, guys," he said, holding a hand over his mouth to hide a small belch.

"Hey, Drake," Bondy said. "How's it looking?" The deputy shrugged his shoulders, unsure of how to answer the question.

"What can I say," he began. "I mean, I wasn't out there, but the civilian who spotted the site said there's nothing but wreckage left. From what I've been told, I would recommend getting the U.S. Coast Guard out here to sweep these waters for any bodies."

Complete wreckage?" Napier said. "I wouldn't be the least surprised that somebody could put enough holes in their vessel by going through some of them rocks, but you make it sound like the whole thing was destroyed." Drake nodded, confirming to Napier that he was not exaggerating.

"No, sir," he said. "The person who spotted the thing told us that the whole area was a floating mass of boat pieces. He said he spotted deck pieces, engine parts, pipes, railing, you name it." Napier looked over at Chief Bondy, who was about to step into the police truck.

"Chief, don't you think that sound's at least a little bit weird?" Napier asked. "I mean, you'd have to really try hard to completely tear the boat apart."

"What are you trying to get at?" Bondy said. He wasn't concerned with any wild ideas or accusations. He was simply in the mood to get to the scene and examine the area.

"I'm not sure," Napier answered. He could tell that the Chief wanted to get a move on, so he quickly got into the passenger seat of the truck. The chubby Deputy hobbled into the office building, preparing himself for numerous reports that he would have to fill out and print.

****

The rippling surface of the ocean surrounding Mako's Center was like a reflective mirror as Bondy throttled the white police yacht away from the southern port. The sunlight beamed down hard, making Napier feel as if he was being cooked inside his black shirt.

"Eight years of post High School Education, Associate of Science degree, Bachelors degree, Masters degree, half of my fucking doctorate, and I was still fucking retarded enough to grab a stupid black shirt in ninety degree weather!" he ranted to himself. Bondy couldn't help but chuckle as he steered the boat toward Mako's Edge.

"Can't say I've never done the same thing," he said, keeping his eye on the big black rock in the middle of the horizon that was the destination. "Then again, our police uniforms used to be dark blue, practically black. We didn't really have a choice. Back in those days we always prayed for winter to come. No snow, obviously, but the cooler temperature helped." Napier carefully bent down under the rail and reached his hand down the side of the moving vessel, allowing some sea water to splash onto his skin. After gathering enough water in his palm, he splashed his face and dipped his hand over the side again to get some more.

"Yeah, well like you said: You didn't have a choice," Napier said, mixing sweat with seawater. "I just got up in the morning, grabbed the first clothes I saw, and threw them on. Some smart scientist I am."

"You ever think about going back and finishing your doctorate?" Bondy asked, embracing the refreshing breeze that pushed in the opposite direction they were traveling.

"Oh here we go," Napier exclaimed. It constantly seemed like that unfinished goal kept coming back to bite him in the ass. "Actually, to my surprise, Jane is the one who actually tries to encourage me to finish it. Hell, when I was her age, I had zero intention of going to college, and honestly couldn't stand it when other people would talk about whether or not they were going, or what they were studying, or whatever. She has a lot of her mother in her."

"You think so?"

"I know so. When my wife Katherine and I were dating during my senior year of high school, she would actually tug on my arm to get me to further my education. She rather enjoyed school, though I never figured out why. I loved learning about science; I just hated to do the stupid research papers. Now Jane, she never enjoyed school as much as Katherine always did, but she certainly likes it a lot more than I do."

"It must be her mother's spirit inside of her," Bondy said with a smile. "She's telling you to do what you do best, man. Succeed and go after things. I mean, hell, I couldn't stand the four years in college that it took to get me into law enforcement, so I can only imagine what it must've been like to go for almost twice that amount."

"It friggin sucks, Chief," Napier said, sparking laughter from the two of them. The smile faded from Bondy's face as the vessel began to approach the jagged island.

"Okay, it's supposed to be closer to the eastern side, so we're gonna have to make a bit of a curve here," he said, steering the boat around the island. The boat swung to the right as the chief turned the wheel. Napier stood at the railing, watching the waves splash violently into the razor sharp rocks.

"Hey, Chief," he called out. "I think Old Hooper was going to take some divers out here today. I guess some scientists are intending to get a look at the cave that's here."

"Yeah, I already talked to him," Bondy answered. "He won't be coming here today. However, that might end up being pushed until tomorrow. Despite my wishes, I can't cut this place off from the fishermen indefinitely. It is a safety hazard, but it technically is still legally fishing ground-- just very risky fishing ground." He saw the deputy police boat, lined with white strips along its sides. The boat was docked between two deadly rocks, but spaced out well enough between them to prevent any damage. Napier and Bondy could see the deputy standing at the railing with a large pole with a round net on the end, scooping up bits of debris.

"I can't see too well from here, but it looks like Deputy What's-his-name might have most of the wreckage collected," Napier said. The Chief's vessel slowed down as it neared the dangerous forest of rocks.

"Oh, that's Deputy Jones," Bondy corrected him. "And you might be right; maybe they did dig up most of the wreckage. There were a couple other boats out helping earlier." He steadily steered the boat closer to the deputy's. With the grouping of rocks growing larger, he decided to drop the anchor. The hauling unit rattled as it lowered the heavy piece of iron to the ocean floor.

With the vessel set in place, Bondy walked to the rail beside Napier, floating about fifteen yards away from the deputy's boat.

"Hey, Jones!" Bondy called out. The deputy looked up from scooping the net through the water. He had seen his boss arriving, but was very concentrated on his work. A few rough pieces of wood drifted in opposite directions around his vessel, but to Napier and Bondy, it appeared as if most of it had been collected.

"Hello, sir," Jones responded. Pushing and pulling the net was hard work, causing the deputy to look like he was in excellent physical shape, when in reality he was about average. Sweat sparkled on his forehead as the sun beamed heavily on him. His skin was beginning to turn slightly red, showing early signs of sunburn. "I'm hoping that I'll be able to come in soon, Chief." He was almost out of breath, since he had been out here for a few hours in the sun.

"Well, it looks like you've almost got this thing finished," Chief Bondy said. "I'm imagining that the other boats that were here had lots of debris on them."

"You would think so," Deputy Jones said. "You see this pile behind me?" Behind the deputy was a stack of deck pieces and pipes that rose to nearly three feet.

"Yeah, we see it," Bondy said. "What about it?"

"This is all we found," Deputy Jones said. Bondy and Napier stood silent, trying to suspend their disbelief.

"That's all you found?" Bondy asked. "I thought the place was covered in wreckage?"

"That's what the guy who originally spotted the wreck told us," Jones answered. "He met us back in port and after about an hour or so we came back out here, seeing maybe a fourth of what he thought he saw." Bondy crossed his arms, feeling a bit frustrated. It wasn't uncommon for civilians who reported a crime or accident to get some of the details wrong.

"Well, that's just great," he said. "He got us all in an uproar over nothing."

"I don't know, sir," Deputy Jones said. "What has me worried is that there's no sign of the main body of the vessel. In water this shallow, it's usually easier to catch any sign of it."

"What kinds of signs would those be?" Napier asked,

interrupting the conversation.

"Anything giving a clue where the boat may be," Bondy said. "Usually in my experience, a fuel leak is one of the most common ones. In areas like this, especially really rocky places, the boat may actually end up lodged against something like a big ass rock, exposing some of it. Usually from damage like this one supposedly had, there would be a clear sign."

"Yeah, but there's not," Deputy Jones said. "I don't know. If there really were more pieces, then it's like something came up from under the water and plucked them."

"Like anything here would do that," Bondy said. After watching the few remaining pieces of wreckage floating on the glassy ocean surface, he decided that there was nothing here for him or Napier to do. "Okay, well this is the plan: I'm gonna head back to port and I'm gonna get a hold of the U.S. Coast Guard and have them investigate the area for a sunken vessel. You just try and get what more you can and then come back in. Who knows, maybe I'll be a nice guy and let you have the rest of the day off."

"Ha!" Jones laughed. "Like you're ever that cool of a chief!" Bondy laughed as he hauled the anchor up, generating another annoying rattling noise that lasted for a few seconds until the large weight was pulled aboard the white police vessel. Bondy then stepped up to the wheel and throttled the boat backwards, away from the rocks. As soon as the water became empty of the hazardous traps of nature, the chief throttled the boat forward, sharply curving it to the left, taking it back to port.

"Fuck this," Deputy Jones said aloud to himself. "I've been out here for long enough. Hell, it took me long enough to squeeze this boat into a good position to collect this shit." He swept his net out into the water, centering another busted piece of wood into its center. He pulled it towards the vessel, allowing himself to hook the net under it to scoop it. He lifted the wood out of the water and swung it onto the deck. Tipping the net downwards, he dropped the piece of wreckage onto the pile before setting the net down on the deck. He stretched his arms outward, attempting to relieve some of the tension. He was ready to leave. He reached into his grey pants pocket, pulling out a set of keys to start the boat engine. With a strong, exhausted exhale, he took another glance at the island bay. Just as he was about to step into the ship's cabin, a strange bubbling in the water caught his eye. He stepped to the railing to get a closer look, lightly grasping the bar. The bubbles were about ten feet away from him, coming up as if someone was releasing oxygen from down below.

"What the hell is this?" he whispered aloud to himself. He knelt down, trying to reach for his net without taking his eyes off the bizarre phenomenon. His hand scrambled aimlessly as it searched for the wooden handle, eventually locating it. He stood up and positioned his hands on the pole to prepare to scoop up what may have been surfacing. After a few more seconds, he could see a white object a few feet under the surface. Suddenly, the net dropped from his hands as he stood in pure shock after witnessing a human forearm emerge from the water. It was severed just above the elbow, drained of blood which gave it a fleshy white color. The skin was hamburger-like, wrinkly, worn, and full of rotting holes where fish had taken bites out of it. A clean, white piece of bone stuck from the center of the meaty wound at the end, appearing chipped at the end where it dislocated from the rest of the body. Bits of muscle tissue dangled in small strands at the large open wound at the end, swaying back and forth like light-pink seaweed. The pinky and the upper half of the middle finger were missing, while the other fingers appeared as if they were boneless, wrinkling with each ripple of water. The arm itself was like a noodle, appearing very flexible in and of itself; the bone within the forearm was busted at numerous points, causing the limb to be held together by skin, wobbling in the water.

Deputy Jones felt as if his stomach was doing somersaults around the rest of his body. His face turned vampire pale as he rushed towards the other side of the boat and hung his upper body over the railing, puking up everything he had for breakfast. Dizziness and nausea overtook him as he held himself at that same position for several minutes. A strong headache pulsed in his skull and his stomach continued to feel as if it had exploded. Steadying his breathing, he slowly backed away from the railing and made his way into the boat cabin, inserting the key into the slot and turned it. The engine roared as he put the floating vehicle into reverse. He looked back to make sure he wasn't backing the boat into any of the rocks, completely ignoring the area of the wreckage to avoid enduring the awful sight of that arm.

"I'm getting the fuck out of here!" he roared, still feeling lightheaded. His heart pounded rapidly and his hands shook as they grasped the throttle and wheel. The boat cleared the rocks and Jones quickly turned the wheel to the left, causing it to swerve away from Mako's Edge. He throttled forward, making his way to port. He took a few deep breaths in an attempt to calm his brief panic. His shaking hand grabbed the radio that laid on a shelf to his right. He pressed a button to get in Chief Bondy's frequency and held the radio to his mouth.

"H-hey Chief! You there?" He waited for a moment as the radio buzzed.

"*Yeah, this is me, Jones. What's going on?*" Bondy responded through the radio. Jones took a couple more breaths.

"S-sir? Y-you won't fucking believe this."

****

A breeze of wind brushed toward the west though Mako's Center, causing numerous small waves to splash to the sandy shore of the northeast side of the island. The sand warmed in the summer heat except where the cooling water splashed onto it, bringing its color from a bright gold to a muddy brown. Several yards from the beach was a grassy hill, where a large white lighthouse stood to provide light for vessels during the night. About a dozen meters north of the lighthouse was a small brown house, resting on the same hill, looking out toward the bay.

Dr. Miranda Sanders sat on a chair on her front porch, holding a pair of binoculars to her eyes as she looked out into the ocean with great interest. A marine biologist for thirty years, she never once lost her fascination for the sea and the secrets it contained. After obtaining her doctorate in Marine Biology when she was twenty-seven, she traveled tirelessly throughout several islands along the Caribbean as well as the south Asian islands, exploring sea life and helping endangered species. A certified instructor, she would return to the United States once in a while to teach a college course for a semester or two. However, being on the mainland was never a typical life for her; she needed to be traveling. She also did some work with film companies; hosting documentaries on underwater sea life in the South Pacific, as well as deep sea life in the Mid-Atlantic. During her travels, she would spend much of her time scuba diving, collecting footage and research for environmental agencies that were concerned about endangered species. And, like many other scientists fascinated by the ocean, she would always wonder about the deep abyss of the ocean; what life existed in those massive bodies of water that man didn't know about?

The front door opened as her twenty-two-year-old son, Ryan, stepped out, dressed in jean shorts and a plain white t-shirt. Pursuing her studies and dreams didn't fare well with her attempts to have a personal life. Dr. Sanders had married twice, but each marriage barely made it over a year. Since her divorce with her second husband, she had Ryan live with her at her island home in Mako's Center during the summer times.

"What are you doing?" he asked, seeing that his mother was looking through some binoculars. "I mean, what are you looking at?" Dr. Sanders gave a small smile as she glanced up at her son before looking back at the binoculars. She appeared very interested in what she was looking at.

"Here!" She said, quickly handing the binoculars over to Ryan. "Take a look out there. Just ahead of us there's a small red fishing buoy. Look about fifty meters ahead of that." Ryan lifted the binoculars to his eyes, scanning the wavy blue water for the buoy.

"I can't see…wait. There it is!" he said.

"You see it?" his mother asked, excitedly. Ryan shook his head.

"I meant I found the buoy," he said. He always did have a fascination of his own for the ocean and nature in general, but it was nothing compared to his mother's. She would write a report on anything from hermit crabs to ancient megalodon sharks.

"Okay," Dr. Sanders said. "Like I said, look about fifty meters beyond it." Ryan went ahead and scanned the scopes up from the red, balloon-shaped buoy, seeing nothing but water at first.

"I'm not seeing what you want me to see," he said, continuing to search. His eyes caught nothing but clear blue water that brushed towards the beach with the tide. He searched the bay until finally his eyes caught a glimpse of a movement that wasn't caused by the waves. He steadied the binoculars as he watched a large, blue dorsal fin slowly cut across the water, followed by a second massive fin that swayed steadily from left to right. He suddenly became interested once he realized what it was.

"You see it?" His mother asked.

"Yeah! I see it!" He said, continuing to watch as a large whale shark slowly swam barely a quarter mile from Mako's Center. From afar, it looked nothing more than a huge bluish shadow moving across the surface of the water. However, with the binoculars, Ryan could see the large white spots that covered its blue skin. Its mouth was open, implying that it was feeding on a group of plankton. Water crashed against its fins and back as the waves rolled over it.

"Isn't it beautiful?" Dr. Sanders asked, smiling happily. Ryan lowered the binoculars.

"It's pretty neat," he said. "I didn't think they would get too close to an island like this."

"Oh, they'll go wherever the dinner is," Sanders said. Watching from the long distance, they could see the dark shape that was the whale shark. From this particular view, they couldn't see any real movement in the creature because it was so far away and so slow moving. During her scuba-diving trips, Sanders had had the pleasure of swimming along one of these ocean giants. They were peaceful creatures; the only danger they ever possessed was an unintentional strike with its tail. Ryan handed the binoculars back to his mother.

"How big do you think that one is?" he asked.

"I'd say it's about as big as they get; about fifty feet," she answered.

"Oh, wow," Ryan said. He took another long glance at the faraway sea creature. "Pretty neat." Thirsty for a soda, he turned and walked back inside. Dr. Sanders remained on her porch seat, bringing the binoculars back up to her eyes. The shark continued to feed on the plankton, waving its large tail slowly to push water through its gills. Finally, the creature's back dipped under the water along with its huge dorsal fin. Sanders continued to watch, seeing the tip of the dorsal fin break the surface every few seconds. After a few minutes, Ryan stepped back out with a blue can of Pepsi in his hand.

"Is it still there?" He asked.

"Yeah," Sanders answered, bring the binoculars down from her eyes to look at her son. "It's gone under, though."

"Awe, damn!" Ryan said. "I was hoping to get a picture of it." His mother chuckled.

"I don't think you'd get a good photograph from way out here," she said. She looked through the binoculars once again. To her surprise, the dorsal fin had reemerged. "Oh, it's still there! I see its dorsal fin." She stopped talking for a moment as she noticed that the fin was strangely moving left and right, rather violently. "Or maybe it's the tail." However, that thought did not last long after she panned right and saw the tail fin behind it, strangely moving left and right in the same bizarre manner. Both fins dipped under and emerged again at rather fast speeds. Sanders held her breath as she tried to understand what may have been happening. Ryan noticed his mother biting her lip in confusion.

"Is everything okay?" He asked, slightly concerned.

"I don't know," she said. She gasped suddenly as she witnessed the creature causing some large splashing in the water. It was twirling its body in a strange manner, as if it was struggling. Its tail rose completely above the surface, flapping violently in every direction. "Son-of-a-bitch!" She said.

"What's going on?" Ryan asked, thoroughly concerned.

"I don't know," Sanders said. "It's behaving funny. It's like it's being…" she took a sudden, long pause. "What the hell was that?!" Ryan stood next to her, almost afraid of whatever it was she was witnessing.

"What?"

"I saw something! I didn't get a good enough look at it. But, I saw something." Ryan tried to look hard without the binoculars, but his vision was already impaired because he didn't have his contacts in. "I don't know what it was!" Sanders continued. "It was like a big snake or something. A big octopus tentacle or… I don't know what that was. It came out of the water and went back in… Oh my God!" Like a massive humpback whale, the whale shark breached the water, exposing its flat head and soft white belly. Sanders' jaw dropped in awe, seeing that the shark's underbelly had been slashed open, exposing its red inner stomach and intestinal regions. The shark crashed down into the water, creating a monstrous red splash. The biologist shrieked as she saw a sudden spout of dark red blood erupt from the chaotic mess of splashing like a giant fountain of death.

"What the hell is going on over there?" Ryan asked, managing to notice even from this far distance that the water was turning red.

"I-- I don't really know," Sanders answered, almost frightened. "The shark-- I think it's being attacked by something." She held her breath once again as the bloody splashing steadily came to an end. The bloody water was quickly dissipating in the bay, bringing the reflective bright image back to the water. Sanders lowered the binoculars and quickly wiped her eyes and took another look at the situation. In the middle of the now calm water was a strange bubbling.

"Is anything happening now?" Ryan asked.

"Again, I don't know," Sanders said. She watched the bubbling continue for a couple seconds before shrieking in fright once again, witnessing a severed blue tail emerge at the surface. There was no sign of the rest of the shark's body. Blood leaked from the open wound as the current pulled on the wavy red strands of flesh that hung from the stub.

CHAPTER 5

A large group of islanders crowded East Port as Chief Bondy, Deputy Drake, and Napier examined the shreds of debris on the deck of the deputy police vessel. Deputy Jones stood at the portside railing, still feeling a bit nauseous. Several questions rose from the crowd, mostly obtaining to the bizarre destruction of the boat. Napier knelt down by the pile of wreckage, picking up a piece at a time, looking at it and tossing it to the side. A cold wind kicked up from the north, where a large grey line of clouds formed.

"Of course, weather always gets to make things easier," Napier said, eyeing the distant storm clouds that approached with the evening hours.

"Yeah, that's why I was quick to get a hold of the Coast Guard," Bondy said. "I want that place searched thoroughly before the wind gets a chance to fuck up the scene."

"What time should they get here?" Deputy Drake asked.

"Inside of an hour," Bondy answered. "They're simply sending a three-person unit due to the fact that it's not considered a huge priority. All they're doing is looking for a sunken boat whose passengers are assumed to be already dead." Napier continued looking at each piece of wood and metal, examining the edges of each piece. One particular plate of metal he examined was a fin from the propeller. It was bent horizontally across the middle, as if something had somehow grabbed the object from top to bottom, pulled inwards, and curved it at the center. The pipes that were brought on board had sustained damage that was equally as strange; the ends of each chunk was jagged and bent at the end, indicating that it had somehow been twisted and pulled apart. The several shards of wood gave the obvious impression that the vessel had been ripped apart.

"This is too weird," Napier said.

"What?" Bondy asked. He knelt down beside the fisherman to look at the debris.

"It's almost like somebody put this ship in some big-ass grinder," Napier replied. "I mean, it's not like this ship had just gotten impaled by some of those rocks. It's literally shredded; torn apart."

"What are you getting at?" Deputy Drake asked.

"I don't know yet," Napier said. "But I have a hard time believing Hogan simply crashed up against the rocks."

"Well, remember Rick," Bondy said, "We don't have the whole vessel here. These are probably just pieces from where it may have hit the rocks."

"I'd agree with you, but the really weird thing is that there are pieces from under the boat, the deck, the cabin, the engine, railing… all in this little pile. I mean, unless Harper's boat got hit by a meteor out there, the debris should only be coming from one general section of the boat," Napier explained. Bondy picked up a chunk of deck from the pile, looking at both of its sides before placing it down and picking up another piece.

"I guess that is a bit strange," Deputy Drake said. "What do you think, Chief?"

"Also, there's that arm that Jones discovered out there," Napier added. As soon as he finished speaking, the attention of all three was drawn to the sound of Deputy Jones coughing up more vomit over the side of the boat. The reminder of the horrible image he had the misfortune to grasp did not fare well with his stomach. Napier turned his attention back to the Chief. "I don't like the description he gave us of how mutilated it was."

"It does seem a bit odd," Bondy said. "However, I'm not making any quick judgments until the Coast Guard unit looks through the area. Which reminds me; Drake you're gonna be out there with them tonight."

"What?" Drake complained, obviously not thrilled about the idea of staying out late.

"You heard what I said," Bondy continued. "I want someone out there to make sure that the Coast Guard doesn't get themselves smashed up on the rocks. Think of it as good overtime pay."

"I don't give a shit," Drake said. "I think the Coast Guard people are more than capable of getting the job done themselves. And I really don't want to see what's left of Harper's body."

"Don't argue with me," Bondy said. "I don't like that they're only sending a few people on this job. I want an extra person over there to lend a hand. It's part of your job, Deputy, so don't argue." Drake slapped his hand against his leg in frustration as he turned away from the Chief, who stood up from looking through the pile. Napier grinned as he resisted the urge to chuckle at Drake's reaction to his own misfortune. However, he had known Hogan and did not find the overall situation very funny. Still curious about the circumstances regarding the wreck, he knelt down and pulled another piece of wood from the pile. The top side of the piece of deck was dark brownish from its decay in the water. He flipped it over to look at the bottom side.

"What the hell..." he said to himself. A strange barb-like object was projecting from the corner of the chunk. He flipped it back over, seeing the pointy tip had pierced through the piece of wood. He grabbed the strange barb and twisted it away from the debris. It had a dark-brown color, but its structure was not like any sort of wood. He rubbed his thumb over the object, feeling a rather smooth sensation, but not similar to steel; it was more like a bone. The tip was almost flawlessly pointy and sharp. "Take a look at this, Bondy."

"What is it?" the Chief asked.

"I have no clue what this is," he answered. "It was stuck in one of the pieces. It's kind of... bony." He handed the object to the Chief.

"Hell, I have no clue what this thing is," Bondy said, eyeing it. "You are right though; it does seem to be a bit bony, doesn't it?"

"Doesn't seem like there's anything normal about this accident, does there?" Napier commented as he stood to his feet. Suddenly, out of the crowd stepped two men, both dressed decently in jeans and short-sleeve shirts. One had brown hair while the other had a buzz cut. Both appeared to be in their mid-thirties with decent muscular builds.

"Hey, Chief!" the one with the brown hair called out. Chief Bondy turned to give his attention to these two strangers whom he had never seen before.

"Yes? How may I help you two?" He asked politely.

"That incident occurred around Mako's Edge, am I correct, sir?" the same person asked.

"Yes," Bondy answered in a flat tone-of-voice. He hated to be interrupted by people who asked questions that had answers that everyone already knew. "And... how may I help you?"

"Well we... well let us introduce ourselves," the man said. "I'm Nic Kelly and this here is my colleague, David Wellers. We're scientists and we were planning on doing some diving in the cave inside Mako's Edge today."

"Well, I'm sorry, sir," Bondy said. "Nobody's going anywhere near that place until the Coast Guard personnel finish their work." Both of the scientists bit their lips, disliking that their project was being delayed.

"Any idea when that'll be?" Wellers asked.

"Listen kid, I wish I knew," Bondy said. "The Guard has some people on their way right now and they'll be working on bringing up what's left of Harper's boat tonight." Deputy Drake could see that the chief clearly had no interest in these two strangers.

"Listen guys," Drake said to the scientists after stepping away from the railing he was leaning up on, "odds are, the Guard won't take very long with their little clean-up operation. It's likely that they'll be done by the end of tonight and you guys will be able to do whatever it is you need to do out there by tomorrow morning."

"Just be careful with your boat out there," Bondy immediately said in a strict tone-of-voice. "As you can see, we've already had an accident and two fatalities-- two more than anyone obviously wants."

"Understood, Chief," Kelly said. Without saying anything else, he and Wellers turned and walked away. Napier grinned after seeing Bondy rolling his eyes.

"What the hell is it with these science freaks?" The chief grumbled. "Are they just attracted to inconvenient timing?"

"I thought they seemed polite enough," Napier said. "I'm actually a little bit surprised that you're letting them do their work over there right after a fatal accident took place." His expression was slightly stern due to the fact that he personally knew Hogan.

"Understand, Rick," Bondy said, "my authority is only here on Mako's Center. Unfortunately, I don't run all of Mako's Ridge. Believe me, if I had the authority, I would make it illegal for any sailor to travel to that island. But, unless there is a known homicide crime that took place around there, I can't shut that area down after the Coast Guard finishes their work." Napier nodded, understanding the chief's reasoning. "Deputy Drake!" the chief barked like a drill sergeant. Drake nearly jumped as he emerged from his own little world.

"Sorry, sir," he said. "What do you need?"

"Let's load this wreckage into the police pickup truck and get it back to the office, where we'll wait for the Guard to contact us," the Chief instructed. He then looked over at Deputy Jones, who was still hanging over the boat railing, green with nausea. "Yo, Jones!" The sickly deputy slowly turned his head to make eye contact with his superior. His eyes were droopy, and his jaw was slightly hung open.

"Y-yes boss?" He asked. His voice sounded almost as if he was turning into a zombie.

"Take the rest of the day off," Bondy ordered. "You're obviously not gonna do me any good the way you are." Jones made a little smile, expressing his gratefulness.

"I guess you are that cool of a chief," he responded, speaking in the same sickly manner. His stomach felt like it weighed a hundred pounds.

"Hey Chief, why don't we grab a couple of burritos with some extra salsa?" Deputy Drake joked, obviously provoking his coworker's upset stomach. Jones' eyes widened and leaked water as he spun back around to lean over the railing. He was immediately coughing and gagging, but there was nothing left in him to come up.

"You… ass--asshole," he moaned painfully. Bondy had to turn away to conceal the fact that he was silently chuckling to Drake's remark. After a few seconds, he managed to bring himself back under control and eliminate his smirk.

"Alright Drake, knock that off," he demanded, but almost in a sarcastic tone-of-voice. "Let's get to work on getting this crap out of here." He glanced towards Napier, who was prepared to leave the law enforcement officers to their job. "Well Rick, I appreciate your help and company today."

The two shook hands.

"No problem at all," he said. "Good luck in figuring this out. Good luck to you, Jones!" As he stepped off the Chief's boat to leave for home, he could see the queasy deputy lift his hand to wave farewell.

****

Water hissed from the kitchen faucet as Jane twisted the warm water knob to fill the sink. Water freefell into the miniature artificial canyon, quickly creating a clear wet layer between the air and the gray marble sink surface. Jane grabbed a triangular shaped plastic bottle, filled with orange dish soap, and pointed it down towards the water. With a light squeeze of the bottle, carroty fluid dripped into the sink, instantly creating bubbling suds that quickly began building up into a mountain shape in the corner. Dishwashing was a chore that Jane didn't mind doing. The kitchen in which she stood in was a mild mess from the late lunch that had just been finished. A blue tiled counter extended nearly six feet from the sink, stopping just before a hallway that led to another bedroom and a laundry room. The floor was covered in a slightly dirty white tile layout, and in the middle of the kitchen was a wooden table, carved in a perfect square shape.

"You know you don't have to take care of my dishes," called a voice from the bedroom in the hallway. Jane didn't care. Her father had raised her to provide any help she had to offer whenever she would spend time at a friend's house.

"Greg, I know you're not going to take care of them," she said. She quickly heard his bare feet graze the floor as he walked from around the hallway corner into the kitchen. She glanced back over her shoulder to see Greg, dressed in a yellow t-shirt and tan khaki shorts, picking up an empty pizza box from the table and shoving it into a brown trash can near the counter. He was a year older than her, had bushy brown hair, and blue eyes.

"Well there may be a little truth to that," he chuckled. Jane grabbed some nearby plates and submerged them in the soapy water. She seemed a bit distant as she worked. Greg could tell there was something on her mind. He walked to her right side and leaned against the counter. "Alright, what's going on in that brain of yours?"

"What do you mean?" Jane asked in a dry tone, expressing the part of her that wanted to avoid this conversation. Greg scoffed at her obviously poor attempt to pretend nothing was wrong. He gently ran a finger through her hair.

"I think you know what I mean," he said. "You're worried that your father will find out about us hanging out together and freak out." Jane sighed and then remained silent as she scrubbed the dishes with the sponge. Greg didn't have much patience for his girlfriend trying to bore him out of this conversation. He had a tendency to be a bit nosy, as well as critical, about other people's personal lives.

"I told my dad that I was going to be spending the day at Amanda's place," she exclaimed. "I'm getting very uncomfortable with constantly lying to him."

"Do you honestly think he'll be that mad when you tell him you're seeing me? Come on, how bad can it be?" Greg said. He was still leaning on the counter as Jane did all the cleaning. The two of them had only been dating for a month and Jane was already beginning to take issue with the laziness she observed from her secret boyfriend.

"He might-- I don't know," she exasperated. "Maybe if you didn't mouth off to him in school and start fights in his classes, then perhaps this would be a lot easier to bring up to him."

"Damn, girl," Greg said. "Look who's suddenly crabby and willing to point out my flaws."

"I'm not pointing out your flaws, other than the fact that you were a jerk to my dad when he worked at the school and you don't ever help me with cleaning your own house when it needs doing," Jane said. She was easily growing frustrated. She rinsed the suds off the newly clean plates and placed them in a drying rack on a counter to her left. With no more dishes to wash, she reached into the warm water and pulled the metal plug from the bottom of the sink. The soapy water made a gurgling sound as it began to sink into the drain. “It’s just that I know my dad will find out about this sooner or later.” Greg handed her a white towel to dry her hands off.

“Hey, listen babe,” he began, “this was your idea. You told me that you were afraid how your dad would react to you seeing me and I supported your decision. If you want to break the news, then go ahead. I just don’t see what the huge deal is. It’s not like you’re telling him that you’re pregnant or anything.”

“I know,” Jane said. She dried her hands with the towel and set it aside. She walked away from the sink over to the kitchen table and took a seat planting her elbow on the edge of the table and resting her chin on her palm. “I’ll wait a little bit. He’s been wanting me to spend a little more time with him. I’ve been rejecting his offers lately so I could spend more time with you.” Greg shot her a stern look, implying that he felt she was blaming him for her lack of quality time with her father. She didn’t mean it this way and immediately saw his expression. “That’s not what I mean, Greg.” She followed with a light smile.

“I understand,” he said. “However, I’m starting to get the impression that you are starting to regret this relationship.” Jane lit up a romantic smile.

“You know that’s not true,” she chuckled. She got up from the chair, walked up to him, and gave him a warm, affectionate hug. “I have no regrets with you.” Greg smiled and kissed her on the forehead.

“I’m very relieved to hear that,” he said.

“You’re not relieved. You knew very well what the answer was,” she said in a giddy voice. “At least, you’d better have known the answer.” She broke away from the hug and walked past him to grab a glass of juice from the counter.

“Of course I knew the answer. That doesn’t mean I’m not relieved to hear it.” he said. “Guys are more sensitive than you think.” Jane drank what little juice was in the glass.

“I guess you’re proof of that,” she said. She strolled past him, into the hallway. Greg heard his bedroom door open.

“What are you doing?” he asked.

“I got to get going,” her voice called from his bedroom. She walked out of the bedroom, holding a couple DVDs that she brought along with her to the house.

"So much for me being sweet, romantic, and sensitive," he teased. She walked out of the kitchen and into the living room, where the front door was located. Greg followed, feeling a bit disappointed that she was leaving. She turned to face him and gave him a quick kiss on the lips, followed by a smile. She knew he was bummed.

"I love it when you're sweet, romantic, and sensitive," she teased back. Greg grinned and gave her a humorous thumbs up. "I'll call you later on tonight."

"I'll be looking forward to it, babe," he said. Both smiles lit up brighter as she walked out the door.

****

"In other news today, tragedy struck Mako's Center as the remains of a fishing vessel was discovered adrift along the rocky coast of Mako's Edge," announced a radio broadcaster on the island's local station, MCBS -- Mako's Center Broadcast Station. The voice had been carrying on from Rick Napier's truck radio as he drove home from East Port. *"So far, the only information known to us is that the vessel was owned by an islander fisherman named Steve Hogan, who is believed to have gone down with the vessel during some late night fishing yesterday evening. It is also believed that his first mate, a forty-one year old fisherman named Burke Harrison, was possibly fishing with him, and may have gone down with the wreck. Chief Bondy has informed us that only pieces of the wreckage have been discovered, while a United States Coast Guard unit is being sent to search for the two fishermen."*

Napier continuously tried to wrap his mind around the events that occurred during the day, especially concentrating on the phenomenon that was the fact that there was no trace of the main body of the vessel to be found. Although the water was deep in certain areas along the coast of Mako's Edge, the vast array of rocks usually would hook a ship that would have run aground on one, resulting in the vessel resting on the slope of the underwater body of the particular rock that impaled it. And then there was that bizarre thorny object that he found speared in a piece of debris. It didn't appear to be a part of the ship, and it didn't resemble any tool or object that would be on any ship. And undoubtedly the strangest and most haunting incident was a fact that was not broadcasted on the radio station, likely for good reasons: the finding of the severed arm. Only the Lord knew whether it once belonged to Steve Hogan or Burke, and a part of Napier wanted it to stay that way.

He coasted his truck through his driveway, bringing it to a stop as it arrived at the edge of the driveway in the front yard. He stepped out of his vehicle and walked to the front door of his house. He grabbed the knob, only to discover, to his surprise, that it was still locked. Jane was still not home. He pulled out his house key from his pocket and let himself in. After grabbing a Coca Cola from the refrigerator, he stepped outside to his front yard. He sipped his soda as he stared out over the arrow-shaped Razortooth Cove into the endless horizon of ocean water. His mind continued to question the sinking of Hogan's vessel and the bizarre circumstances surrounding it. In addition to his immense curiosity of the occurrence, his mind was also consumed by his worries of his fishing nets that were still adrift in their respective locations. The next morning, he and Wayne Michaels would go out aboard the *Catcher* to go out and pull in the nets. Napier simply prayed silently that they would have a better day in regard to quantity of fish caught than yesterday.

"Hey, Dad!" he heard Jane's voice call from behind him.

"Damn," he stuttered. "You scared the crap out of me." Jane laughed as she walked around the front of the truck to the front door. Napier followed her in, freeing his mind from all that was concerning him. He glanced at his watch, reading the time. "It's almost seven," he said. "You were with Amanda all day?"

"Y-yeah," Jane answered, not restraining her voice from sounding confused to the interrogating tone of her father. "You'd be surprised what us chicks can come up with doing when we hang out." She entered the house and Napier followed her in and headed back toward the kitchen and dining room.

"I will not challenge you there," he said as he picked up the day's newspaper. He had brought it in earlier, but did not get a chance to look at it. "So, how was your day?" he asked. "What did you and Amanda do?" He unfolded the paper and skimmed over the first few headings. It was mostly economic and political garbage that just got repeated a dozen times over. There was an election coming up for a mayor of Mako's Center, and seeing as the island was U.S. property, it obviously would spice up a new feud between republicans and democrats. There were a few headlines that listed news regarding issues in the fishing industry. He went ahead and began to read the article.

Fishermen in Mako's Center are enraged as they discover that the fishing has gone down in the last couple of days. Reports from around the North and East sides of the island have indicated that several fishermen had reeled in their nets, not only to find that there was hardly any catch, but that their nets had literally been torn to shreds. This shocking phenomenon has been reported by eleven fishermen so far, and there are rumors speculating that these events could be the result of a possible perpetrator who has been personally cutting holes in the nets. So far, there has been no comment by law enforcement personnel regarding this issue.

"Holy shit," Napier said aloud to himself. He instantly recalled the incident in which Old Hooper had complained of his net being destroyed. Napier assumed that it was just bad luck: Old Hooper never did take great care of his materials. But this newspaper article reported that eleven fishermen had suffered the same problem. "This is just great," he said aloud to himself under his breath, "this better not have happened to my nets. With prices going up, sales going down, and buyers getting extra nervous, the last thing I need is my nets to be torn to shreds." He quickly flipped the page, now trying desperately to get his mind off this particular topic. As his eyes skimmed the articles, he realized that Jane had not responded to his question of her day. Perhaps she didn't hear him.

"So what did you and Amanda do all day?" He repeated the question. He tried to make sure that he didn't sound as if he was trying to pry into her business.

"We just--," her voice paused for a moment. "We just… we shopped around town for a bit." Napier tightened his lips, trying not to look up from the paper. His lips mouthed the word *"nice"* in a derisive manner. It seemed that she had no true interest in talking about her day-- which was normal for a person her age. However, it did seem slightly strange: It was as if she was making things up. Napier inhaled deeply and ended with a strong exhale. It was just another thing for him to *try not to think about*. It had been too long a day, and he just wanted to relax, try to sleep, and have a good fishing day tomorrow. He skimmed the headlines on the second and third page of the paper, finding one article that was moderately interesting: "*Famous Shark Hunter returns to Mako's Ridge.*"

Most people are familiar with the famous shark killing character Quinn from the classic 1975 blockbuster "Jaws", who set out on his vessel to do battle with the awe inspiring monster legend of cinema history. Imagine if that character were real. Today, a true legendary shark hunter, Ryan Rein has come to one of his temporary homes on Mako's Center. And unlike the ill-fated encounter between Quinn and the 30-foot shark from "Jaws", Rein has never lost an encounter between him and the creatures of the deep which he hunts. Mr. Rein reports that the reason he comes home to Mako's Center this time is to get his fishing vessel repaired, after it was damaged during a recent excursion with two twenty-foot great white sharks that were reported to have been lurking off of the Florida Coast. He hopes to be back on the open water soon to continue his adventures.

"Whatever," he scoffed at the article. He didn't see the glory in poaching sea creatures for the sake of the glory. He felt that was a rather sick thing to do. Finally, he folded up the newspaper and set it down on the table. A quick glance out the window was enough to tell him that another storm was about to set down upon the island. "Sucks to be those Coast Guard guys," he said. He walked into the living room and snatched up the television remote. As he sat down into his comfortable brown chair, Jane walked by to go to the kitchen.

"So what about *your* day?" she asked. Napier's lips tightened once again.

"It's a long story," he said. "I helped Chief Bondy in an investigation. Steve Hogan's boat sank near Mako's Edge. The

Coast Guard is taking over tonight." Jane responded with a semi-interested 'hmmm' and a nod. She didn't know who Hogan was, nor was she familiar with any of the island's fishermen beyond her father and Wayne. Napier turned the television on. The audio immediately came on while the picture took a few seconds to come into focus. The first channel to be seen was, of course, the local news channel. According to the audio of a story the reporters were just finishing off on, it appeared that they were talking about Steve Hogan's sinking vessel; a story that would likely flood tomorrow's newspaper. On the bottom of the news screen, there was a scrolling bar that carried information from right to left of the screen, usually full of secondary news that people would find less important. However, one of these new listings did catch Napier's eye, causing him to lean forward for a closer view:

"*Marine Biologist reports claims of a sea monster off the northeastern corner of Mako's Center.*"

This was too weird of a day, he thought to himself.

CHAPTER 6

Deputy Drake sipped his black coffee from his brown mug as he stood along the railing on the starboard side of the law enforcement vessel, which was anchored off the coast of Mako's Edge. About twenty feet away was the Coast Guard vessel *Arthur Bishop.* Though it had the same basic design, this ship was considerably over twice as large as the small police boat. Both vessels were pointed toward the main body of the island, which was about eight hundred yards from where they were anchored. On the port side of the *Arthur Bishop* stood Corporal Robert Arness, almost mirroring Deputy Drake's posture in the way he stood with coffee in hand. The time was nearing eight o'clock and the sun was on its path to setting. It was already darkening because of the storm clouds that were rolling in from the north, now nearly overhead, turning the sky into a gloomy shade of gray.

"I hope they find it quick," Deputy Drake said, looking up at the ugly overcast of clouds. "I don't want to be out here in this weather."

"Doesn't make a difference to me anymore," Corporal Arness said. Knowing how long it would take to get back to base in the Gulf of Mexico, he knew he would be driving through some of this weather at some point. From Drake's view, Arness looked like a giant, standing six-feet-seven-inches tall and wearing a yellow jacket over his blue uniform trousers and short-sleeve shirt. He kept his eyes on the water, specifically the intense blockade of razor sharp rocks that made Mako's Edge so notorious. "I hope I'll never have to drive a boat anywhere near this place ever again," he remarked.

"I don't blame you," Drake said. He looked down into the water, noticing air bubbles popping up on the water's surface. "Are they on their way up?" he asked, referring to the two Coast

Guard divers who were busy searching for the lost wreckage.

"They might be," Arness replied. On the bow of the *Arthur Bishop* was a large crane-like mechanism with a large black cable. Arness grew anxious about the time it was taking for them to locate Steve Hogan's vessel. If it got too dark, the divers would have a difficult time hooking up the cables so the Corporal would be able to operate the winch and tow the boat up to the surface. On the bow of the deputy's vessel was a small pile of floating wreckage that the divers had collected from the surface. Other than that, there was no sign of any intact vessel.

"Have you ever had anything like this happen before?" Drake asked. "I mean, have you ever had a ship just disappear like this, minus the bit of debris?"

"Son, we're the Coast Guard. We deal with situations similar to this almost every day," Corporal Arness explained. "In one case, there was a fishing vessel a few miles off the coast of Bermuda, in which the fishermen were packing dynamite on the boat."

"What?" Drake's eyes flared. "Why the hell were they shipping that stuff? Were they trying to start a war?"

Arness shrugged his shoulders and shook his head, expressing his lack of a definite answer. "Hard to say," he said. "But, that was one case in which there was no real wreckage to bring to the surface. Just pieces. Except just a hell of a lot more than we've found here, which is how I know this is not a similar case; not to mention that much of the debris contained evidence of powder burns." He sipped his coffee a bit. It was fresh out of the pot, so it was still scorching hot. He looked up at the sky after hearing another roll of thunder rumble through the clouds. He could hear the rain drizzling in the ocean to the northeast, knowing that it was only a matter of minutes before it would start pouring where they were at. The amount of sunlight was steadily decreasing, as if somebody was slowly pulling a curtain over the sun. He stepped away from the edge of the boat and walked into the cabin. On the right side wall of the cabin was a white switch. He flicked it up, and the spotlights on the front side of the boat came on, reflecting off the water and rocks. He walked out of the cabin and saw Deputy Drake still standing in the same location.

"Well, if you need something to do, Deputy, you may want to

put on the lights on your boat," he suggested. "It's getting dark, and as you may have figured out for yourself, the wind is picking up."

"That might not be such a bad idea," Drake said. What the corporal was saying was true. The storm was bringing in plenty of wind along with the rain, and this could be seen in the steady rising of the waves. Drake looked up at the corporal. "Will you guys be able to work in this storm? The waves are steady at the moment, but they're gonna be kicking up soon."

"The Lieutenant will probably have us throw in the towel after this," Arness answered. "It won't be the first time a wreck wasn't completely brought up. Sometimes, nature just needs to have its mysteries. We may never know what caused it to disappear like this." His coffee finally cooled down enough so he could finally begin swallowing it. Like Drake, he drank it black. There was no need for him to sweeten it with cream or sugar. As he brushed his jacket sleeve over his lips, he noticed a much more steady array of air bubbles coming up to the surface, only about ten feet from the bow. "That's them coming up right now," he said to Drake. The deputy quickly rushed into the cabin of his small vessel and switched on the spotlights and pointed them down to give more illumination to the water. After they were set, he hurried back to the starboard railing. He arrived just in time to see the heads of two individuals emerge from the water. One of them quickly pulled the mouthpiece out, taking in a breath of fresh air before looking up at the corporal who stood nice and dry on the large vessel. The diver then pulled off her mask, revealing her face. It was Lieutenant Lisa Thompson, a thirty-four-year-old redhead. Behind her was Officer Jake Denning, who didn't bother to take any gear off in case they decided to take one last dip.

"Is there anything else?" Corporal Arness called down. He could tell the Lieutenant was frustrated, which meant they didn't have much luck.

"I think what we've already found is all there is," she called back. She looked up, immediately taking notice of the harsh weather conditions. "Can't say I didn't see this coming," she said.

"What do you want to do?" Arness asked.

"Are you sure you can't find anything down there?" The

deputy called down to the divers, interrupting Thompson's opportunity to answer the corporal's question. The lieutenant shot the deputy a rather pissed off look, expressing her disconcert over him asking a redundant question. Drake clenched his teeth upon seeing her eyes digging holes into his face.

"Why, no. I'm only on my five-hundred-thirty-fourth dive and I'm not yet sure if I know how to find a fucking downed sea vessel," she retorted. Lieutenant Thompson was certainly a woman with a short temper, whose patience gradually got shorter and shorter as she got older and moved up in the ranks of her career. Her father was a homicide detective in Chicago and her mother was a correctional sergeant in a medium security prison for female inmates in that same city. Attitude ran well in the family. When noticing the feisty character in Thompson, some friends of the family would wonder if the strong attitude was genetic.

"I don't mean to point out the obvious, but we do have a storm coming in," Officer Denning said. "As the lieutenant and I clearly know, the water is on the verge of getting rough and I really don't want to be swimming down here in it." As soon as he had finished speaking, the drumming of rainfall finally came down on them in a steady drizzle. "Great!"

"It's up to you, Lieutenant," Arness said. Thompson thought about it for a moment, looking south past the stern of the two vessels. She then looked back at Denning.

"Alright," she began. "We're gonna take five minutes more. I'd like to shine my flashlight a little more over that way. If we don't find anything, then we're out of here and we'll report to the commander. If he still wants it found, then he'll just have to keep a better eye on the weather." Even though Denning's face was covered in his diving mask and goggles, Thompson could read his dissatisfied expression. Denning was a predictable person in his behavior. However, he followed orders to the letter, no matter how he personally felt about them.

"Whatever you say, boss," he said with an exaggerated sigh. Thompson shook her goggles clean of water, then spat in them to remove the fogginess before putting them back on her face. With her mouth piece in hand, she looked up once more at the corporal, who continued to lean on the railing. Of course, there wasn't anything better for him to do.

"Five minutes," the lieutenant said, as if confirming the plan. She put her mouth piece in and checked to make sure all her gear was intact, before she and Denning sank into the depths, shining their flashlights into the deep, making them appear as if they were spacecrafts traveling in the dark of space.

****

It funneled water through its various sacks that oxygenated its blood as it channeled into a brief blackout. It had spent precious energy hours earlier as it had finally slaughtered prey that finally brought its hunger to a temporary satisfaction. It could barely remember the killing, but its tiny brain could still recall a sense of fulfillment that came from slaughtering another creature nearly equal to its own size. It didn't replay the fading memories in its limited mind, nor did it try to analyze the content feeling it was experiencing. The memories didn't matter, nor did their meanings.

Its snake-like tentacles curled tightly against its body, clutching any nearby rocks to help anchor itself to the sea bottom. It intended to rest for the night. There was no need for it to hunt, as its nutritional needs were met for the time being. There was no need to branch out and seek new territory, as it felt happily secluded in this otherworldly home. It entered a deep sleep, separating itself from the events of this day, allowing the memories of its accomplishment to be lost from its mind, like a drop of rain in the open ocean. Once awakened, only instinct would take over, with only a particle remaining of satisfied attainment, just enough to motivate it to rise and do it again.

Sensory receivers in its bulb-shaped eyes suddenly sent signals to its brain, bringing a halt to the intended slumber. A bizarre illumination under the water triggered automatic electrical impulses, resulting in the creature taking a defensive position. Its tentacles, along with other appendages, supported its bulk as it came out of its restful state. Sensory receptors on its thick shell detected vibrations humming through the water, as if some form of communication had been taking place. Also detected by these vibrations was movement by more than one intruder. If the creature had a real attitude like that of a human, it would be considered very angry. It had declared this entire region to be its habitat, and any creature to wander upon it was meant to be destroyed. However, instinct drove the creature to move along the water carefully, altering the coloring of its outer shell to assume the appearance of the rocks in which it traveled along. With each arm, it slowly pulled itself along the rocky forest, carefully nearing the fateful encounter with its new enemy.

****

Denning and Thompson stayed close together. Visibility was quickly shortening, even with the help of the flashlights in their hands and the spotlights from the two vessels overhead. Thompson knew this wasn't the brightest decision she'd made in her fourteen year career. It was specifically mentioned in her training not to waste precious time and resources looking for something that couldn't be found, or wasn't worth finding. In this case, the missing vessel applied to her as both. She wasn't a cold hearted woman. She understood that the loss of these two people must be affecting someone, somewhere, but the reality she recognized was the fact that they clearly were gone, and whether or not the remains of the vessel are discovered should not make any difference.

They were already down for three minutes, and Denning was considerably more than anxious to head back up to the boat. Thompson never really sympathized with his reasons for wanting to return to base, knowing that he was just looking forward to a night of poker with his friends. He was no good at the game, but he enjoyed trying his luck. He had no wife or girlfriend waiting for him, and his immediate family was all the way up in Salt Lake City, Utah. He enjoyed womanizing way too much to settle down, and the idea of women being used as personal gimmicks did not float well with Thompson. While she was not married, she didn't go for the outrageous lifestyle of her diving partner. There was one particular individual in Maine that had her attention for a short time, and even lead to marriage. However, that only lasted seemingly five minutes when he turned out to be hanging out at strip clubs on Friday and Saturday evenings behind her back. Luckily for her, she was already being ordered to a new post in Bermuda at the time, so that made it easy for her to knock out two of his teeth and be out of the state before anyone really had any clue of what happened between them. Luckily, the divorce was quick and easy. Now she was here in Mako's Ridge, looking for a fishing vessel, with her reliable but despicable diving partner, along with Arness. There wasn't much for her to know about him. They first worked together when they were stationed in Bermuda, and they seemed to enjoy each other's company. Like Denning, he took orders well, but unlike Denning, he lived a rather low-key personal life-- less playboy-like.

Denning steadily paddled his flippers, keeping pace about seven feet to the right of Thompson. With the flashlight in his left hand, he shined a light down into the rocky abyss, where it diminished into darkness in the distance. The stormy weather made the skies darker, which in turn took away what little visibility that was left under the water. Denning was not comfortable with this at all. Swimming in these conditions with nearly no visibility was not Coast Guard protocol. However, he was under Thompson's command, and getting her pissed was not something that was easily undone. He shined his light downward and then to his left. There was nothing. There wasn't even any fish. It was a barren wasteland underwater.

Did Steve Hogan actually expect to catch anything out here? Denning thought to himself. He shined his flashlight over to his right and continued paddling forward. The visibility was the same as before. The light shined into darkness, and then there'd be a large rock. After the light moved past that rock there'd be darkness again, and finally another massive formation. This formation was much different from the other rocks in the area, which took more of a pointed stake-like form. This one in particular was more oval, somewhat resembling the shape of a giant pancake. The light generated just enough illumination to catch the overall shape of the structure. Just before he shined the flashlight away, something else caught his eye. Something had moved. He shined the flashlight back toward the rock, but this time he couldn't see anything else. In his mind, he tried to envision what he saw. Whatever it was, it was much thinner than the rock formations, and also it appeared flexible, like a hose. His heart seemed to jump in his chest as his mind came up with a theory for what it was. Perhaps it could be the net used by Hogan and Burke, which supposedly was hooked onto the boat that sunk. Under the water, the net could have got tangled in any bizarre form.

He exhaled; releasing several bubbles to escape to the surface, and then took another breath from his re-breather. He looked to his left to look for Thompson, but she wasn't there. He shined his light ahead of him and realized he must have slowed his pace accidentally because she had gotten ahead of him. At this point, he didn't care. He figured that in the worst case scenario, if they got separated, they'd just swim to the surface where'd they'd meet back at the *Arthur Bishop*. She'd be pissed that they got separated, but Denning was aware that he always got on her nerves anyway. He turned and swam toward the strange formation. With each kick, the massive structure began to take more shape. Whatever coloring he could make out was the same as the rest of the rocks. He also was surprised at how huge this rock was. It was probably sixty feet in diameter, and its surface was different than the other rock formations. Its surface appeared to be…spiny.

****

It lay close to the bottom of the seabed and remained stationary, allowing itself to blend in to its environment. It had found a suitable place to observe the life forms that had awoken it. One intruder dared approach. It was tiny in comparison. The bizarre illumination increased as the enemy drew near, flaring the receptors in its eyes, which had adjusted to the dark space-like environment. The intruder continued to move in and flashed its blinding offensive behavior. It positioned its legs for its ambush strategy and coiled its tentacles like springs. It didn't desire to feed: It desired to kill.

****

Denning neared closer. He was barely twenty yards over the rock by now. Swimming made it harder to get a good look at the object, especially with the darkening water. Now that he found a decent position to observe, he shined his light around the rock formation for the moving object that caught his eye a few moments earlier. He panned it around, but there was no sign of the vessel. He then illuminated the front of the large rock. The front of the massive oval object caught his attention. It wasn't like any rock structure he'd seen. Separated by a number of yards were two huge round formations, like joints, that each connected the main body to smaller, narrower formations that took a curled position, tucked into the front of the rock. He then focused his light in-between the two 'joints'. There were two small objects, each the size of a soccer ball attached to the rock by what appeared to be a pair of antenna. Directly below that was another bizarre feature, which Denning's mind could only compare to the alien mandibles in the movie *Predator.* In the center of these large objects was a large bony formation, which resembled the beak of an eagle. Under his mask, Denning could begin to feel himself sweat…as the beak opened and closed, and the large rock body began to shift.

Just as he was about to turn to swim away, his eyes took notice of one more thing to the side of the object. A moment passed before he realized that that 'one more thing' was actually four more things, each coiled like springs and pointed at him. As quickly as he had taken notice of them, they uncoiled and tore through the water at him, flailing like the many heads of an angry hydra. Denning opened his mouth to shriek, but his voice was muffled by the sound of dozens of air bubbles escaping his lungs into the water. He paddled his arms and kicked his legs to bring himself upward, but the terrifying snake-like arms already encircled him. The next thing he knew, there was a pressure along his waist and abdomen, as one of the huge arms wrapped itself around him like an anaconda. With the flashlight still in hand, he flailed his arms in panic, creating a vast display of light flashes that began to resemble the effects of a flying saucer. The pressure increased, cracking the bottom of Denning's ribcage. After that came a shooting pain from all sides, as something sharp was piercing into him. The arm pulled him downward toward the large mass, which seemed to have moved, and strangely appeared to be looking at him through those large round…eyes. The objects connected to it by use of those 'joints' also began to move and take shape, like huge arms. The end of each arm was a jointed, toothy appendage that opened and closed like pincers, like that of a scorpion…

Or a crab.

The pincers opened and closed repeatedly, as if the ungodly life form was consciously preparing for an attack. And it was. Muffled by the water, Denning released a dull scream which didn't last for long, as the pincers and tentacles tore his body apart like a paper shredder. There was no effort to it. The tentacles pulled his legs from his abdomen, popping them off at the joints, while the pincers repeatedly chopped up his torso like scissors.

****

Lieutenant Thompson had already turned around when she had realized that her diving partner was nowhere to be seen. In her mind she cursed him for disobeying her rules, which required divers to stick with their partners. She could see his light in the distance, and for a while it appeared that he was examining something in particular. For a few minutes as she neared him, Denning's light maintained the same position, moving only as he moved. She knew how little Denning cared for this assignment to begin with, much less the extra minutes they were putting into the dive, so the fact that he appeared to be investigating something intrigued her. From her distance at ninety feet, she could only see a massive rocky structure ahead of him.

Perhaps he found the wreck? She thought to herself. As she got closer, something suddenly changed. The stream of light had gone into a spasm, spinning in every direction possible. Adrenaline fueled her body and she kicked her feet up and down to gain speed. After closing an additional ten yards, she was less than fifty feet away. She slowed to a stop when the light ended its frantic display. Something wasn't right. The light was still moving in circular motions, but much slower, and it appeared to be sinking. Thinking Denning may have dropped it, Thompson shined her own flashlight into the location where Denning was just moments ago. There was nobody there, however there was something else that was strange. She saw that the water where she illuminated was full of a cloudy substance that she could not identify. It was a dark color, but not black like dirt or sludge. She couldn't be certain, but it almost appeared red. In the mist of the cloudy substance was a large quantity of debris. She slowly paddled forward to get a closer look. There was no wood in this debris. Rather, it appeared to be made up of shredded clothing material. She held her light on the mass array of floating substance. As her eyes examined the scene, another object passed by her sights. It was an oxygen tank, the same one Denning was using. Immediately passing by her view was another piece of debris, one of which Thompson could not immediately identify. But after noticing the five jointed digits, as well as the tissue dangling from a round stub, reality struck that it was a hand severed at the wrist. Air bubbles exploded around her mouth piece as she shrieked at the sight.

Her mind had barely any time to comprehend what she had just seen as another thing caught her eye. She noticed movement within the cloud of blood and guts. There was something moving about within them. Multiple something's. They were long and moved like monstrous snakes rising vertically from the bottom of the seabed. Thompson's eyes traced along these long organisms, looking down to their roots of origin: that strange rock formation. It had arms. It had eyes. It moved. It moved towards her. She released another muffled shriek of terror and bolted for the surface.

****

"They should've been back by now," Deputy Drake said. He was still leaning on the railing the stern of his vessel, this time with no coffee. The wind was picking up, and the sky was officially black. Rain was showering down and pounding on his black raincoat. "Do you think they may have found the wreck?"

he asked Arness, who was also beginning to look worried.

"If they did, they'd immediately notify us," he said. "She wouldn't waste her time admiring the scenery." A crack of thunder echoed throughout the night sky. Arness looked at his watch. It had been ten minutes since they went back under. Thompson was always on schedule. This wasn't like her to be late. The bad weather wasn't helping Arness' anxiety which was steadily getting worse. He cursed himself for not voicing the opinion that they should just dock in East Port, spend the night in Mako's Center, and just try again in the morning. Finally, after numerous long moments, his eyes caught sight of light from a flashlight in the distance. It was waving back and forth madly, as if to get their attention. "There it is!" He pointed out to it.

"I see it," Drake said. There was a brief pause, while both men recognized Thompson's voice in the distance, screaming out to them. They couldn't yet make out any words, but immediately knew it was urgent. Without saying a word to each other, they both withdrew to their cabins and electronically pulled up their anchors. Free of the weight that bolted their vessels from the sea floor, both men propelled their boats forward. For communication, each of them clicked their radios. "Could you hear what she was saying?" Drake asked through.

"*Negative,*" Arness responded through radio traffic. "*I only see Thompson. No sign of Denning.*" Within twenty seconds, the boats pulled up near Thompson, who quickly made her way to the nearest one. She was still yelling frantically, almost in a panic. Both Arness and Drake hurried out onto their decks, surprised to see Thompson grabbing the ladder of the Police Vessel, which was nearest to her. Without the distance between them, her panicked screams finally took the form of words:

"THERE'S SOMETHING IN THE WATER!"

She launched herself onto the deck. She had already thrown off her other gear while waiting for the vessels to approach-- she didn't want any extra weight slowing her down.

"Let's get out of here!" She ordered. "Turn the boats around and head for Port!"

"Lieutenant!" Arness yelled from the *Arthur Bishop.* "Where the hell is Denning?"

"Denning's dead!" Thompson shouted back. Both Arness and Drake appeared to freeze in position. All at once, they hysterically responded back:

"What the hell are you talking about?"

"What do you mean he's dead?"

"What the fuck happened down there?"

Thompson's heart pounded harder, and her temper flared under the tremendous pressure and fright. "God damn it, something killed him. I don't know what it is, but it's fucking huge! We need to get out of here now!"

"What the hell are you talking about, Lieut--" Drake's question was silenced with a gasp as he braced himself against the railing after the vessel reared up a few feet. Something had made an impact on the bottom. Whatever it was, it was big. "Holy mother of God!" he exclaimed as he rushed for the cabin. Once inside, he wasted no time pushing the motor to its max, speeding the boat forward and away. Once the vessel was in motion, Drake looked behind him to make sure the *Arthur Bishop* was leaving the scene. And it was, propelling away with intense speed. Maintaining their velocity, both vessels began speeding their way to East Port.

CHAPTER 7

"Did you sleep well, sir?" Napier remarked as he watched Wayne pull into the driveway, late again as usual. He stood on board the upper deck of the *Catcher* with his arms crossed while he leaned against the railing. There was a bit of a breeze in the air left over by the storm that passed over during the previous night, which also caused a drop in the morning temperature. Napier compensated by wearing his old grey sweater. He stood and waited as Wayne took his sweet time walking towards the vessel. He tapped his left hand against his elbow repeatedly, as if this would somehow quench the anxiety he was experiencing. He had spent the early morning looking over his bills, and he barely had enough money in his account to make his truck payment. The small catch made during the past Saturday certainly did not help the matter. It was July, and in a month Jane would be going back to school for her senior year, which would mean she would be in need of school supplies. He still needed a winch for the *Catcher* to reel in the nets, but unfortunately that would have to wait until his other priorities were taken care of. Now he was plenty anxious to see the results in his nets this morning. Mondays were usually good days because they always had an extra day, Sunday, to bring in some catch. And Napier needed a good day. His savings account only held so much money.

"Howdy," Wayne said as he climbed aboard the stern of the vessel. He wore the same damn jeans, t-shirt, and cap, all covered in fish-gut stains, mud, and seaweed. The only thing different was a navy-blue hoodie that he wore over his shirt, and it too had the same signs of dirtiness.

"Morning," Napier said. He throttled his vessel forward out of the dock, aiming it for his buoy in Razortooth Cove. The breeze grew stronger as they pressed against it, and Napier was grateful for this. Wayne had lit a fresh cigarette, and the wind blew the smoke and smell away. *At least I've gotten one blessing today,* Napier thought to himself.

****

"Good Lord, I can't wait until that winch is fixed!" Wayne cursed as both men finished tugging the net on board the deck, unhooking the fish and tossing them into the large rectangular holding container. The net contained as much catch as every other Monday, which brought a mild feeling of relief for Napier. However this was a small net that contained a small fraction of the day's earnings. And he never experienced any trouble with this net; it was the other two that were lacking in results on Saturday, and he was anxious to see what they held today.

"I hope you're not too sore," Napier said. "The other two should be a lot heavier to bring in."

"Well, as long as nobody decided to cut those nets up as well," Wayne remarked. "Have you read the newspapers? I guess Old Hooper's not the only one to find his drift nets torn apart."

"Don't jinx it," Napier said. The two spent the next half-hour laying out a fresh net and marked it with the same buoy. After that work was finished, Napier climbed into the cabin and throttled the *Catcher* out of the cove. Once they were clear, he turned the vessel towards the southeast buoy.

****

"I don't understand it," Napier complained as he climbed back up to the upper deck, leaving Wayne alone with the southeast net, which still had some of its bait still strung to it. There was even less fish than before. Napier's hopes were already dry, as he expected the eastern net to return similar results. He stepped into his cabin and stared through his front window into the open ocean. Was it possible that the fish were migrating elsewhere? Was this his punishment for using driftnets, which he used despite how much he despised them? He pushed away this superstitious thought from his mind. His nets were strategically placed so they would only catch what they were meant to, and they never failed at their goal. Most other fisherman abused the driftnet exemption law that Mako's Center possessed, resulting in the killing of numerous sea creatures that had no value in the local markets.

"Yo, Captain," Wayne called out. "You asleep up there?" Napier realized he was sharing too much time with his thoughts and hadn't throttled the vessel yet.

"My bad," he said. He pressed the throttle forward, causing the engine to rumble as the propellers pushed the *Catcher* in a northern direction toward the east buoy. He continued to stare out into the ocean as he drove the vessel. The sky had finally begun to clear up, and the wind had subsided. His thoughts were interrupted by the sound of Wayne climbing up the ladder behind him. He didn't bother to look back as his fishing partner stepped onto the upper deck and opened the door to the small cabin.

"No need to fall on your sword, Rick," Wayne said, trying to sound somewhat philosophical. He knew what was on Napier's mind…at least he knew some of the things. "These things happen to every fisherman at some point. Just give it enough time. You'll get your boat fixed up and we'll be back to our normal fishing routines instead of using these drift nets." Napier didn't say anything back for a couple of minutes, as he thought over Wayne's words, 'these things happen to every fisherman'… That was one of Napier's troubles; he wasn't meant to be a fisherman. While he was definitely meant to be out on his boat in the ocean, it was to be studying sea life, not trapping it in nets for a store owner to cut up. He didn't begrudge the fishing industry, it just wasn't what he felt he was born to do. He continued to stare into the horizon and drive the vessel.

It wasn't a very long trip from the southeastern buoy to the eastern one. Napier always saved this one for last, as it was the closest one to East Port, where he would meet up with Mr. Gary to make their transaction. Wayne had stepped outside onto the deck as they neared their destination. Both fishermen looked ahead and saw the black buoy bobbing within the water, signaling the location of the net. However, their eyes went beyond the buoy into the distant horizon, beholding the sight of a Coast Guard Cutter anchored nearly a half-mile off of Mako's Center's east coast. The cutter, labeled on the port side as the *USCGC Ryback,* was a National Security Cutter, stretching over three-hundred feet from bow to stern. On the deck was a large cannon; a Bofors 57mm gun, a weapon capable of tearing a ship of equal size to bits. To their view, the enormous ship almost looked like a silver grain of rice in the light blue blanket of water. The sound of multiple boat engines caught their attention, and both men were surprised to see several smaller Coast Guard vessels, roughly the same size as the *Catcher*, cruising the northeast corner of the island. Napier's mind was no longer dwelling on his problems; rather he was dying to know what such a large Coast Guard unit was doing in Mako's Ridge.

"What in the hell is this?" he said. Wayne stepped back into the cabin.

"I don't have a single clue," he said. He looked westward toward the island. East Port was almost visible from their location, and it appeared a couple of the Coast Guard vessels were approaching that area. "There might be something happening on the island."

"Could be," Napier said. He watched as a couple vessels were clearly heading northeast. There was only one thing of interest northeast of Mako's Center, and that was Mako's Edge. Then a thought suddenly lit up in his mind. "There was a Coast Guard vessel that was working with our police department in an effort to locate Hogan's boat," he said. "I wonder if this has something to do with that."

"Oh, hell," Wayne cursed. "What if that vessel hit a rock and sunk too? We'll have the Guard here for a week." Napier shook his head in disagreement.

"They wouldn't send a cutter for that," he explained. His curiosity was getting the better of him. He wanted to head into port to find out what was going on. "Let's hurry up and bring in this net. Then we'll figure out what this is all about."

****

Napier didn't dwell on the fact that the east net contained even less catch than the other net, which would result in another tiny paycheck when money was needed the most. This particular occurrence with the Coast Guard had really intrigued him, and he wanted to get in touch with Chief Bondy. He steered the *Catcher* into its usual position in East Port, and after bringing it to a stop he realized Mr. Gary was nowhere to be seen. Then it struck him that he forgot to give him a phone call stating that he was on his way into the dock. He was too interested in what was going on around the island. He could see the chief's black police pickup in the large square-shaped parking area. Down in the sandy area was the chief himself, talking to a gentleman in a white uniform. Throughout the beach were other individuals, wearing blue uniforms, who appeared to be keeping curious onlookers at bay. Napier stepped out of the cabin and looked down at Wayne, who stood on the main deck.

"Hey Wayne," he called down. Wayne looked up at him, giving his attention. "Would you give Mr. Gary a call for me please and tell him we're ready for him to pick up these fish. It totally slipped my mind."

"Sure thing," Wayne said. He knew his boss was curious as to what was going on. Napier climbed down his ladder and stepped onto the dock that he parked next to. He began to approach Bondy, but carefully due to the fact that he wasn't sure if he'd be stopped by any Coast Guard personnel. Not standing too far away from the chief was Deputy Drake, who was standing beside two Coast Guard personnel, one of which was a woman with red hair. The other was a towering individual who stood nearly a foot taller than the deputy. Even at the distance he was away from them, Napier could see the tired expressions in each person's face, implying they had either had a long night, or simply didn't get their morning coffee. Napier neared to within twenty feet of Bondy when two Coast Guard personnel stepped in front of him from the left, seemingly out of nowhere. Both men had a large muscular physique, and appeared more like bouncers working in a local bar had it not been for the Coast Guard uniforms they wore. They each held up a hand, signaling for Napier to stop.

"Excuse us, sir," one of them said. "We're going to have to ask you to turn back, please. There is official business being conducted here."

"He's okay! Let him pass!" Bondy's voice called out. The two men stepped aside and allowed Napier to continue walking up to the chief. The other individual appeared to be a high ranking member of the Coast Guard. He looked to be aging around fifty, had a thick mustache, stood at about six foot even, and wore several medals on the left breast of his white uniform jacket.

"Good afternoon, gentlemen," Napier said. He immediately noticed the serious expressions in both men before any words were spoken by either one. The Coast Guard individual gave Napier a strict stare, wondering why a civilian was interfering with a formal discussion.

"Who the hell is this?" he demanded to know from Bondy.

"Commander," the chief began, "this is Rick Napier. He's a unique fisherman around these parts with a distinct knowledge of the sea. I suppose you can say I've unofficially deputized him. He's helped me on occasions in which I've been shorthanded." He turned to face Rick. "This is Commander James Tracy."

"How do you do, sir?" Napier extended his hand.

"Hello, Mr. Napier," Commander Tracy greeted back. "I hope you'll pardon my rudeness a second ago. I didn't realize you were a helping hand to the Chief here."

"Don't worry about it," Napier said. "So what's going on here? Why all the Coast Guard boats, as well as a Coast Guard cutter?" There was a brief moment of silence, as if Bondy and Tracy were trying to decide who should answer.

"There was another unfortunate incident last night at Mako's Edge," Bondy spoke up. "One of the divers that was searching for Hogan's boat was killed."

"My goodness," Napier exclaimed. "What in the hell happened?"

"Your guess is as good as mine," Tracy said.

"Did the other divers give any testimony as to what happened?" Napier said. There was another pause from the Commander and the Chief. Tracy crossed his arms and breathed a deep sigh.

"I suppose you could say that," he said. He glanced over at the individuals standing near Deputy Drake, particularly the woman. His eyes returned to their stern expression. He looked back to

Napier. “But I don’t suppose it’s anything we can go on.” His tone clearly indicated that the debriefing he received of the incident was insufficient to his liking. Napier was almost nervous to ask his next question.

“Well…what did they say?” he looked to Bondy to answer this one. He too appeared disgruntled as to what the answer was.

“According to the Lieutenant, they continued diving late into the night. They were supposedly wrapping up their search when one of the divers…” he stopped, as if he didn’t want to finish the story. Both his and Tracy’s facial expressions spelled disbelief for what he was going to explain next. “The Lieutenant thinks she saw some sort of sea creature under the water in Mako’s Edge. She claims it was like an octopus or something.”

“The word ‘Behemoth’ was used,” Tracy added. “Personally, I think it’s all horseshit. They had already been out way longer than they should have. And in those weather conditions, they should’ve called off the search sooner anyway.”

“But that’s why we have so many vessels out here,” said Bondy. “The high ranking U.S. military officials freaked when they heard the report of a massive object under the water. And who was even more freaked were the politicians. Apparently they’re more worried that it could be a North Korean submarine, or something-- even though these waters are a bit too shallow for something like that. But that’s Washington for you.” Finally, it made sense to Napier why there was a massive Coast Guard cutter off the coast of Mako’s Center.

“We’ve got several cruisers out there doing a radar scope of the area,” Tracy continued. “So far, nothing’s been reported.” Napier now understood why the Commander appeared aggravated by this whole event, beyond the obvious fact that a lost Coast Guard diver was no laughing matter. The story given by the Lieutenant of last night’s operation sparked a massive Coast Guard investigation that required many expensive resources, including the cutter. And now it was beginning to appear that it was all for nothing. A commotion from the crowd gathered the attention from the three individuals. The crowd had split in half to make way for the mayor and his suited staff, who walked from the parking lot onto the sandy beach. Mayor Chuck Graford was just a bit older than the Commander, but his features made him appear much older. His head was balding, leaving a horseshoe shaped curve of hair on the sides and back of his head. He wore a grey suit and blue tie, and didn't seem to mind getting sand onto his black dress shoes.

"Good afternoon, gentlemen," he greeted.

"Hello, sir," Bondy said. "Sir, I'd like to introduce to you Commander James Tracy. He's in charge of the operation." Bondy always took a very formal tone when around the mayor, who was the very individual who appointed him chief and was the only person who had any real authority over him on the island.

"Pleasure to meet you, Commander," Mayor Graford said. He always had a very enthusiastic tone to his voice. Bondy always figured he thought of himself as a celebrity entertainer rather than a town politician. He shook the Commander's hand and then observed the Coast Guard vessels in the area. "So is there anything to report regarding this?" This question was directed at Bondy.

"So far, nothing," the chief said. The mayor looked to the Commander.

"How much longer do you think you'll need, Commander?" he asked. "We've got a big week ahead of us, business-wise. There is a fishing tournament taking place tomorrow. We'll have many fishermen from all over the world coming to this location to snag the big one. In addition, they'll be bringing their families, which means the beaches are going to be flooding with tourists." The Commander had to keep his composure when dealing with politicians, especially ones who couldn't seem to take into account the reason behind the investigation.

"We'll probably move out by the end of the day," Tracy said.

"Sir," Bondy cut in. "Just to be on the safe side, I'm gonna have all of my deputies on duty tomorrow." The mayor chuckled.

"That's perfectly fine," he said. "Well, as long as this is over with by tonight, then tomorrow's event will be perfectly set to go. Keep up the good work, gentlemen." He turned around and headed back to his limousine, followed by his staff. It was common for him to make these brief appearances. Just enough time for someone to snap a picture for the local newspaper and make it appear he was doing all he could to assist in the investigation. Commander Tracy continued his bitter stare even after Graford was out of sight.

"Of course he doesn't give a shit that someone is dead," he said. Bondy, on the other hand, had no problem expressing his relief that the mayor took off.

"I'm just happy he didn't stick around long enough for us to have to explain Lieutenant Lisa Thompson's report." Napier, who had stepped aside when the mayor arrived to speak with the two officials, suddenly looked up with extreme interest. There was familiarity with that name, Lisa Thompson.

"Excuse me," he interrupted, "You said 'Lisa Thompson'?"

"That's correct," Tracy said, pointing in her direction. She was the redhead Coast Guard woman standing near Drake. Napier immediately recognized her. Memories flooded back into Napier's mind. Thompson was his high school sweetheart, before Katherine. They had dated throughout most of his four years of high school, up until prom, during which he took a somewhat adulterous turn in his life when he dumped her to be with Katherine. Seeing Lisa as a mature woman rather than a teenage girlfriend in high school was...different. She appeared... almost more beautiful.

"Wow," he said. Luckily, Tracy and Bondy were caught up in their own conversation, and didn't seem to notice Napier's silent staring. "I'm going to talk to Deputy Drake," he said. It was really just an excuse to get closer to the Lieutenant. A quiet voice in his mind warned him that there was no luck to be had. After dumping her for Katherine the way he did, it wouldn't be surprising if Lisa wouldn't be too pleased to see him. He remembered their breakup. It mainly consisted of a sobbing Lisa Thompson throwing things at him after learning of his unfaithfulness to the relationship. He mentally argued against that voice in his brain. *I was young. I was a damned teenager. Plus, I ended up marrying the woman I left her for, so therefore I have no regrets.* "Hello, Deputy," he called out to Drake, although his attention was mainly on Thompson.

"Hi, Rick," Drake said.

"So I hear you've had a rough night. Finding sea monsters out near Mako's Edge are we?" he joked. Immediately, he mentally scolded himself for making that remark, as he momentarily forgot it was Lisa's debriefing that suggested that the diver had been killed by a creature in the water. *Not exactly what I had in mind to start this out,* he thought. Deputy Drake leaned in close, trying to keep his voice down as to not offend the Lieutenant.

"I'm honestly clueless as to what happened," he said. "One minute we're getting ready to come on home, the next minute she's screaming that something in the water killed Denning."

"Hey jackass!" Thompson shouted out. Neither Drake nor Napier was certain which of them she was yelling at. "What about the thing that hit your boat?!"

"Listen, Lieutenant," Drake started. "Did you even pay attention to the waters surrounding Mako's Edge? I'm lucky I didn't smash into any rocks in my hurry to get you out of the water."

"You hit a rock?" Napier said, surprised. "Is your boat okay?"

"Damn you," Thompson exclaimed, angrily. "That was no rock. I saw something down there, and whatever it was, it was enormous and alive." While Napier was intrigued by what she was saying, he was more curious as to whether or not she recognized him. Deputy Drake shrugged his shoulders. He didn't know what to say. Suddenly he heard the chief call out to him, ordering him over by where he was standing. He quickly followed his orders, and happily. It got him away from the lieutenant, whom he thought was losing her mind. Napier suddenly found himself without an excuse to be near his old girlfriend. He figured there was nothing to gain and thought about heading back to his boat, being as Mr. Gary should be arriving any minute. As he was about to leave, he noticed Thompson making a beeline right towards him. He wasn't sure what to say, so he figured he'd try a formal approach.

"Is there anything I can do to help--" his words were stopped suddenly by a sharp smack to the face. It was a damned vicious impact too, causing Napier to stumble back a couple steps. "Holy mother of ass!"

"I see you're as much of a dick as you were back in school!" She said, barely keeping her voice below a shout. Napier kept his cool, which was not something he was good at. She recognized him alright. He thought of their high school breakup, which was probably his best practice at being calm in tense situations.

"I'm sorry for my remark about the sea monster," he said. "I just was making conversation with Deputy Dra--" Another smack struck him on the right cheek, again catching him off guard. He could feel his temper brewing within him. His interest in Thompson was quickly diminishing. "Okay," he said, holding his hand to his jaw. He kept his words slow and spaced apart. "Don't you think this could get you in trouble with your superiors, slapping me like this? A civilian?"

"I'm probably facing court-martial anyway," she said, darting toward him. Napier braced for another smack, but instead she walked past him. To his surprise, he wasn't feeling anger towards her, rather sympathy. A person died under her supervision, and due to her testimony, everyone in the Coast Guard was beginning to think of her as a lunatic. Her reputation and career were at stake. And the worst part of it was she knew she saw something, and for some reason the Coast Guard wasn't able to locate it on radar. He stood silent for a minute and watched her walk away. As he looked in the distance, he noticed a pickup truck parked near the *Catcher*.

"Oh shit," he said. He made his way to the boat after recognizing Mr. Gary, who was waiting patiently to make their transaction.

CHAPTER 8

Dr. Isaac Wallack sat alone, smoking a six-inch long, curved pipe, shaped like a rippling sea serpent. The cauldron end of the pipe where the tobacco burned was shaped like the mouth of a dragon, while the rest of the pipe resembled its scaly body up to the mouthpiece. He sat alone in his private office, purposely secluding himself from the rest of the world. His maple desk had several papers scattered about, mostly notes dedicated to his hybrid specimens which he had been working on for years in the Atlantic Warren Laboratory, up until recently. After the recent incident in one of the lab chambers, which resulted in the escape of the most expensive hybrid experiment, Colonel Richard Salkil demanded the funds be eliminated from Wallack's projects. One terrible accident had left the ambitious scientist without any money, making further progress nearly impossible. The United States Government provided all of the funding and resources to make his dreams a reality, but unfortunately the Colonel didn't see eye-to-eye with him, and filed a report to Washington to shut down the project. Even the massive laboratory was taken away from him. He would have to start over completely, and the worst part was he didn't have the funds or resources. The doctor thought about Project 241, wondering what became of it. Colonel Salkil was convinced it had died at sea, due to the fact that it was never able to test its instincts and fend for itself. It was always given the nutrients it needed by its creators, and Salkil believed it wasn't able to hunt food for itself. Wallack knew better. However, after an extensive naval radar hunt for the specimen produced no results, he too began to believe that Project 241 had perished to the bottom of the sea.

A knock on his office door quickly drew Wallack's attention. "Come in." The door opened, revealing a man in his late thirties, dressed in a white dress shirt tucked into black pants, not wearing any tie. It was the doctor's general assistant, Jeb Keith. He held a newspaper tucked under his right arm. After the military confiscated everything, Jeb continued to work at Wallack's side. It was as if he had sworn allegiance to the scientist. He had assisted him throughout the years on board the Atlantic Warren Laboratory, and was one of the few people who took his ideas seriously, after several others laughed at the prospect of what Wallack believed he could accomplish. Jeb took a step into the office, taking a few quick glances at the numerous photographs on the walls, which almost appeared as a diagram illustrating the progress they had made with the hybrids. He saw his employer, or at least a broken shell of him, slumped at his desk staring at his hundreds of pages of notes. In the midst of those scattered papers were two empty beer bottles, and a third rested in Wallack's hand. However, Jeb believed he carried news that would bring back that hope and ambition to the doctor once again.

"What is it?" Wallack said half-heartedly through a few puffs of his pipe. His words had slowed, perhaps a combined effect of the alcohol and broken spirit.

"Sir, you may want to read this," Jeb said as he placed the newspaper on the desk. The doctor didn't budge. He simply looked down at the paper, unwilling to gather the tiny amount of energy and focus to pick it up and read the article.

"What's so important?" he grumbled. He took another puff of his pipe, blowing smoke rings that clouded the small office. Jeb sighed and picked up the newspaper.

"There was a incident in Mako's Ridge regarding a sunken vessel. It sank near the island of Mako's Edge, and there was a report that a Coast Guard diver was killed during the search for it," he explained, holding the front of the article up to his mentor. Wallack's expression remained about the same: Detached and depressed. Jeb wasn't sure if it was the alcohol or the disconnection from reality, but he immediately knew the doctor wasn't able to piece together what he was getting at with this news. Finally he threw the newspaper back on the desk, dispersing several pages of the notes. "Just read the damn thing!" he demanded. Wallack's expression finally changed. His eyes widened in brief shock, and he scooted a few inches back into his seat. It wasn't like Jeb to speak to him in this manner. Wallack decided not to challenge his younger assistant. He overcame his detached state-of-mind and picked up the newspaper. The title was in a large bold font: **More Tragedy Strikes Mako's Ridge!**

He read the article, which recapped the bizarre wreckage of Steve Hogan's fishing vessel. The article continued on to describe the Coast Guard operation to locate the vessel and any possible bodies, which resulted in the death of Officer Denning. Jeb watched Wallack's facial expression suddenly become alive, and he knew he was reading the section of the article summing up Lieutenant Lisa Thompson's report of what she saw. The doctor now summed up what his assistant had been trying to explain to him. These strange incidents were happening at Mako's Edge, the location in which the secondary laboratory was located to house Project 241.

"Oh my God," he said with excitement. He looked up to Jeb, who was also smiling. "It found its way home! It's there! It's alive!" It made so much sense. As a much smaller creature, it nearly escaped into the rocky waters of Mako's Edge. It appeared to treat the area as its natural habitat, blending into the rough environment. "Why didn't I think of it before?" He stood up with the paper still in hand.

"We need to contact the government," Jeb said. "If we can recapture *Architeuthis Brachyura*, perhaps we can get our funding back from the government. Then we'll be able to continue your experiments." Wallack stood quietly for a few moments, thinking over the prospect.

"Thanks to the Colonel, that's not likely to happen," he explained. "When he arrived at the laboratory for his inspection, he immediately detested 241 after I explained it to him. He didn't think the military was ready for such a massive hybrid, rather, he didn't think it could be controlled."

"So what do we do?" Jeb asked. Wallack already had the

answer in mind before Jeb even asked his question.

"We're going to place a call to Redford Gibson," he said. He searched his pockets for his cell phone, but could not remember where he had placed it. He had been an isolated, unsocial, drunken wreck for the last few days. "Get me the phone," he demanded from Jeb, who quickly left the office to retrieve a cordless phone from the lobby. Without military assistance, Wallack was forced to resort to his own resources to track down his creation and hopefully recapture it. He had plenty of his own money saved, enough to hire a team of mercenaries to complete the mission.

Redford Gibson was a hardened ex-marine whom Wallack had hired previously to do his 'dirty work'. Nearly a year ago, a team of Nigerian cartel members stole precious materials from a small vulnerable supply ship that didn't contain security personnel. When the government took too long to begin an operation to resolve the matter, Gibson and his tough-as-nails team of ex-military gun-for-hires were quick to track down the Nigerians before they reached their destination. Not one was spared, which Wallack intended to serve as a warning to anyone who dared to attempt to interfere with his projects. For the right price, Gibson was more than willing to attempt any assignment. And Wallack believed he had just the right amount of money. He was going to recapture his creation, or go broke trying.

"Sir?" Jeb said, gaining Wallack's attention as he walked back into the office. "We may be able to afford the mercenaries, but we may not be able to acquire other resources for this particular mission. We won't have a large enough boat to hunt down the specimen."

"Don't worry about that," Wallack said. He took the phone from his assistant. "We'll conduct personal checks on the locals living in Mako's Center. Sadly, there are times that it's necessary to just take what you need from those who have it." He dialed a series of numbers on the phone and held it to his ear. It rang twice before a rough grizzled voice answered on the other line. Wallack's lips formed a devilish smile. "Mr. Gibson? It's Dr. Isaac Wallack from Atlantic Warren Laboratory. I have a proposition for you..."

CHAPTER 9

Nic Kelly took a swig of his root beer while his colleague, David Wellers sat across from him, looking over a dinner menu. It had been suggested to them by many of the island residents that the restaurant, Fast Fillet, was a great place for tourists to dine. Kelly and Wellers didn't think of themselves as tourists, as they had come to Mako's Ridge to check out the newly discovered cave in Mako's Edge. The Geology Institute of Georgia, in conjunction with the University of Florida, requested research be conducted of the new discovery. While they appeared more like young thrill seekers than scientists, both Kelly and Wellers held Master Degrees in Speleology, with a particular interest in underground and underwater caves. Both men had exceptional experience in scuba diving. They explored underwater caves located in Alaska, such as the El Capitan Cave, which was the largest in that state. In addition, they explored countless locations in South America, such as Cueva de los Tayos in the Morona-Santiago province of Ecuador, and Toca da Boa Vista in Brazil, which was the largest known cave in the southern hemisphere. Now they were excited to be the first to dive into the unnamed cave leading into Mako's Edge, despite the delays resulting from the incidents taking place at the rocky island which prevented them from doing their job the last two days. The Coast Guard had cleared out, and by the looks of it, the two explorers would finally be able to conduct their search tomorrow.

The Fast Fillet was a privately owned restaurant located almost in the dead center of town. Like most food service businesses on the island, it served mainly seafood recipes. Chicken and beef meals were also on the menu, but at a higher retail price than in the mainland. The restaurant was particularly crowded this evening. Several sporting fishermen had come to the island for the Annual Bailey Fishing Tournament, a yearly event which brought many thousands of dollars to the local businesses in Mako's Center. Each year, hundreds of sportsmen fish off the coast of the island in a competition to get the biggest fish. Last year, the competition was won by an Australian contestant who hooked a four-hundred pound marlin on the north side, creating a new record.

"I hope he gets here soon," Nic said, referring to Old Hooper. The cranky old fisherman was due to briefly meet them here at the restaurant to specify terms of tomorrow's trip, namely the time of departure and the length of time he would have to wait as they begun studying the underwater geography. In addition, they both had a suspicion that the bastard would also try to renegotiate to increase his pay. Old Hooper didn't have a cell phone, so the discussions had to be made in person.

"He'll show," David said. He placed his menu down on the rectangular shaped table, having decided what he was going to order.

"Talking about me?" A deep, croaky voice called out from the crowded restaurant aisle. Both scientists took notice of Old Hooper as he walked to their table from the bar area. He was dressed in his usual: muddy old Carhart vest over a black long-sleeve shirt, which thanks to his beer gut was barely tucked into his blue jeans. They were barely blue due to the amount of dirt that covered them. His face wasn't much better. He clearly hadn't shaved in two weeks, and he didn't spout a good beard. It was patchy, with plenty of empty areas. The stains of dirt on his face only added to the filth. He held a beer in hand, dripping from the tip of the bottle as he held it nearly horizontally. Both scientists were not thrilled with the idea of hiring him for the job, but unfortunately, he was the only one who didn't mind driving his boat into the rocky waters of Mako's Edge.

"Hi," Nic greeted. Normally he shook a man's hand on these occasions, but the stench made him think otherwise. However, it was in his nature to be as polite as possible. "You may take a seat at our table if you like." Old Hooper advanced for the seat opposite Nic. David had no intention of sitting next to this human waste bucket. He quickly slid out of his seat and scooted to Nic's side of the table, just as Hooper sat down.

"Let's make this quick," the old fisherman said. *Yes please,* David mouthed the words to himself.

"Okay," Nic began. "We'd like to be at the location by noon. It is supposed to be a nice sunny day tomorrow, so the extra illumination will help us locate the exact position of the cave. We're going to have to get as close to the island as we can to minimize the amount we'll have to swim."

"I can't make you any guarantees there, boy," Hooper spat out a few suds from his mouth. "I may be crazy enough to go out there, but the rocks get worse the closer you get to the island itself. So if you want to *minimize* the likeliness you'll have to swim back here to Mako's Center if we sink, you'll just have to deal with the fact that I can only get you within two hundred yards." Nic struggled to keep himself from cussing the old fisherman out. *Why does this prick have to be our only boating option?* He pleaded with God in his mind. Hooper took another slug of his beer, which was going on empty. He nearly slammed it down on the table, as if he was slugging shots at a drinking competition. "Unless you have the coin," he concluded his statement.

"Dude," David spoke up. "We're already paying you a thousand dollars."

"That's the fee for any kind of regular diving," Hooper argued. "This is a different matter. My boat, and subsequently my life, is in jeopardy with this job. Therefore, I'm upping the cost. Unless you want to try your luck with the other fishermen on this island." Both scientists knew very well that he didn't care one bit about the risks. He took the exact same risks just to make a few extra bucks netting fish off the island. Nic exhaled sharply.

"We can increase your pay up to fifteen hundred," he bargained. "It's not going any higher than that. The institute simply won't allow it." Hooper chuckled.

"Obviously the *institute*," he held up both of his hands and formed quote signs with his middle and index fingers, "doesn't give a shit about your stupid explorer thing." He took a long pause, waiting for Nic to up the offer. When nothing was said, Hooper finally decided to put his terms to plain English. "Two grand is the deal."

"The hell with you!" David accidentally let his tongue slip. Nic's whole body notably tensed for a moment, resulting from his colleague's mishap. Hooper began to stand up.

"Well, you know how where to find me if you change your mind," he said.

"Whoa, hold on there a sec, friend," called another voice from the crowd. Old Hooper and the scientists looked to the man who stepped up to their table, whom none of them recognized. He was dressed rather fashionably, with blue Wrangler jeans along with a dark green shirt under a brown sleeveless leather vest, along with brown cowboy boots and a black safari hat. He wore a necklace which contained an inch-and-a-half long white ivory shark tooth, resembling that of a great white.

"Who the hell are you?" Old Hooper immediately shot his mouth off. His trailing voice gathered the attention of numerous people dining around them, who looked in their direction as if they expected a fight to go down. The stranger, dressed like Crocodile Dundee, simply lit up a big smile.

"Perhaps you've heard of me," he said. Nic and David were both surprised that his accent was purely American, when they were expecting it to be Australian. "My name is Rein. Ryan Rein."

"Are you supposed to be a movie star?" Hooper's tone remained aggressive.

"Shark hunter guy," David identified him.

"Poacher," Nic whispered under his breath, concealing his words with a cough. Rein lit up another celebrity-style smile.

"I wouldn't use the word poacher there, sir," he said to Nic, who sat silent, slightly embarrassed that his voice was still heard. "Sorry, I just have a good ear. Goes with the nature of hunting." Rein continued.

"What can we do for you, Mr. Rein?" Nic asked, not too successful in hiding his disinterest in the poacher's presence.

"I'll get right to it. I understand you gentlemen have a transaction to go to Mako's Edge." Nic stared down at the table, unsure on how to answer that based on their recent conversation with Old Hooper.

"How do you know that?" Old Hooper cut in.

"Mako's Center isn't a big place, bud. I've been around town, and fishermen around here talk... a lot," Rein said. "Also, I couldn't help but overhear what you chaps were talking about just a minute ago. Like I said a minute ago: Good ear."

"Damn pricks can't mind their own damn business," Hooper nearly shouted, more to himself. "It doesn't matter. These boys here don't seem to want to withdraw the proper amount of money from their mattresses."

"Whoa, give them a break, chief," Rein said. "I understand that these guys are working on a strict budget. There's only so much they can pay you."

"Then there's only so much service I'm willing to provide," Old Hooper glared at Nic, whose face was beginning to turn red with anger.

"Before we get hasty," Rein said, noticing the increasing tension at the table, "How would you like it if I put down three thousand dollars, in addition to the grand they were initially gonna pay you?" Suddenly all three sets of eyes turned to the shark hunter, each expressing pure amazement.

"Four grand, huh?" Old Hooper smirked.

"What's the catch here?" Nic asked. Under the table, David kicked his shoe into his colleague's leg, mouthing the words *Shut up! What are you doing?* He didn't care why this semi-celebrity was assisting them, he was just glad he was doing it.

"The catch is..." he paused, as if for effect, "I'll be going with you." Old Hooper's normal response to any request like this would be 'go fuck yourself,' but a large offer of cash money made him think otherwise.

"Why do you need to tag along with this expedition?" Nic asked.

"Damned great whites chewed up a third of my beloved vessel," Rein said. "She's now in the shop."

"I think Nic meant, 'what is your reason?'" David decided to pitch in. Rein chuckled.

"Didn't you hear the news? The Coast Guard lady said

something was living under the water over there. I've been dying for a good hunt lately, and I think it's lurking over in those waters. Whatever it is, it tore a Coast Guard diver to shreds, and I want to find it for myself and put a harpoon through its eye." Old Hooper couldn't care less for what he was saying, as long as the money was real. Nic, on the other hand, already thought this poacher was out of his mind.

"I don't think there's anything over there," he said. "The Coast Guard already did a search…"

"They were looking for submersibles, genius!" Rein's voice rose a bit. "All they took away from the commanding officer's testimony was that there was a large object moving under the water, which caused the government to act like morons once again."

"Listen," Old Hooper interrupted. "Let's cut the bullshit. I really don't care about sea monsters or submarines or friggin underwater caves. If you have the money, then according to these two schoolboys," he pointed at the scientists, "we'll be leaving at noon tomorrow. But there'd better be some cash up front…" Rein slapped a small brick of cash on the table in front of the old grimy fisherman.

"That's half," he said. "You'll get the rest from me when we get back from our trip."

"Wait," Nic held up his hands. "How is this gonna work tomorrow?"

"It's easy," Rein explained. "Old Hooper here will drive us on out there in his fishing boat. You guys go do your cave swimming, while I do myself a bit of monster fishing."

"Enough of this," Old Hooper stood up. "East Port, tomorrow at noon, all three of you. Don't be late." He walked away, stopping at the bar table for another beer before exiting the restaurant. Ryan Rein also began walking away, but not before giving a small salute to the scientists.

"You're welcome," he said to them. Nic and David sat silently, not noticing the waitress approaching to take their order.

CHAPTER 10

Napier sat at his kitchen table, wiping the sleep from his eyes as he looked over his stack of bills, which piled nearly a foot high. At 10:30 P.M., the red mug of black coffee was not effective in keeping him from getting drowsy. Jane, being a teenager, was wide awake in her bedroom surfing the internet on her laptop. Napier yawned and wished he still had some of that young energy to stay up and focus on his budgeting. But what he wished for more than that was a way out of his struggling payments. Today had been another bad fishing day, and unfortunately there was no money to be made tomorrow, as no drift nets were allowed to be set up along the island for the duration of the fishing tournament. He had already converted much of his savings account money into his checking account to pay for many of these bills, and now he was concerned as to whether he would have enough to pay through the next month. He always vowed to keep away from credit cards, due to having witnessed many friends and family fall into a seemingly endless pit of debt by using them. But now he was beginning to fear that he may have to turn to those malignant cards to keep afloat. There was also the option of moving, which he also hated. He had grown to love Mako's Center, and he also knew Jane would be upset if they moved. He quietly continued sitting, resting his chin on his hand, and stared at the white envelope pile through glassy eyes. Sleep was moving in on him like a siege, and his resistance to it was nearly gone.

"*These things happen to every fisherman at some point,*" he quoted Wayne aloud to himself. He brushed the electric and propane bills to the side, brushing them past the large stack. This did nothing to ease his frustration, nor his financial concerns. However, those downbeat feelings were able to be cast aside when a sudden knock on the front door shocked Napier out of his daze. He quickly shuffled out of his seat and walked into the living room area where the front door was located. "Who's knocking after ten-friggin-thirty at night?" he vented as he twisted the knob. The door swung outward, and there stood Lieutenant Lisa Thompson. She was dressed in civilian clothes, which included Wrangler jeans, brown boots, and a red tank top, which outlined her womanly features. Napier reacted with a flabbergasted "whoa" upon first sight. For a moment, he wondered if he had actually dozed off and was dreaming. "Uhh, hi," he managed to get some words out.

"Hi," Lisa said. Her voice was low and disheartened, which also showed in her facial expressions. "Long day, huh?" There was a minor slur in her words, which led Napier to believe she had consumed a bit of alcohol.

"Yes, I'd say it was-- still is," Napier said, still surprised to see her at his front step. He wasn't quite sure what else to say. Rather, his mind was trying to figure out why a high school sweetheart who hated his guts was now suddenly at his house at ten-forty in the evening. He glanced at a clock that was visible in the kitchen. "Listen, are you aware of what time it is?"

"Only ten-forty," she said. Without warning, she stepped through the doorway past Napier into the house. He stood like a statue, continuing to look out the open doorway, his confusion illustrated in his facial expression.

"Come in," he whispered under his breath. He shut the door and then saw that Thompson had taken a seat on a couch in the living room. *You've got to be kidding me!* He nearly screamed in his mind. He figured there was nothing to look forward to from this visit. Ever since his senior year, a clear-headed Thompson certainly wanted nothing to do with him, except perhaps slap him some more. And now this time he figured she was intoxicated, which would make her hate him even more if he 'took advantage' of any drunken behavior. With all of this in mind, he knew there was nothing to gain from this visit. All he wanted was to go to his bedroom and sleep soundly until the next morning. "Yes, it is ten-forty," he said. "That's twenty minutes to eleven. Does that help with the time clock in your head?" Lisa laughed, almost hard, while trying to keep sitting up straight.

"You were always a night owl," she continued to laugh. Napier bit his lip.

"Yeah okay, when we dated eighteen years ago…as *teenagers*, I may have been one." He briefly paused to mentally arrange his sentences. "But now I'm a grown-up. One who likes to go to bed around nine-thirty at night, rather than one-in-the-morning. One who doesn't like people barging their way in when he'd like to be asleep." The sound of footsteps interrupted him, and he looked up the stairway to see Jane coming down. She obviously heard the commotion downstairs, and wondered who was in the living room with her father. Wearing a long white t-shirt and small blue shorts, she quickly shot her dad a puzzled look upon seeing Thompson sitting on the living room couch.

"Ummm…hi," she muttered after a long pause.

"Hi, Jane," Napier said. He gestured to the lieutenant. "Jane, this is Lieutenant Lisa Thompson." He then gestured to his daughter. "Lieutenant, this is my lovely daughter Jane." Thompson looked up to Jane, with a surprising sharp concentration.

"Hello, Jane," she said while struggling to suppress her troubling thoughts. She forced a smile. "It's so nice to meet you." Jane also forced a smile in the midst of the awkwardness.

"Nice to meet you too," she said. Her eyes went to her dad, which sent a message without words: *Why do you have a woman here so late, I wonder?* Napier knew the inappropriate thoughts his daughter was thinking, and quickly shot her a look in return, which she understood as meaning: *No, you little brat, it's nothing like that!*

"Ummm… listen Jane," he said. "Go ahead and do…whatever it is you do in your room upstairs. I need to talk to this lady." *And get her out of my house,* his thoughts finished the sentence. Jane turned and went back upstairs, covering her mouth with her hand to conceal her laughter. With his daughter back in her room, Napier felt he could now focus on getting Thompson out of his house. He turned to face her, prepared to simply say 'listen, I'd appreciate it if you would be on your merry way'. But when he noticed her sadness, it stopped him in his tracks. "Well…" he searched for something to say. “Umm, Lisa? Listen, it’s late, and…”

“So that’s your daughter,” she interrupted. Napier didn’t say anything. Thompson took a deep breath and wiped her eyes. “I guess life led you down a suitable path. You’ve got a family. A job, a kid, a wife.” Napier struggled to understand her babbling. “I guess it worked out for you, leaving me for that…” she maintained just enough conscious control to stop herself from referring to Katherine as a whore, “that other woman.” She paused again and scanned her eyes throughout the room, as if searching for something. “Where is she, anyway?”

“I beg your pardon?” Napier said.

“That wife, whom you left me for. Is she home? I’d hate to get you in trouble.” Napier didn’t find this funny.

“What the hell are you talking about?” he said, keeping his voice low enough not to alert his daughter. “Is this some kind of sick joke?! By-the-way, how the hell did you find out where I live?” Thompson laughed out loud.

“Everyone in Mako’s Center knows you, Rick. It wasn’t hard,” she leaned back into the sofa. “So what’s the wife up to?”

“Can you get off that subject? High school was a hell of a long time ago.”

“What? You don’t know where she is?” Thompson started to laugh drunkenly again. Napier’s temper flared like a box of fireworks.

“She died! Okay? Does that fucking amuse you?!” He barely kept himself from screaming. In the blink of an eye, the lieutenant’s facial expression went from solid drunken amusement to a combination of sorrow, embarrassment, and most notably shame. She leaned forward and buried her hands in her face. Even though she didn’t yet cry, she was clearly upset.

“Oh fuck,” she mumbled. “Oh fuck. Oh shit. Jesus help me.” She looked up at Napier, teary eyed. “God… I’m so sorry. I really didn’t know.” She stood up and started for the door. With the first step she immediately stumbled, due to the loss of coordination from the alcohol. Napier quickly stepped in and caught her, wrapping his arms around her shoulders.

“Okay, okay,” he said. “Go ahead and sit down again.” He

helped her back onto the couch. Even though there was a chair in the nearby corner of the room, he didn't feel comfortable enough to be sitting during this bizarre situation. Therefore, he decided to stand in the middle of the room as before. Thompson continued to mumble about how sorry she was. Napier's anger had already subsided, especially after remembering that she was not in the most balanced state of mind.

"God, I'm just so stupid," she continued. Napier shrugged his shoulders and tightened his lips.

"Don't worry about it. It could happen to anyone." He squinted as if in pain after hearing himself make that stupid remark. "Listen, don't worry about it. It's alright." Thompson shook her head.

"God," she groaned. She closed her eyes and leaned back, dwelling on her misfortunes. "I don't know what the hell I'm doing." She opened her eyes and looked at Napier. "It hasn't been the greatest day for me, can't you tell?" She added a fake chuckle.

"Well how bad could it be?" Napier said, finally taking a seat in his chair. "Should I make you some coffee?" He asked, suddenly thinking that would help with her buzz. She ignored the offer.

"Well, for starters, I got one of my men killed last night." She paused for a sigh. "My statement to my superiors led to a massive Coast Guard operation that turned up nothing. Now…" she stared off into the distance for a moment, "Well I'm up for a court martial. It's not yet scheduled, but they told me that I'm off duty until the whole shebang is underway. And it looks like it'll lead to a dishonorable discharge, which of course destroys any future I thought I had." Napier didn't know what to say, although his mind was reeling off thoughts. *Shit, no wonder she had a date with the booze tonight.*

"Damn," he finally said. "I'm……sorry."

"He'd still be alive if I just did what I was supposed to do," she continued. "He was a douchbag, but he didn't deserve that. He didn't even want to keep diving, but of course I thought we could still find the wreck. Now everyone I know thinks I'm insane."

"You're not insane," Napier tried to sound comforting. Lisa chuckled.

"I know I'm not insane, but that doesn't mean I don't feel like I am," her voice broke a bit as she fought to hold back tears. "There's something in the water over there, Rick. I'm telling you I saw it. It had a huge, rigid body, and several long arms. It was like a large, I don't know, a Kraken, or something. I don't know what it is, but it's there." Napier sat quietly, processing her words in his mind. It seemed extremely unfathomable that there was something in the water like what she claimed. However, to his surprise, she didn't come off as crazy to him. There was a strong conviction in her voice and a sure sign of terror in her eyes as she reflected back on the dive. In addition, there had been a lot of bizarre things happening around the island chain over the last few days. Fishing suddenly decreased almost overnight; Steve Hogan's boat disappearing almost without a trace; the bizarre disappearance of the Coast Guard diver Denning; the destruction of fishermen's nets; bizarre unconfirmed sightings on the news. Somehow, with everything going on in Mako's Ridge, the lieutenant didn't sound crazy to him.

"Perhaps, if you'll still be in town for the next few days, we can take my boat out if you'd like," he said aloud while still in his thoughts. The lack of response from Lisa snapped him back into reality. She had passed out on his sofa. "Oh, you've got to be kidding me!" He cursed any existing higher power. He got up out of his seat and walked out of the living room through the kitchen and into the laundry room, where he pulled a freshly cleaned fleece blanket out of the dryer. Back in the living room, he helped position Thompson into a lying position on her back, placing the sofa's pillow behind her head and covering her body with the blanket. With an exhausted sigh, he headed up the stairs to his bedroom, where he felt he could sleep for a month.

CHAPTER 11

The creature concealed itself in a state of hibernation within the dark habitat. Instinct dictated that it remain hidden in its tunnel, due to several intruders that had been lurking about in the area throughout the previous day. Normally, it would fight off any life form to invade its habitat, but the sheer number of intruders caused its small brain to reconsider any offensive maneuver. It balled all of its appendages into its body, becoming an inanimate object resembling a massive pebble within the deep dark passageway.

Now, even as it was still in a state of unconsciousness, its brain slowly began punching minor energy sparks throughout its body. Hunger was now settling in. It hadn't ingested anything more than a few small fish throughout the previous day. Its monstrous size required an intense amount of energy, and that energy required organic fuel. Being in this natural environment required spending more energy than it was used to before, accelerating its metabolic rate. Within a short period of time it would awaken again, and immediately afterwards its instinct will drive the leviathan to kill and keep killing.

****

"What the hell," Lisa Thompson moaned as she woke up and reviewed her surroundings. It took her a few whole minutes for her memory to start trickling back from the previous night, which answered her mental question of where she was. "Oh, shit!" she exclaimed upon realizing she was on her ex-boyfriend's living room couch. She was still dressed in her civilian jeans and tank top, and her other belongings were at a motel in town. She stood up and searched the house for a bathroom, which she found near the laundry room. After relieving herself, she washed her hands in the sink and then splashed water over her face. She walked to the front door, which had a window view of the cove. Looking out, she could also see the driveway off to the side of the house, which reminded her that she had no vehicle. In her drunkenness, she had hitched a taxi-ride to Napier's home, and eliminated the possibility of leaving quickly.

The sound of footsteps made her jump. She looked to the stairway and saw Napier coming down, wearing a red t-shirt and blue jeans. Halfway down the stairs he stopped after making eye contact with Thompson.

"Well, I can't say this isn't awkward," she said with a nervous chuckle. Napier tittered as well.

"I wouldn't worry about it," he said. Thompson struggled to maintain her false smile as she struggled to recall the complete events of yesterday. Napier noticed the serious look in her face. "Umm, you're not planning to slap me again, are you?"

"No, no," she quickly answered. "Wha-- what happened last night?" She looked at the couch, and then checked herself, noting how perfectly dressed she was. "It's safe to assume you and I didn't--" she made a squiggly gesture.

"Oh, no," Napier said with another friendly laugh. "I knew once you were in your right mind, you'd murder me if I'd let that happen."

"Yeah, you aren't wrong--" she stopped and thought for a moment. "Wait, 'not in my right mind'? Please don't tell me I wasn't a complete idiot." Her voice sounded as if she was pleading to a jury.

"No, just upset. You know, because of the court martial coming up and everything." He finished coming down the stairs.

"Oh, wonderful," Thompson said in distaste. "Well, you probably learned my whole life's story."

"Oh yeah," he said. He walked past her and headed into the kitchen. "Want some coffee?"

"Please," she answered. "One spoonful of creamer if you can spare some."

"Yes, ma'am." Napier sounded like a waiter. He came back into the living room with a large white mug for her. The coffee took on a brownish color after the creamer dissolved into it.

"Thanks," she said. "Listen…I'm sorry about yesterday….well, yesterday and last night to be more specific. With a particular emphasis on slapping you in East Port."

"Oh don't give it any thought," Napier said after sipping some of his hot black coffee. "I kinda deserved it."

"No you didn't," she said. They both took a seat at the dining room table. "Your daughter's very pretty."

"Well I see you remember her," Napier joked. "Yes she is, thank you. She's sleeping in right now." After a couple of minutes they were both finished with their coffees. Napier took the mugs and placed them in the dishwasher.

"Hey, Rick, I hate to be a pest after all of this, but could I ask a favor of you?" Lisa asked.

"Absolutely," he said. "There's no fishing today because of the tournament, so I'm free all day." Telling her that just reminded him once again that today was a no-paycheck day.

"Oh excellent," she said. "If you wouldn't mind, I could use a ride to the Harrison Motel. That's where my things are, and I need to grab a shower and change."

"No problem," Rick said. "I'm ready to go whenever you are. Let me grab my keys."

"Thanks so much," she said as he went upstairs to collect his wallet and keys. Little was she consciously aware that she was checking him out as he walked up the stairs.

****

At six in the morning, the Annual Bailey Fishing Tournament had commenced with the sound of a screeching blow horn. As the horn blasted, countless fishing vessels launched from East Port, as if it were a race. In some sense, it was a race: everyone wanted to be the first to get to the good fishing spots around the island. With local fishing shut down for the day, the entire island was fair game to them, with the exception of the beach areas, that way tourists could enjoy a nice swim for the day. The methods of fishing that this tournament allowed were spear fishing and line-fishing, the latter of which was the most popular in this tournament.

Now that the competition had commenced, the air was already cumulating with foul dialogue from the contestants mocking and insulting each other from the safety of their boats. The police department had all officers, what few they had, on duty, including their reserve officers. It was a busy day for the police, as they had to keep an eye on the numerous boaters and make sure everyone stayed above water, was fishing legally, and was respecting the environment. It was common for some of the sportsmen to toss their beer cans into the ocean, amongst other garbage. The tournament would be a day-long affair. The rules required all participants check in by seven P.M.

Chief Bondy had set up a command-post at Palm's Beach on the northeast corner of the island. He arrived there at five in the morning, and knew it was going to be a long day.

****

"Glad to see you made it," Old Hooper said to the two scientists, who arrived at East Port by taxi precisely at noon. Nic wore a white t-shirt with khaki shorts and grey tennis shoes, and David was dressed in a blue tank top and khaki shorts and sandals. Each cave diver carried his own large case, which contained their expensive scuba equipment. Both men also wore large waterproof cameras strung over their shoulders. They looked up to the cranky fisherman, who wore his normal sloppy attire. He stood on the stern of his vessel like a king. Kneeling on the center of the deck was Ryan Rein, who was sorting out his equipment.

"I'm sorry, but number one: we're not late," Nic said, "and number two: I'm not the one who's being paid four grand to be here." They climbed onto the stern and began to sort their luggage. Ryan Rein looked up from his large brown cases.

"Howdy," he greeted, sporting his usual Hollywood smile. He wore blue jeans and a brown leather vest, exposing his tan hairy chest. His shark tooth necklace hung from his neck. "I don't know about you guys, but I'm more than ready to go on this trip."

"Exactly what do you expect to hunt out there?" Nic asked.

"That's part of the thrill: I don't know," he said. "But whatever it is, it did a number on that Coast Guard diver."

"Wha-?" Nic said. "Exactly how do you know that? There was no body recovered."

"The other diver said she discovered tons of blood in the water, with bits and pieces of the dead guy floating about," Ryan Rein explained. His voice was very enthusiastic. "And from what I heard, she got scared shitless! Can't say I blame her."

"So, you're basing this on some nut job diver who claims she saw a sea monster?" David tapped Nic on the shoulder to divert his attention.

"Hey," he spoke in a whisper in order to prevent being heard by the poacher. "Listen, this guy may be crazy, but he's the reason we're able to get Hooper to take us out to the cave. So let's just do our job, and let this guy do whatever he wants."

"Your friend is smart," Rein said. Being a lifelong hunter, his hearing was truly excellent, and it would take more than quiet talk to keep him from eavesdropping. He looked at the cabin, which like the rest of the vessel, was in need of a remodel. Inside of it was Old Hooper, who didn't bother to conceal a glass bottle of whiskey. "We're ready to head on out whenever you are, Captain." The engine of the *Thunderhead* bellowed, and within a few minutes, the old fishing vessel was traveling northeast.

****

"Here's a question," Napier asked while he waited in the motel room.

"What's that?" Lisa's voice called from the bathroom, slightly muffled by the closed door.

"So why are you staying here in Mako's Center? Don't you have a base or something where the military gives you housing?" The question he really wanted to ask was whether or not she was married or seeing anybody, but he wasn't sure how to come across asking that.

"I do," Lisa opened the door and came out, newly dressed in light blue jeans and a green tank top, with her wet red hair hung over her right shoulder. Like her previous outfit, it outlined her fit body perfectly, and caused Napier to struggle not to stare. There was no ring on the left hand, making it likely she was unmarried.

But that didn‘t eliminate the possibility of her already having a boyfriend. “But right now, I thought it’d be good to be away from everybody.” She sighed and looked out the window. “Maybe I’m paranoid, but I have a feeling they think I’ve gone crazy. But I do know that they blame me for the death of Denning, and deservingly so. He had quite a few friends on the base.”

“What exactly do you think you saw down there?”

“I’m not sure. Every time I attempt to describe it, I feel like I’m describing something from a science fiction movie.”

Napier took a seat at the coffee table in the room. “Why don’t you give it a shot? I’m curious.”

“Why do you care?” She kept looking out the window.

“Well I did go through nearly eight years of college studying oceanography,” Napier smiled. “Plus, there are all these weird occurrences happening lately. I’m starting to suspect they’re all connected. Fishing vessels don’t just vanish in waters like those along Mako’s Edge. You stated you saw--” he searched for the best way to phrase his next sentence, “what was left of Denning.” He wasn’t sure if those were the proper words. He decided to continue. “Plus, there’s something going on with the fishing. It’s like they’re moving out of the area.”

“Don’t fish migrate?” Thompson asked.

“This is a breeding area. Fish from miles around come here almost all year long. And even if they were changing territory, there would be signs of it. They wouldn’t be moving away so many at once. It’s almost as if something is scaring them from the breeding grounds. In addition, it seems like several fishermen are finding their drift nets torn to shreds lately…”

“Like something is after their catch?”

“Exactly,” Napier said. “So, honestly, after all of this stuff going on, you’re debriefing statement doesn’t sound too crazy to me.” While what he said was true, he also said it that way to sound like a nice guy. Thompson turned and took a seat at the other side of the coffee table.

“I think I told you last night, if I remember correctly?” Thompson said.

“The Kraken thing? I wasn’t sure if that was what you actually saw, or if that was the booze talking.”

Thompson chuckled briefly, but her expression went serious after replaying that horrible memory. "No, that's what it was. All I saw were these wiggly…tentacle things. It was dark and murky, I didn't get a good look…but I barely saw an outline of the body."

"Like a squid?" Napier asked.

"It was…but it wasn't," Thompson said, with a shrug of her shoulders. "Like I said, it was dark and I couldn't see too well. But one thing is for sure… it was huge." The room went silent for a moment. "It's not like there's anything we can do about it," she said. "We're not investigators. Just a couple of down-on-our-luck folks. You've wasted over a decade of your life pursuing a career that led you nearly bankrupt from college debt, with a job that barely puts food on the table. And me, well I was doing good up to now. Then this whole accident happens, and now I'm likely to get a dishonorable discharge. That's not a good strong point on a résumé."

"I'm sure you'll be fine," Napier tried to sound comforting again. Thompson laughed in a mocking way.

"I appreciate it," she said. "But that's how it's gonna play out." Napier's mind went back to debating whether or not she was single. *Cut it out dumbass, she's not interested in you. Or is she? Damn, but you've got to figure out if she's single. Just be subtle.*

"It'll all work out in the end. I'm sure your boyfriend has a good job." *Real subtle. You've just suggested she go home and play stay-at-home housewife for the rest of her life! And the casual mentioning of a boyfriend?! Oldest, most obvious damn trick in the book.* "Just kidding," he immediately followed up his remark for damage control. Luckily, Thompson didn't appear to think anything of it. She stood up out of the chair and begun to put on a pair of boots. "So, if you don't mind me asking, what were you planning to do today?"

"I'll be enjoying myself a little mini-vacation," she said. "I just need a little bit of time alone. Luckily it's not costing me any pocket money. I think all I need right now is a day at the beach, maybe with a margarita. Maybe go on a date or something. Just something to get my mind off things."

"Oh." Napier felt his spirits deflate. *I guess there's my answer.* "You won't need a ride or anything?"

"No, thank you," she said. After tying her boots, she grabbed a small bag containing her swimsuit and opened the motel room door. Napier, lost in his thoughts, was still seated at the coffee table. "You planning on staying in my motel room?" She remarked sarcastically.

"Oh!" Napier stuttered. "Uh- yeah…NO!" He nervously faked a chuckle. "Haha, no, of course not." He got up and walked out while Lisa held the door open. She closed and locked it.

"Well, listen," she said. "Sorry again about last night. And thanks for the favors."

"Ah, no problem," he said. His fake smile was overly big, which almost betrayed the concealment of his disappointment. "Hey, feel free to stop by if you wish. You know where I live."

"Appreciate it." She turned around and started walking. "Bye." Napier stood and watched for a moment. *Damn, that conversation was going so well. Then she just ends it like in the blink of an eye."*

"So much for that," he whispered to himself. "She never liked me much anyway." Exhaling an exasperated sigh, he climbed into his truck and started the engine.

Carrying her beach bag, Lisa walked into town, releasing a sigh of her own. "Damn, I had the chance and I blew it!" She cursed herself. Her mind continued the scolding. *Who cares if he cheated on you in high school? You had one good thing going for you and you blew it.* She glanced back, but Napier was already pulling out of the driveway. She continued walking, now trying to think of a clever way to run into him again. *I'll just have to think of it while I tan myself up at the beach.*

****

"This is as close as I can go," Old Hooper said after he dropped the anchor. The *Thunderhead* bobbed with the jagged current caused from the tight grouping of rocks, nearly a hundred and fifty feet away from the south side of the island's main body. On the deck, all three of Hooper's 'clients' were preparing to make their dives. David and Nic each had dark grey wetsuits with bright green lining on the sides, along with red flippers. They had completed the safety checks on their air tanks and snorkels, and had made sure their cameras and waterproof flashlights were working properly.

Ryan Rein had his own wet suit, a bright red one with black flippers. The choice of color was intentional, as Rein's most useful bait to lure dangerous underwater predators proved to be himself. Kneeling on the deck, he held up his weapon of choice, a Rival's PR-12 harpoon rifle. This model was a custom design by Rein, made to fire a four-foot steel harpoon at 80-feet per second, with enough force to penetrate an inch of steel. But Rein didn't stop there to make this the perfect weapon to hunt underwater creatures. He designed the tip of each harpoon to be laced with a thin canister of poison, which would quickly stop the heart once in the bloodstream of his wildlife opponent. While Rein loved the life-or-death thrill of the hunt, he had no problem keeping an advantage over his prey.

"You ready?" Nic asked David, who was triple-checking the lens of his video camera.

"Yeah, I'm all set," he answered. The sight of Rein aiming his spear gun over the wooden railing caught his attention. "Good God, what do you think is down there?"

"I don't know... and that's what I find most exciting," he sported his Hollywood smile.

"What's in the other case?" Nic asked, pointing down at a large brown clamp case. The poacher un-clicked the latches and flipped the top open like a clam. In the case was a large brown rifle, a M309-30.06 caliber Rifle. "Holy shit! What were you looking to hunt with that? A whale?"

"Again...dunno," Rein said as he closed the case.

"Hey," Old Hooper interrupted. "I thought you guys were here to dive. Not fuss over Steve Irwin's toys here." Nic refrained from cussing the old sailor out, and instead positioned himself at the stern ladder, followed by his colleague.

"Okay, bud," he said to David, "Let's meet at the stone wall, and then we'll make our way to the mouth of the cave." David, who already had his mouthpiece in, simply nodded in agreement. Nic spit into his goggles before putting them on. He stepped on the ladder and a moment later, splashed into the water. David waited for him to clear the way before he entered the water.

Rein held his spear gun in his right arm and eyeballed the ocean. He embraced the chilling sensation he always felt along his spine seconds before embarking on a fresh hunt.

"Nice suit. Good choice of color," Old Hooper commented. "Damn boy, haven't you ever watched *Star Trek*?" Rein chuckled.

"Well, red seems to give me the opposite luck," he said. He moved to the end of the deck and cleared his goggles with saliva. "Okay, Captain, God-willing, your vessel will be the next to tow the corpse of my latest kill."

"As long as I'm paid when we get back," Hooper snorted in his cabin like a sea lion. Rein gave him a thumbs up before stepping over the ladder and hopped into the water. Instead of swimming towards the island structure, he headed west and gradually went deep. Aiming the tip of his gun forward, he guided himself through the forest of rocks. With any luck, he'd find whatever killed the Coast Guard diver and drive a poison spear through its heart. What Ryan Rein perceived as luck, most people would view as a curse.

****

Water splashed into his face repeatedly as Nic waited for David at the stone wall of Mako's Edge. *Today, please,* his mind lectured. After another long minute David finally swam over. Nic held his head out of the water long enough to briefly remove his mouthpiece.

"You were always a slow swimmer," he remarked. David smirked behind his snorkel and held up his right hand, flashing the finger. "Thank you, I am number 1," Nic joked again before replacing his mouthpiece. He then pointed west, indicating that they needed to move alongside the structure. David gave a thumbs up to signal he understood, and both scientists began kicking west. After swimming about one-hundred feet, they took a dive and aimed their flashlights. The lights scanned the wall of the island before locating a massive round section of dark black. They had reached the mouth of the cave.

Holy friggin crap! David thought. *This bitch is huge!* His heart thumped with excitement as they slowly approached the cave's edge.

****

Dressed in jean shorts and a flannel short-sleeve shirt, Jane tapped her bare feet on the property deck as she stared out into Razertooth Cove. She knew her dad was out and about, which would make this the perfect opportunity for Greg to pick her up on his new boat. It was a pleasant sunny day and she was excited to be spending the day alone with her boyfriend. Her secret boyfriend. The mental reminder of this fact bothered her. She didn't like that her father didn't know about Greg, and felt guilty for always turning down his offers to take her out for a day on the *Catcher*, especially now that she was going out on her boyfriend's boat.

In the distance, she saw a small speck of white. *Is it Greg's boat? Or is it some fisherman trying to catch himself a trophy?* The white grain gradually grew bigger as it approached, and began to take form. It was her boyfriend's twenty foot long boat, brand new off the line. It demonstrated to Jane just how spoiled Greg was, coming from a wealthy background. She took after her father in believing that becoming wealthy was a good thing, especially if an individual works hard at doing so. However, being spoiled to this extent without putting forth any self-effort was annoying to them. Jane tried to put these feelings aside in order to focus on having a pleasant time with her boyfriend. Greg controlled the small vessel from within its tiny cabin, steering it beside the *Catcher*.

"Damn!" he exclaimed as he looked up at the large fishing vessel that dwarfed his own. "I never realized how big your dad's boat was until now."

"Gonna get your parents to buy you one like that next?" Jane's remark slipped. She kept a straight face and didn't look him in the eye, resisting the impulse to cover her mouth after realizing what she'd said. Luckily, Greg was unable to tell whether or not she was kidding. She forced a chuckle and climbed aboard his boat from the dock. The deck of his vessel had a small bench on the port and starboard sides and a small coffee table in the middle. On the table rested a portable battery-operated television set. He had a red cooler located near the cabin entrance stashed with packaged sandwiches and soda all smothered in ice. *Wow,* Jane thought after viewing her surroundings, *He may be spoiled rotten to the point where he doesn't have to do a damn thing for himself, but I'm sure as heck gonna take advantage of that today!* Greg reversed his boat away from the dock, turned it around, and headed toward the opening of the cove.

"Ready for a little sunbathing?" He turned and smiled at his girlfriend. She wrapped her hands around the back of his head and pressed her lips to his for a long minute. "I'll take that as a yes."

****

Lisa Thompson was still dressed in her day clothes while she sat on a sprawled out towel on the beach. After arriving, she quickly lost interest in getting in her bathing suit and sunning herself. Her mind was on Napier, and she hated it. She'd spent so many of these years resenting him for what he did back when they were teenage lovers, and the fact that she could sense herself having any feelings for him almost felt like sacrilege. In her mind, she knew she was meant to never see him again, and if he were to reappear in her life, he'd be the same womanizing loser he was when she left him. But instead, he did reappear in her life, and he was almost the opposite of what she'd expected. He was much more mature in his behavior than she had expected him to be, possibly a result from having a child. Financially, he definitely wasn't the perfect choice, but Thompson had learned from her previous marriage that money was not the key thing to a relationship. In addition to her thoughts of Napier, her mind was also dwelling on the likely end of her military career. She loved the adventure, the skills she learned, the companions she made, the places she saw. And now, after a single incident, it appeared she was going to lose it all.

As she rested on the sandy beach, she tried to distract herself by watching the vacationing tourists doing various activities. The beach was dotted with hundreds of people, with most of the men wearing nothing but swim trunks and the majority of the women wearing bikini outfits, which revealed golden skin. Over a hundred people were swimming in the water, some as far out as forty meters, while on the sand, several vacationers played games such as volleyball and football, and others simply enjoyed sun tanning. The air was filled with joyful screams and shouts as people of both genders kicked up sand playing their games, which grew louder when a score was made. Thompson continued scanning the beach and saw a high thirty-foot life-guard tower where a muscular gentleman wearing red swim trunks and a white t-shirt with a red cross symbol was seated on top with a pair of binoculars, keeping a close eye on the events in the water. About twenty feet behind the tower was Chief Bondy, dressed in his usual police uniform. He was standing next to a wooden picnic table, underneath a tarp held up by four large posts set up in a square formation. He was communicating with his deputies by radio, probably issuing instructions to them. She redirected her attention to the horizon, watching numerous fishing vessels moving to-and-fro in the distance. From her position, the boats looked like little grains of rice scattered about the ocean's surface. *If the fishing around here is as bad as Rick claims, then these fishing guys are in for a boring day,* she thought. Her mental reference to Rick brought him back to her thoughts, and reminded her of how much she enjoyed being in his company. And of course she couldn't help but think of how handsome-looking he turned out to be.

"Damn it!" she cursed under her breath. *Why must I keep thinking about him?* She sighed and balanced her chin in the palm of her hand. Suddenly a quote from her father played in her mind like a tape recording.

"*Never pass up a good thing. And sometimes, you may not immediately recognize that good thing for what it is. But once you do, hang on to it.*" Thompson cracked a smile, the first real one she had in days.

"You're the best, Dad," she thanked her late father's spirit. She decided she was going to try to meet up with Rick. Only this time, she wasn't going to be under the influence. But the question was how to get in touch with him. She didn't want to just surprise him again at his house, and who knows if he was even home? Then an idea lit up her brain like a Christmas tree. Rick was friends with the chief, who would be able to help her get in touch with him. And the chief conveniently happened to be right there. She quickly got up from her spot on the beach and made her way over to Bondy. *Time to go out on that boat of his like he suggested last night,* she thought with a smile.

****

In the name of all that is good and holy... Nic thought as he peered into the monstrous mouth of the cave. The opening was larger than the institution had estimated, and it probably ran deep. Possibly through the entire island. He sank at a steady pace before paddling his feet to level himself out at the center of the dark opening. He pointed the beam of his flashlight into the darkness, but the light didn't capture any images, rather it was consumed by the black tunnel. David quickly leveled himself out nearby, a little to Nic's left. He too shined his flashlight into the cave, but still he couldn't see much more than some small bits of muck and seaweed floating about in the water. He and Nic made eye contact, the latter pointing into the cave, which signaled that he was about to enter. As he approached, he aimed himself toward the left corner of the cave, that way he could examine the wall of the tunnel while they explored. David took the right side. The two scientists moved in, and were quickly swallowed by the darkness that blanketed the inside of the cave, with only their flashlights and instincts to guide them.

****

Sensory receptors in its solid exoskeleton picked up small vibrations and electrical activity occurring within the habitat. Its brain began clicking signals at a steadier pace, stirring the creature fully awake from its state of hibernation. Immediately, instinct assigned a priority to the beast: to feed. The electrical signals in the water informed the creature that prey was already nearby, infiltrating its habitat. It was as territorial as it was carnivorous. It contracted its eight tentacles, pumping blood into them. The suction cups on each leathery arm swelled, and the muscle in the center of each one which contained spear-like barbs inside began to pulse. The bulb-shaped eyes stimulated, giving the creature sight in the shadowy surroundings. It stretched its mandibles and clipped the water with its bird-like beak while it opened and shut its two large pincers like a couple pairs of scissors. Despite the immense size difference compared to the smaller prey approaching, instinct still drove the creature to use stealth. It didn't just want to remove the threat to its habitat, it wanted to feed. And it would take a lot to satisfy it this time.

****

To the northeast corner of Mako's Center, most of the fishing vessels had cleared out due to a lack of progress in that area, in an attempt to produce more favorable results on the northwest side of the island. The outcome was a vast overcrowding of fishing boats, all fighting for space to conduct their fishing. Within the floating crowd were two white vessels, riding parallel to the north.

"I didn't pay three grand for this shit!" Ray Dillard nearly shouted as he clenched his fingers around his pole. He was seated on a chair attached to the deck of his thirty-foot long boat, which he personally titled *Babe Magnet.* Wearing a red-yellow Hawaiian shirt with khaki shorts, the thirty-two year old playboy was simply a bank manager in his regular life in California, where he nearly lost his job twice due to flirtations with clients, sometimes while on shift. Some of those incidents led to much more than simple fun flirting, which in turn led to the end of his marriage, something he didn't value that much to begin with. Lucky for him, the ex-wife was happy enough with the divorce and decided not to burden him with alimony.

With him on the deck was a date from the island: a golden skinned nineteen-year old woman sporting a new white bikini. She was lying face down on a towel, sunning her back while Dillard cast the baited twenty-eight pound line thirty yards out. After the two-pound weight made its splash, he glanced over his shoulder at the controls, where his cousin Tom Frost drove the vessel forward to begin dragging the line.

"And we're off again," Tom said. The thirty-year-olds voice lacked the enthusiasm that it had at the beginning of the competition. There was hardly any catch to be had, and to make matters worse, his whole upper torso was getting sunburnt where his white tank top didn't cover him. His legs fared better, thanks to the white exercise pants he wore.

"What the hell happened to all the fish around here?" Dillard complained.

"Hey baby," his young date smiled from her stretched out position on the deck. "You'll get something this time." He looked down at her and smiled back. However, as he eyeballed her nearly bare back, it was obvious that it wasn't her words of confidence that made him grin.

"Tom!" he called out like a Marine sergeant. "Make sure we don't run into this hotshot's boat over there off the port side. Asshole wants our space." He pointed to the white vessel trailing along left of the *Babe Magnet.* Strapped to a fishing chair on its deck was a woman, who clutched a pole similar to Dillard's. He saw this, and in his mind it was competition. *Okay lady, think you're gonna steal my fish? Joke's gonna be on you.*

"Aye aye, Captain," Tom said.

****

The breeze cut through Thompson's hair as she stood on the upper deck of the *Catcher*, while Napier steered the boat out east away from the popular fishing areas. The sky was nearly empty of clouds, save for the occasional isolated cirrus floating in the light-blue world above. The ocean was flat like a sheet of glass, with reflections of the sun sparkling like golden holiday decorations. The sun was hot, but the ocean breeze helped to moderate Thompson's temperature. The *Catcher*'s engine hardly made any noise as Napier throttled it forward. In the cabin, he tried to focus on the blue, beautiful horizon. However, his eyes often drifted to the window on his left, where Lisa stood. He couldn't help but wonder what was on her mind. The butterflies in his stomach were beginning to flap their wings as he contemplated what could result from hanging out with his high school sweetheart.

Once again, after watching the horizon for a minute, his eye drifted toward her again. She had an athletic figure, beautiful red hair that freely hung just beneath her shoulders, tan skin, and lovely blue eyes. He didn't know what she saw in him…if she even did see anything in him. He figured he was a graduate school dropout with an iffy 'career' as a fisherman, with plain brown eyes, pale-white skin beside his perfect farmer's tan on his forearms. On top of that, he was the one who cheated on her in high school, dumping her for another senior for the prom dance. To Napier, he wasn't sure if that still mattered after all of these years, but then again he knew most women's minds worked differently. Quickly, his glance, or what was meant to be a glance, turned into a long drawn out stare. For a few moments, she simply stared ahead, with a small grin on her face. Then she turned and looked at him. Napier didn't bother to hide the fact that he was looking at her. Without saying anything, he gave a smile and a wave. Instead of return the friendly gesture, Lisa pointed a finger toward the front of the boat and began to say something: "You trying to run this guy over?"

Napier's eyes returned ahead to the *Catcher*'s path, intersecting with the path of a much smaller police cruiser which was moving in from the starboard side. "Crap!" He quickly eased off the throttle and steadily veered his vessel to the right, steering it behind the stern of the cruiser. He brought the *Catcher* to a stop and stepped out of the cabin. He looked out to the port side at the cruiser, standing next to a visibly amused Lisa. Standing on the deck of the police vessel were two uniformed officers, one standing at the stern railing, and another near the control booth. He recognized the latter to be Deputy Jones, and he waved down to him.

"Hello!" Napier said. "Sorry about nearly running you over."

"No problem. Just keep your eyes on the road," Jones chuckled. "Hey, Rick, you're not out here fishing are you?"

"Heck no," Napier shook his head. "Just taking the boat out, enjoying a little bit of sunshine." Jones cracked a smile as he focused on Napier standing next to Thompson.

"Oh…. I see now," he said, barely containing his own laughter.

Napier gave him a questioning look, not understanding what the deputy was getting at. "I'll leave the two of you alone." The othe deputy had already failed to contain his laughter, despite covering his mouth with his hand.

"Wha-?" Napier stared quizzing for a moment, then gave a quick glance at the beautiful Lieutenant Lisa Thompson who stood next to him, and then his mind quickly did the math. He shot Deputy Jones a wide eye look. "Oh…No no no! It's not wha you think!"

Great! Pleading like this will definitely convince them. Hi mind once again scolded him.

"Okay, okay," Jones said, holding his hands up, as i beseeching surrender. "So what are the two of you doing ou here…alone?" His contained laughter was forcing him to crack monstrous smile. Napier opened his mouth to answer, but failed t produce any words.

Okay, what exactly are we doing? Lisa wanted to come ou here and… spend time on the boat? Hell, I don't even know.

"Well, uh…we're…taking the boat for a…ride." *Nice choice o words.* Lisa was also laughing, and beginning to blush, whic didn't help Napier's current situation. "We're just, fuck! It's n what you think!" Jones' colleague was nearly cracking up, ar Jones himself wasn't far behind.

"Sure it's not!" he laughed. "Don't worry, I'll place a messag through the radio to alert all units to avoid the *Catcher*! Don want you charged with indecent exposure!" Laughing at his ov remark, he returned to the cruiser's controls, turning back once wave farewell to Napier. "See you later!" He throttled the cruis north, its engine slightly muffling the uncontrolled laughter fro the deputies. Napier bit his lip as he watched them leave.

"Assholes," he said with a smirk. He looked over at Lisa w was smiling and looking out at the ocean, admiring its beauty. " there anywhere specific you wanted to go? You never did t me." He asked.

"I think this is a nice place," she said, looking into his ey Napier returned the smile.

"As you wish," he said. Quietly, they stood side-by-side at railing, staring out into the horizon.

****

Ryan Rein had begun to double back, as his search through the murky waters proved ineffective in locating any predatory creatures. As a matter of fact, there was nothing to be seen. The waters around Mako's Edge were a dead zone, which was very strange because in the weeks prior, fishermen like Old Hooper had reported that this particular area was home to large population of fish. Rein, enthusiastic about stalking whatever killed Denning, took the barren area as a sign that something had frightened the populations from the area. As he explored the possibilities in his mind, he grew excited, knowing that this unknown life form would make a great hunt. However, it was nowhere to be seen. The light strapped to his spear gun acted like headlights on a vehicle, pointing whichever direction Rein swam. He had been swimming toward the *Thunderhead* when his eyes caught the sight of the large mouth of the unnamed cave. Its immense size caused Rein to consider a new possibility: that the 'something' he was hunting could have made this cave its habitat. He changed his direction and took a few slow paddles toward it, contemplating going inside. However, he knew that Nic and David were also exploring the structure, and knew it would bring him misfortune if he were to accidentally injure either of the two scientists.

He waited for a few minutes, keeping track of his position between the cave, nearly sixty feet ahead of him, and Old Hooper's vessel, which remained a little over a hundred feet behind him. His instincts screamed at him to head into the cave and continue his hunt, while his conscience urged him to leave the scientists to their work.

****

Damn, this is unbelievable! Nic thought as he paddled his way through the mysterious dark cave. If he was above water, he'd be shouting at the top of his lungs in pure excitement. *There is no doubt that this cave runs through the whole island. And I'm the first one to explore it! That'll look good on a resume.* He had

taken numerous pictures of the rocky structures within the tunnel, the flash of the camera briefly giving form to the cave's interiors. The wall was composed of countless jagged forms of rocks compressed into one lengthy structure. Several pointed cone-shaped formations were aimed upward from the bottom, while others hung from the cave's 'ceiling', pointing downward. Nic snapped a photo per every few meters he moved inward. His flashlight barely provided enough light for him to see where he was going. Looking to his right, he could see the shimmer of David's flashlight, as well as the quick light flashes from his camera as he moved parallel on the opposite side of the cave.

David checked his waterproof watch. They had been in the cave for nearly fifteen minutes. He clutched a bulging rock on the 'wall' to maintain his depth while he did the math in his mind to determine how far within the cave they had traveled. He figured three feet per paddle, one paddle per second-and-a-half, pausing every ten seconds to position for taking pictures, possibly an average of fifteen seconds to complete that task… approximately one thousand-twelve feet into the cave. *Not too bad.* He figured he'd continue for another fifteen minutes before attempting to meet up with Nic. As he attempted to kick off the wall of the cave, his grip on the rock slipped, sinking him suddenly into the dark abyss. His reflexes immediately kicked in, and he leveled himself out. But he quickly realized something was wrong: the camera was no longer in his possession. *Shit!* He attempted to verbalize his anger, but the profanity was stifled by the watery gurgle of air bubbles. He frantically shined his flashlight through the darkness surrounding him, seeing nothing. He then aimed it downward. *There it is!* His light barely caught the image of the camera sinking to the bottom before darkness consumed it. *Great! I better go get it, or else Nic'll freakin kill me.* Continuing to point the light downward, he steadily descended to the floor of the tunnel.

On the left side of the tunnel, Nic continued moving forward after having just taken a few pictures along the side of the cave. He paused after glancing in David's direction, seeing his light aiming downward. It appeared that he was descending, rather than moving inward. *Perhaps he's gonna try and get a few pictures of the bottom?* He wondered. He decided not to think about it and kept moving forward. He paddled forward for a few moments, keeping his light aimed forward. The glow of the wall was captured by his light's radiance, while the middle area of the tunnel continued to be empty darkness. He paddled a few more strokes and distanced himself from the side of the tunnel by a few feet. Suddenly he stopped, as his light began to capture the image of a large structure in the middle of the tunnel. *What the heck is this?* It looked like a bizarre rock formation, nearly forty feet long. Other than an estimate of the size and basic oval shape of the object, Nic was not entirely sure what it was. Logic directed him to assume it was just another rock formation, being as that was what the whole island was composed of. *Whatever it is, it should make a good photograph.* Getting his camera ready, he moved toward the strange object.

****

The creature remained motionless, successfully luring the prey closer. Its sensory receptors continued picking up the electrical signals in the water, alerting the creature that there were two small life forms intruding upon its habitat. In addition, it picked up other signals coming from outside the cave: one coming from a smaller organism the same size as the approaching prey, and another signal coming from a larger intruder. All four didn't match its size and strength, nor could they compare to its ferocity. The creature tightened the muscles within its multiple appendages as it prepared to capture its prey.

****

Nic paddled closer to the large object, closing the distance by another ten yards. He secured his flashlight to a strap on his belt in order to hold on to the expensive camera with both hands. He allowed himself to sink a few feet to get a better angle of the strange formation. He took a breath through his regulator and held the sights of his camera up to his goggled eyes. After steadying the camera, he pressed his thumb on a round button on the right side of the square shaped device, releasing a series of bright flashes.

The brief flashes from the camera momentarily provided more than three times the span of illumination as his flashlight, and it brought the object into form. His mouth nearly gaped open from a combination of shock, amazement, and fear, the last of the three to be the dominating sensation. This 'rock' had a main body with a shape Nic's mind could only describe as similar as to the head of a goblin. It was clearly hard and rigid, with several curled appendages extending from its sides. These snake-like 'legs' did not appear to have a solid exterior, rather they appeared leathery. Towards the front, it had two larger, bulkier appendages with the same rocky exterior as the main body. At the ends of these two 'arms' were two scissor-shaped structures. Between these two arms were two bulbs, each the size of a bowling ball…eyes. And they were focused on him.

****

The small prey had positioned itself directly in front of the creature, settling a few meters above its position. As the creature tensed to strike, its sensitive eyes were pained by a strange series of flashing lights coming from the intruder. Its brain sparked electrical signals throughout its body, which acted as adrenaline, as instinct declared that this activity was an offensive action. The tense muscles immediately went loose, springing from their tight positions toward the prey like a praying mantis.

****

Even if he hadn't been underwater, there'd be no time to scream or run away. One of the slimy, leathery appendages wrapped around his waist like an anaconda. Nic grunted and gagged under his face mask, losing his regulator in the process. His right hand, which still held the camera, flailed, while his left armed was pinned to his body by the constricting tentacle. The camera flashed almost non-stop, creating a visual rendering of his own demise. He felt his ribs and hipbones begin to crack from the increasing pressure. Fluid from that portion of his body was squeezed into his upper torso, bursting blood vessels. As a result, his nose and mouth begun to bleed. In addition to the immense pressure, he suddenly experienced several intense stabbing pains. Something…many something's…were piercing deep into his abdomen. With the camera still flashing, the tentacle pulled him closer the creature's main body like a fishing line. The flashing of the camera captured the last bloody moments of Nic's life, and illuminated the giant mandibles peel open like pedals on a flower, exposing a massive beak-like object. The rigid 'mouth' of the creature opened, and in a single moment, Nic's existence was torn to bloody shreds as the beak clamped down on his body.

****

From several meters back, David didn't know exactly what it was he was watching. He had located his camera at the floor of the cave and had intended to pick up where he left off when he saw his colleague taking a few pictures of something deeper in the tunnel. The next thing David saw was a continuous, uncoordinated series of flashes which for several brief moments brought a bizarre object into view. From his position, all David could see was a huge mass in the middle of the tunnel, with several snake-like objects protruding from it. One of these huge limbs had a hold of Nic and was pulling him closer.

David didn't stick around to watch the creature to consume his friend. He quickly turned around and kicked for the mouth of the cave. Air bubbles burst from his regulator as he hyperventilated from the sudden panic he was experiencing. He didn't have a clue what it was that killed his colleague, but knowing what it was wasn't a concern at the moment. The concern was escape.

****

The quarry which it had just swallowed did almost nothing to satisfy its now intense hunger. The vibrations coming from the other intruder within the cave had suddenly increased, signaling that it was on the retreat. The creature pumped its sacks, lined along the joints where its tentacles attached to the body, with water. As soon as these balloon-like sacks were full, all at once they contracted with tremendous force, spewing water behind the creature. This force launched its massive body forward. Within seconds it had already closed the distance on the distressed prey, and reached one of its enormous pincers at it, guided by a haze of tentacles.

****

David kicked and stroked as hard and as fast as his muscles would allow. He had been an excellent swimmer all of his life, but in this moment he couldn't possibly be good enough for his liking. He believed he maintained a meter per kick speed, and he strained to make it faster. He could see the opening of the cave, and the sunlight that crept through. Sunshine never looked so good.

Suddenly he felt a strange vibration from within the tunnel, like a jet propulsion. He didn't think about it, nor did he look to see what it was. He kept his eyes on the target. However, just a few moments after the strange echo, he suddenly felt the presence of an enormous mass coming up from behind him. He clenched his teeth, nearly biting through his mouthpiece in the process. His body tensed as the dark tunnel suddenly became darker, as the shadow of the monster overtook him.

Still, he didn't look back. He kept stroking and kicking. Another stroke; a few feet. Another kick; nothing. He kicked again; no further distance. He suddenly felt very light headed, and began to experience a bizarre, indescribable pain beneath his stomach. Quickly experiencing a lack of energy, he looked down to examine himself, only to find that his lower half was missing, replaced by a haze of blood that freely leaked along with entrails from his open wound. Before the life left his eyes, he caught one final sight: His dangling legs, still perfectly attached to the hip, clutched in a huge pincer. It was illuminated by the flashlight, which was still strapped to his belt.

One of the tentacles grabbed a hold of David's lifeless upper body, and pulled it in towards its huge bird-like beak. The creature fed while it approached the mouth of the cave for further kills.

****

Rein sensed a pulsation rippling through the water, seemingly originating from the mouth of the cave. He recognized these sensations from past underwater hunts, when larger animals created vicious moments. However, these sensations were stronger than what he was used to. An amateur would be able to detect them, and for the first time in several years, Rein felt himself getting nervous. Stronger pulsations meant a bigger predator. He pointed his spear gun and flashlight toward the cave, and steadily back paddled toward Hooper's vessel. He kept his eyes forward, and felt his own pulse nearly go haywire as the darkness in the cave took formation; a formation he wouldn't be able to comprehend until now. It had an enormous body, slightly narrow and pointed to the back like a tusk, while in the front it was more rounded. What shocked him as much as the immense shape and size were the snake-like tentacles, four protruding from each side of the creature's body. They acted like legs, guiding it in whichever direction it moved. In the front were two large knobs, which Rein determined to be shoulder joints, which attached to two large thick, arms. Each of these arms could bend at elbow joints, and each contained a jagged set of ten foot long pincers, which could easily sever a man in half. And the worst realization Rein had: they already had. On the left claw were bits of swimsuit and some other bloody material…or tissue. Between the two shoulder joints were the creature's eyes, which appeared like light bulbs, impossible to know what they were looking at. He allowed himself to kick back a little faster, but keeping himself steady.

****

It emerged from the dark tunnel into the vastness of the ocean. It stopped moving for a moment, allowing its eyes to adjust to the change in illumination. As it paused, its sensory receptors detected the heartbeats and movements of another small organism nearby. The sting in its eyes vanished, and finally the creature's vision was as clear as crystal. The prey's color made it very easy to spot in the murky water. Its body demanded more sustenance, driving the creature forward.

****

Son of a bitch! Rein cursed in his mind as the creature moved in his direction. And it was moving fast! For the first time in his life, he wished he wasn't wearing his bright red wetsuit. He'd only created another twenty feet worth of space from back paddling, and the vessel was still fifty feet away, resting on the surface. He didn't have time to think; just act. He pointed the spear gun and squeezed the trigger. A sharp hissing sound seeped through the water as the large arrow shot from the gun with the speed of a bullet, quickly making its way to the creature, where it bounced off the thick rigid shell on the left shoulder. Rein didn't wait to see whether it did any good as he slid the straps of his air tank off his shoulders. Freeing it, he held the tank upside down in front of him. He looked forward. The creature had gone into a wild spasm, springing all eight tentacles at him. The spear didn't do any damage, but it clearly threatened it. Rein pried his flashlight from the spear gun, which then freely sank to the ocean bottom. With the flashlight, he slammed it against a valve on the end of the tank, and then quickly held on tight. The pressurized air exploded out of the open valve, turning the tank into an underwater rocket. As if it were the thruster for a NASA space vessel, it quickly shot Rein to the surface of the water, just as the mass of the creature engulfed his previous position, attacking the empty section of water. Rein looked up to the surface. Forty feet; twenty feet, five feet. He let go of the tank, which continued to rise out of the air, before curving like a cruise missile and landing back in the water. Mild decompression symptoms immediately began setting in as nitrogen bubbled in his blood vessels. His nose and ears began bleeding as he quickly paddled to the *Thunderhead.* The ride along the air tank had lifted him at an angle, bringing him up only fifteen feet from the vessel. After a few desperate strokes, he grabbed a firm hold of the ladder and pulled himself clear of the water, landing on his back as he collapsed onto the deck. He rolled himself to his hands and knees and saw his brown case, as Old Hooper stepped out of his cabin.

"Boy, what in the hell's wrong with you?"

"Get us the fuck out of here!" Rein called out in a cracking voice. With quivering hands, he pried his case open, revealing the large 30.06 caliber rifle. Old Hooper looked out into the sea.

"Where are the two science boys?" He asked.

"They're dead! Now get us out of here?" Old Hooper's eyes went bloodshot. He pulled his whiskey bottle from a dirty pocket in his vest and took a long slug while Rein pulled the bolt open in his rifle, pushed in a large cartridge, and slammed it into the chamber.

"Have you gone apeshit!" he yelled. "What the hell happened down there?!"

"I don't have time to expl…" Both men's eyes went to the stern, where the water churned violently. Old Hooper nearly went limp, letting the bottle slip from his hand and shatter on the wood deck upon seeing the multiple leathery tentacles splashing about in the water, surrounding an unrecognizable form that began to bulge from the surface. He turned and reached for the wheel.

****

The creature grew furious. Its own prey had attacked *it*, and had nearly escaped by climbing onto the strange inedible life form on the surface. It filled its sacks with seawater and propelled itself to the surface, reaching up with its tentacles. While it still intended to devour the smaller creatures, its primary mission was to eliminate any intruder from its claimed territory.

****

With quivering hands, Rein raised the butt of the rifle to his shoulder and pointed the barrel at the creature's center mass. A metallic squeal pierced his eardrums, as Hooper reeled the anchor back into the boat. As he did that, he started the *Thunderhead's* engine. It made a few dry revs, sounding like long V's, until finally it ignited and roared. Rein attempted to steady the rifle as best he could, through the excessive bleeding, pulsing headache, and the rocking of the boat. He squeezed off a shot, sending a bullet to hit the monster in the back, only for it to be stopped cold by the solid shell.

****

The smaller life form had attacked it once again. The creature felt no pain, but recognized the offensive actions taken against it. What little consciousness it had now turned into a spiraling rage. In the frame of its limited mind, the prey had no right to defend itself. The creature had no awareness to the rights, sanctity, or worth of any single thing on the planet, other than its own self. It felt an outrage, and its newly evolved instinct dictated that it destroy any other life form that dare come near it.

****

Rein did his best to chamber another round. Suddenly, he stumbled forward, toward the edge of the stern as the vessel began dipping backward. Hooper grabbed onto the wheel, seeing the bow of his vessel beginning to point at an upward angle. He looked back and saw that the creature had at least two tentacles clutching the stern railing of the boat, pushing downward. Water began to seep onto the deck and onto Rein as he fumbled for control of his weapon, which he nearly lost his grip on. Without aiming, he fired a shot, causing a round to crush itself into a mushroom shape after impacting the creature's shell casing. The creature didn't hesitate to retaliate. Rein felt one enormous, slimy tentacle wrap itself under his right armpit, enfolding around his whole upper arm, while a second tentacle snatched him by the waist. He felt his body become weightless as he was lifted from the deck and held in the air like a kite in the wind. Old Hooper, even in his state of panic, couldn't take his eyes off the infamous Ryan Rein. The famous hunter was now the hunted. Worse; he was the trophy.

Rein squealed as the barbs hidden within the tentacle's suckers, unknown to him, began piercing their way into his gut. As this painful action was taking place, the other tentacle around his arm began to pull away…with his limb. Rein let out a blood curdling scream as his shoulder bones dislocated. The muscles and tendons pulled apart, followed by the skin and blood vessels, creating a spewing of red fluids as Rein's right arm detached from his body. Rein fell into a state of shock as he looked at his limbless shoulder, now looking like the top of an open ketchup bottle. Before he could lose consciousness, at least two other tentacles rose from the sea to engulf him. All he could feel was one of the slithery limbs folding over his head. His last sensations included a crushing pressure around his skull, followed by a tugging feeling on his neck and legs, as the tentacles pulled them from his body. The many pieces of his corpse were lowered into the bloody red water and into the huge beak of the creature.

Old Hooper cursed several f-bombs as he throttled the vessel immediately into its fastest speed. The propellers kicked on, kicking up water behind the stern. The *Thunderhead* heaved forward, causing its railings to snap off due to the creature's unrelenting grasp on them. The front of the vessel splashed into the water as the tension behind it released, allowing it to rocket ahead like a slingshot. Free from the 'thing', Old Hooper looked back at the enormous mass feeding on Rein's body in the water behind him. He redirected his attention to the path ahead of him, just in time to see the tip of a large rock just a few feet ahead of him. His reflexes took over and he spun the boat's wheel in the starboard direction. However, the vessel's speed had caused it to immediately close the distance, and the *Thunderhead* bounced upward as the nearly submerged rock punched a massive hole in the bottom of the port side, raking away shards of wood as the propellers continued pushing the vehicle forward. Old Hooper didn't bother to stop and check for damage. He had only one goal; to get the hell away from Mako's Edge. He kept the throttle up to speed and aimed for the safe refuge of Mako's Center, ignoring the fact that seawater flowed freely into the ship's engine.

****

The creature felt a sense of satisfaction from tearing apart its smaller, inferior enemy before feeding on it. But now, the larger, inedible intruder had begun to retreat. It had no intention of letting this other enemy escape, especially after discovering that it carried yet another small life form which it could feed upon. Its sacks inhaled several gallons of seawater each, taking only about a second to do so. And within the next moment, it spewed the water out, launching itself after the enemy, and leaving behind a murky trail of water.

The violent zone of ocean soon went calm again as if nothing ever happened. The remains of blood and human tissue spread apart and seemingly dissolved in the water. The only evidence remaining was an inch-and-a-half long great white shark tooth attached to a loop of string, which slowly spiraled in circles as it sank to the bottom of the sea.

****

"Come on, baby," Ray Dillard spoke to the ocean, as if trying to entice it. "Bring me the big one. Make me famous." He bounced in his seat, growing impatient with each pass. He occasionally glanced to the right at the other vessel, which appeared to be keeping pace with his. He didn't think much of it, and simply waited for the familiar tug on his twenty-eight pound line. His much younger date, Jesse, rolled over onto her back to allow the sun to beam down on her tight stomach and chest areas. She released a strong exhale, looking up to the sky through purple sunglasses. She had grown bored.

"Want to keep treading this way?" His buddy Tom asked. He was slumped on the boat's steering wheel, also bored. Dillard didn't look back at him.

"Yes!" His voice expressed his frustration. "I'm telling you, dude, I have a gut feeling. The winning fish is down here somewhere." He clutched his pole and kept his eyes on the blue ocean surface.

Several minutes passed. The *Babe Magnet* slowly moved forward. Jesse and Tom both began to grow more and more impatient. Dillard didn't care. He remained focused on the water, and the fishing line that extended from his pole. He felt himself beginning to grow excited, feeling that any minute he'd feel the massive tug against his line.

"Hey look!" Tom called out, pointing to the port side. Dillard ignored him, and kept his eyes on the stern. A few seconds later, Jesse stood up.

"Oh cool!" She exclaimed. Once again, Dillard forcefully ignored them. He didn't care about anything else at this point. However, the distant sound of a large splash, followed by the cheer of the female on the nearby vessel finally drew his attention. He bit his lip and slowly turned his eyes away from his line, and witnessed the dreaded reality, just as a five-hundred pound marlin leapt from sea, holding a horizontal pose for nearly two whole seconds before crashing back down into the sea. Once again, the sound of a woman cheering echoed through the air, as the female on the deck of the white vessel tugged on her pole and reeled in her line.

This can't be friggin happening, Dillard thought to himself. He forced himself not to cuss the woman out. Instead, he simply stared with a resentful gaze as the lady fought the fish up to the aft of her boat. With each tug of the line, he prayed for it to snap, which would at least prevent her from taking away all of the day's glory. *His* glory. However, his wishes were not met, as he watched the woman, with the help of a muscular man on board, haul the marlin onto the deck of the boat and strap a chain through its gill slit. He then felt his own vessel begin to change direction. He looked back at Tom, who was spinning the wheel to port.

"Tom! What the hell are you doing?!" He barked.

"Gonna congratulate this person!" Tom said. He had a much better sense of sportsmanship than his self-centered friend. Dillard simply leaned back in his chair, sulking like a child. "Hey," Tom said to him. "At least you were right about the winning fish being in this area!"

"You wanna swim back to the island?" Dillard threatened. Tom simply laughed as he steered closer to the other vessel. Jesse stood, anxiously waiting to get a closer look at the likely winning catch. The sun sparkled on her golden skin. Tom slowed the *Babe Magnet* within twenty feet of the other vessel, titled the *Comanche,* and began whistling cheers for the other competitors. Finally, Dillard forced himself to see his opposition with what he still perceived as rightfully *his* fish. A few moments ago, he didn't think his day could be more miserable. He was wrong. On that deck of the *Comanche* was a woman in her early thirties, with golden hair, beautiful tan skin, wearing a white tank top and jean shorts. Dillard recognized everything from the hair to the jeans, and his blood pressure suddenly went through the roof. The hairs on the back of his neck stood on end, and his teeth clenched tightly after seeing his ex-wife, Rebecca, standing twenty feet away from him on her own vessel, basking in the glory of catching the enormous blue marlin. *His* marlin!

"No…no…NO!" He nearly screamed. The anger was boiling. But what was more overwhelming was the pure disbelief of the reality of what just happened. He turned and kicked his fisherman's chair, bellowing in frustration. "I hate that bitch! I hate her! This is the worst fucking day in my whole life! The worst fucking day! And I paid three thousand dollars for this fucking day!"

"Holy crap, dude," Tom said. "Relax. It's part of the sport. Besides, we still have the rest of the day to go."

"Unfortunately," Jesse rolled her eyes. She began to wish she was on board the *Comanche*.

"Oh my god!" Rebecca called out from her vessel. Dillard turned around, knowing his ex-wife had recognized him. He tightened his lips to prevent himself from saying anything rude. He took a deep breath and simply waved.

"Hi there," he unenthusiastically replied. Rebecca crossed her arms, exposing a victorious smile.

"I thought that ranting coming from your boat sounded familiar," she remarked. Tom turned away to attempt to hide his laughter. Even though Dillard was his friend, he knew he was also a bit of a jerk, and didn't feel very sorry for him on this occasion. When he saw Dillard give him a glare, he pretended to be clearing his throat. His deception didn't work. Dillard flipped him the finger before he looked back to his ex-wife.

"Good to see you too." *God, kill me now.*

****

Old Hooper's heart raced as he kept racing the *Thunderhead* at its top speed. The rusty vessel had moved a little over two-thirds of a mile away from the rocky island, which now served as a gravesite for his clients. He frequently looked back over his shoulder, attempting to find out if the monster was chasing him, but unfortunately couldn't see anything but water. Looking ahead, he could see the northeast side of Mako's Center in the distance. In front of the large lump of land were numerous sea vessels, appearing just a little larger than white specks to his perspective. In his panic-stricken state of mind, Old Hooper ignored the smoke that billowed from the exhaust pipes, as well as the drag caused from the *Thunderhead*'s added weight.

****

The creature pursued, like a cannonball in water. Its enemy initially had great speed and had created several yards of distance, but now it appeared as if it was slowing down. The creature began nearing the injured prey, quickly jetting forward with bursts of water from its numerous sacks. Its bony beak clicked rapidly, thirsty for more blood. Within the beak was a tongue, lined with rows of razor sharp teeth. Tissue-thin strands of flesh and inorganic material hung from some of these teeth, soon to be washed down the gullet with a bite from the creature's next meal. With another explosive burst of water, the creature was nearly upon its prey. Its tentacles lashed out, nearly curving around the fleeing life form, which was barely out of reach. The creature filled its sacks again, ready to make another killer attempt.

****

The engine of the *Thunderhead* had begun rattling, resembling the sound of a rock being shaken inside of a tin can. Old Hooper heard the sound, and choked on the black smoke which had nearly engulfed the whole vessel. Despite all of the agony on his vessel, he didn't ease off on the throttle, keeping the boat directed at Mako's Center. While the island got closer, with each passing moment it was feeling further away. The vessels participating in the fishing tournament could now be clearly seen in the distance, particularly two white vessels that drifted side-by-side nearly two-hundred yards away. He could feel the presence of the leviathan in the sea, and his veins ached for another long slug of alcohol.

"When I get back on that island I'm getting so shitfaced drunk," he said aloud to himself. He forced a chuckle in an attempt to calm his nerves. It didn't work. Especially after he felt the shockwave within his boat, resulting from the engine exploding. The metal exterior of the hull peeled outward, where smoke rose in a long narrow form, almost resembling a cobra. The extra weight created by the seeping seawater had taken its toll on the vessel's buoyancy, causing it to slowly sink. Old Hooper stood motionless in his cabin. "This can't be happening!" He hissed. The stern of the vessel dipped under the water, allowing water to cover the deck like a blanket. The bow began pointing upward, causing the vessel to resemble a miniature Titanic. And finally Old Hooper beheld the worst as he stepped out of the cabin. The front of the creature emerged from the churning sea, even larger than the *Thunderhead.* Two tentacles smacked the sides of the railing, constricting anything they could to maintain a grasp on the boat. Old Hooper squealed as he forced his way back into the cabin, fumbling his cabinet drawers open as he located his loaded Taurus pocket .38 Special revolver. Just as he grabbed the five-shot weapon, he collapsed to the floor as he heard the roof of the cabin creaking. The creature had lifted one of its huge pincers from the water. The bony appendage opened like the mouth of a Tyrannosaurus-Rex, and chomped down on the corner of the cabin, bending the metal pillars and splintering the rotting wooden roof. Pieces of debris rained down on Old Hooper, who covered his face with his arms. He looked up again and screamed at the sight of the huge claw hovering above him, wreaking havoc on his vessel. Without any strategy of defense or plan of escape, he pointed the two-inch barrel of his revolver at the towering arm and fired off all five rounds. Each bullet proved useless, as they all were reduced to crushed lumps of lead. His finger continued squeezing the trigger, resulting in a useless click from the firing pin.

In the midst of this madness, Hooper didn't take notice that the creature had wrapped several of its thick tentacles around the vessel, and had begun constricting, splintering the structure of the *Thunderhead.* The fisherman looked down past his feet to see the spot where the door of his cabin used to be, looking into the antenna like eyes of the creature. A purplish-red tentacle slithered its way from the submerged rear of the deck up the incline, all the way to Hooper. He clicked the now useless firearm at the slimy invader. He panted heavily, and screamed once again as the tentacle coiled itself around his feet, continuing up the rest of his body. His eyes bulged as the tentacle draped around his entire body like a Twizzler. The tip of the leathery appendage slapped on his face, placing a round suction cup perfectly over his right eye. He attempted to squeeze his eyes shut, but couldn't. The gooey suction cup had his eyelid pressed open, leaving him helpless to look into the disgustingly soft flesh lined with red veins and arteries. He couldn't scream, as his mouth was pressed shut. All he could do was groan in pain, as the tentacle began squeezing tightly. However, for Old Hooper, that wasn't nearly the worst of it. He felt the donut shaped suction cup pulse against his sweaty skin, and his eye caught the sight of a pointed barb centered in the flesh of his captor. And it moved closer with each pulse. With his eyelid pressed open by the position of the suction cup, Hooper was forced to witness the tip of the barb sink into the cornea of his eye. He attempted to flail in agony, only succeeding in getting his mummified body to rock right and left as his body was pierced by the barbs on the other tentacles.

It dragged him down from the cabin area and down the deck before splashing him into the water. His already muffled screams were forever silenced as the tentacle released him to the beak, where the tooth layered tongue peeled the flesh off his bones like a cheese grater, as the jaws closed down on his body. The creature released his grip on the *Thunderhead*, allowing the crushed vessel to freely sink into the depths.

****

"Holy shit!" Tom called out, pointing to the northwest. Everyone on the *Babe Magnet* and *Comanche* followed his direction, and witnessed the stern of an old rusty fishing vessel rise upward as the bow sank beneath the depths. The enormous fog of black smoke coming from the exploded engine clouded their vision as to exactly what was happening, but they were able to see that the vessel appeared to be breaking apart.

"Oh my God!" Rebecca almost screamed from her boat. "We've got to help the people on that boat."

"You want to help them? Be my guest," Dillard said. Rebecca shot her ex-husband a stern look. This moment was a reminder of why she left him.

"Go to hell, Ray," she said. She hurried to the wheel and throttled the *Comanche* towards the sinking vessel. The muscular individual with her, Doug, who was dressed in sandals and athletic shorts and no shirt, began sorting out the contents of a large box to look for a first aid kit. Dillard sat back down in his fisherman's chair and bitterly watched as they sped away. In his selfish state of mind, even in the midst of a nearby crisis, all he could think about was how that 'bitch' stole his fish. He nearly jumped out of his seat in surprise when he heard the *Magnet's* engine ignite. He looked back to Tom, who had begun to steer the boat.

"Hey, Tom! What do you think you're doing?"

"What the hell do you think I'm doing? I'm trying to help," Tom replied. He was growing tired of his friend's absurdity. Dillard stood up out of the chair.

"Don't think so!" he demanded. "Let that idiot take care of this. If I wanted to save sinking ships I would've joined the Coast Guard!" Tom ignored his instructions. Dillard tensed with frustration with the insubordination. "Hey! Didn't you hear what I said?!"

"Shut up before I break your jaw!" Tom threatened. Dillard froze. He'd never been threatened by his friend before. To his surprise, it was quite intimidating. He stayed quiet and sank back into his chair. Tom grabbed a radio that was hanging on the wall and turned up the volume. "Mayday, mayday! Local Law Enforcement, this is the yacht *B--...*" he paused, embarrassed about the stupid name of Dillard's boat, "the... *the Magnet.* We've got a fishing vessel nearly a click northeast of East Port. It's emitting black smoke and appears to be sinking fast. Over."

"This is Chief of Police Geoff Bondy," a voice answered from the radio. *"I'm sending a unit right away. Are there any injuries?"*

"Unknown," Tom answered. "I'll keep you updated."

Meanwhile, Rebecca steered her yacht closer to the site of the incident. The vessel had disappeared beneath the surface, leaving behind a trail of debris. The smoke had begun to clear, making it easier for her to examine the scene. The area of water was dark, due to the pollution from the accident.

"Oh God!" She held her hand to her mouth. There was no sign of life. Her companion held a rope in a loop, as if he was going to lasso any survivors like a cowboy.

"I don't see anyone," he said.

****

It had just finished slaughtering the life form that had led it on a rigorous chase. It remained submerged, watching the inedible carcass sink beneath the waves, never to be seen again. It was about to move along, when another strange organism approached along the surface. It was of the same species of that which it had just killed. The creature responded to its instincts, which demanded to kill this one as well. It tilted itself upward and held both of its monstrous pincers toward the sky. It filled its sacks once again, their individual loads adding up to nearly a ton of seawater. Simultaneously, they released the pressure. The creature launched upward like a bottle rocket, directly underneath the enemy organism.

****

"Is there anyone out there?!" Rebecca called out. She looked out over the side along with her friend Doug. Her heart was pounding and sweat was beading down her forehead. Aside from the dark water, receding smoke, and the large amount of floating pieces wood, there was no sign of life.

"I don't see anything," Doug said. He began to make his way to the radio. "We need to get in touch with the Coast G--" He bit his tongue nearly in two as his body, along with the rest of the

Comanche was rammed upward by a tremendous unknown force from below. After being airborne for a brief moment of time, both he and Rebecca crashed down on the deck. The rear of the vessel had mysteriously lifted from the water, and the disaster only got worse from there. Rebecca, who clutched the railing at the port side aft, watched as the middle of the *Comanche* splintered and cracked upward vehemently. Her throat went numb, preventing her from screaming as she witnessed several large narrow, pointed objects erupt from within her boat, crumbling the entire front half into an unrecognizable form. Metal, wood, and plastic sprinkled into the water, and smoke began to hiss from the fracturing engine. As the strange objects broke through the vessel, they took greater form. At first Rebecca would have described them as spears, but after rising from the innards of her boat, she realized they actually had more of a scissor shape, as if they belonged to a gigantic crustacean. No longer supported by the huge pincers, the elevated rear half of the vessel crashed into the water and immediately begun sinking.

Rebecca quickly began flailing in the water to kick away from the disaster as quickly as possible, followed by Doug. A terrible scream from the muscular man forced her to look back, which she immediately regretted. One of the huge pincers had sunk underneath the surface after decapitating the vessel. As they fled, that same pincer rose from the sea once again, this time under Doug. He had been skewered through the abdomen by one of the pointed figures and lifted out of the ocean. As he was pushed ten feet out of the water, his arms still reaching down toward Rebecca, as if he hoped she could pull him away. With a deathful grunt, his mouth vomited a pint of blood, and his body was dragged into the water by the enormous appendage.

The intensity, shock, and terror had been too much for Rebecca's fracturing mind to handle. After screaming in reaction to what she had just witnessed, her eyes closed and her tense body loosened as she fainted to a quiet peacefulness, floating amongst the debris.

****

It fed once again, clamping its beak and mandibles on the small fleshy prey. Around it were pieces of the large inedible creature that it slaughtered, sinking into the depths below. It took no notice, as its attention was currently on another small organism. While it resembled the other ones, this particular organism didn't move. It simply floated at the surface, amongst the pieces of wreckage. Perhaps it was already dead? The creature's sensory receptors were picking up trace signals, likely being heartbeats. Dead or not, it was an edible object, and the creature prepared to reach out with a tentacle to consume it. However, its attention was grabbed by the presence of yet another floating organism, which approached at great speed. The shelled creature took this approach as a sign of aggression, and even though it knew it could not consume the strange life form's 'flesh', it would not back down from any challenge. In addition, the creature's had learned that these floating challengers carried the smaller, edible life forms, and there was further reward in slaughtering more of them.

****

Deputy Jones stood in the cabin, holding a hand-held radio to his ear as Chief Bondy laid out instructions to him. There had been a report of a fishing vessel sinking a little over a mile north of his position.

"Get over there ASAP and get a report of what happened," Bondy's voice instructed over the radio. *"Don't worry about the boat itself, because by the sound of it, it can't be saved. I'll notify the Coast Guard.*" Jones looked over to the reserve deputy with him, twenty-eight year old Deputy Ted Burg, who stood a short five-foot-six, with a buzzed cut head. He was inexperienced and was more than eager to investigate this particular incident. He stood at the stern while Jones hit a switch near the wheel, turning on the red and blue emergency lights, and also ignited the vessel's siren.

"Ten-four," he answered the chief. "*Forty-nine-eight* is on route." He hooked the radio to his belt and throttled the vessel forward.

A quarter mile behind them was the *Catcher,* which was

anchored facing the east in the same position it was when it encountered Jones' vessel. Napier and Thompson stood side by side on the upper deck, reflecting on their past lives. Napier had listened intently as Thompson spoke of her brief marriage which took place in Maine. She admitted it had happened too fast and were the acts of a young woman who thought she found the right one. In her book, that was the second time she thought she'd found the right guy, who in turn, fooled around with other women. This made Rick feel a bit guilty, as he was the first guy to do that to her. He talked a little bit about Jane, and the difficulties of life after his wife died. He refrained to speak too much about the marriage itself, due to the awkward fact that it spawned from an affair during his high school relationship with Thompson. Still, it made him happy to be able to open up to someone, and she felt the same way.

However, it quickly came to a stop when Napier overheard police traffic on the radio, which he left on Bondy's channel. He overheard the conversation regarding a sinking ship, and tried to resist the urge to pull up the anchor and help the deputies. Lisa could see his eyes on the cabin radio.

"Hey," she said. "You shouldn't have to worry about it. The police here have jobs to do, and I'm sure they're capable of doing it." Napier smiled.

"I suppose you're right," he said. A subtle breeze kicked through the air, picking up a few strands of Thompson's hair. Napier's mind went from debating whether to assist the police situation to her beauty. Unbeknownst to him, Lisa's mind was consumed with thoughts of how charming, and surprisingly mature, Napier had become. He was a different person than before. *Age and experience will do that to someone,* she thought. They shared a quiet moment, both feeling the intense urge to plant a kiss on the other's lips. Looking into each other's eyes, without blinking, they slowly felt themselves lose control, and simultaneously leaned towards one another--

--Just as the radio buzzed again.

"*Police Central Command, this is the... same person who contacted you before. I'm at the scene, and now... something just sunk a second boat. I mean... It just tore it to shreds in like a few seconds. Please send help, there's a woman in the water, and she appears to be unconscious! I think there's something in the water."*

"This is the Chief of Police. I'm sending in all of my units. Someone will be there momentarily. Please remain calm. Do you know what happened to the second vessel?"

"I think there's something in the water! I don't know what, but I think there's something big swimming around over here. I'm near the woman, and I can try to get her on board."

"...Okay, you may proceed. All units, please report to that location. Forty-nine-eight? Are you on scene yet?"

"Negative. But we're nearing. Stand by, please."

Napier and Thompson looked into one another's eyes once again. This time, it wasn't a feeling of calm and kindliness. They were both feeling alert, and now Thompson's instincts as a Coast Guard diver kicked in.

"Let's go," she said. Napier didn't argue as he quickly rushed into the cabin and clicked a switch to bring up the anchor. After that task was complete, he throttled the *Catcher,* turning it to a northerly direction, following the sirens from Deputy Jones' vessel.

****

Tom steered the *Babe Magnet* as close to Rebecca as he possibly could. Chunks of the *Comanche* bounced off of the hull as he entered the scene of the disaster. It was like a graveyard at sea. Next to Tom stood a hysterical Jesse, who shivered from the sight of Doug being impaled by what appeared to be an enormous claw. She had pleaded with Tom to simply steer the boat away and head for shore. But he couldn't live with himself if he left the area knowing a living person was still in the water. He argued with himself mentally. He saw the same thing Jesse did. However, he debated if it was what they thought it was. *We were several yards away, so we didn't have the best perception. Perhaps it was a large stake of wood or a pole from the boat. It was breaking apart, into several bizarrely shaped pieces. Perhaps an air bubble or something forced a broken piece of the vessel toward the surface, where Doug happened to be.* He knew his mind's rationalization for what possibly happened didn't make much sense. Whatever killed Rebecca's friend appeared very much alive, and there was no other explanation as to what wrecked her vessel so fiercely and so fast. It was almost as if it had hit a mine. He forced himself to quit thinking about it for a moment so he could concentrate on rescuing the helpless Rebecca. Pulling the *Babe Magnet* a yard-and-a-half away from her on the starboard side, he looked back to Dillard.

"Ray!" he called out. "Hurry and grab her!" Ray bit his lip. Never in his life did he expect this day to get so strange. Even in this moment of calamity, his selfish behavior begged to take over. He hated the fact that he was reaching out to save his ex-wife. He remembered all the nagging, or at least what he perceived to be nagging; the arguments that he blamed her for, despite the fact that he started most of them; and finally, the lack of sex, again his fault-- affairs don't usually put wives in the mood. He ducked under the railing and held his arm out for Rebecca. However, he didn't reach out to his fullest extent. His selfish behavior had succeeded. He knew if he hung out further over the side and stretched his reach to its maximum while holding the railing, he'd be able to grab her wrist and pull her up. Instead, he decided to make it appear as if he was doing all he could. He decided he'd rather leave her in the water. Dillard was never a saint. He was barely decent. But this was the worst from him.

"I can't reach!" he lied. "Let's just get out of here. You guys said there was something in the water, so let's leave before it gets us!" He didn't see the creature that Jesse claimed destroyed the *Comanche.* Except for what he said on the radio to the police, Tom didn't confirm or deny that there was something beneath the surface. Dillard simply thought they were both crazy, but he figured he could at least use that to his advantage.

"Try harder, Ray!" Tom ordered. He saw his friend wasn't trying hard enough, but chose not to believe what he suspected that meant. Jesse rushed to the railing where Dillard kneeled.

"Come on, Ray! Just grab her please!" she pleaded. She could also tell he wasn't trying very hard. Dillard bit his lip. He was being bossed around on his own boat, and he was resenting every second of it.

"You try it!" he yelled and stepped away. Jesse's jaw dropped open in distress to his egotism. She knew there wasn't much time to waste, so she hung over the railing and reached out as far as she could. Rebecca floated face up, still unconscious and just out of her reach. Jesse was a smaller person than Dillard, and didn't quite have the range that he did. Her heart pounded and she began to tear up.

"Damn it, Ray. Please grab her! You have a better reach than I do!" She pleaded. Dillard looked at her, and then looked to Tom, who was about to step out of the cabin. And the look on Tom's face implied that he was going to kick his ass. Dillard exhaled an exaggerated sigh and he reached out over the deck. He quickly snatched Rebecca's wrist, and with a mighty tug he lifted her over the railing onto the deck. Tom and Jesse pulled her to the middle and checked her vitals. She was alive. Dillard leaned back on the starboard side and crossed his arms.

"Good. You can tell her that her ex-husband saved her ass," he said. "Now get us out of here." Both Tom and Jesse looked up at him.

"Listen you jackass! I know what you were trying to do--" Tom's voice went silent as he and Jesse witnessed a purplish-red, worm-like tentacle wiggle out of the ocean, right behind Dillard. He could hear the splashing behind him, and could smell the awful odor coming off the slimy leathery flesh. He didn't have enough time to turn around to see what was behind him; the tentacle had found its target and had coiled around his torso, pinning his arms to his sides, and immediately began to constrict him. His eyes literally bulged, as did his tongue from his mouth as the pressure snapped his arms like toothpicks and crushed his ribcage. He couldn't gather any breath to scream. Instead, blood simply oozed from his mouth, nose, and ears. As quickly as it appeared, the tentacle returned to the surface with a yank, taking Dillard to the depths. Jesse threw her arms across her eyes and screamed for her life and Tom jumped to his feet and dashed for the wheel. He quickly thrust the throttle to its highest speed. The propellers kicked up buckets of water as they twisted like circular saws. The *Babe Magnet* began pushing forward, but following a loud popping sound from under the boat, it suddenly ceased to accelerate. Tom looked back and saw that the propellers were kicking up water. *Why aren't we moving?*

The answer to that question lied in the hull, where the creature had impaled the exterior of the underbelly with its pincers, clamping down on the innards of the vessel. The engine began to emit smoke, and soon enough, the propellers shut down. Several of its tentacles lifted from the surface and began slapping at the boat. Jesse shrieked at each loud clapping noise, and shivered when she saw the boneless invertebrate-like appendages slither onto the deck, as if they were searching for her. On their bottom side was a layer of suction cups, which pressed against the deck. Jesse could see the tip of the barbs that were hidden within the middle of each of these cups, scraping against the deck floor. She held on to Rebecca and scooted back against the cabin, away from the slithery killers that were just feet away from them. Her eyes then went to the port side, and her eyes beheld further terror. The massive body of… 'whatever it was' began to emerge. Water rolled off its huge spiny shell like numerous raging rivers. Its eyes, resembling balloons, appeared to float over its mandibles as they stared at the helpless vessel. Its bony shell creaked like door hinges as the creature rose a massive arm from the water, snapping its pincer in the air.

Jesse whimpered as she began scooting toward the other end of the deck to get away from the creature. Just as she reached the starboard side edge, she felt Rebecca stirring in her lap. The redhead wiped her eyes, momentarily oblivious to her situation, before seeing the tentacles thrashing about in the water as if in a feeding frenzy. Her body was still a bit jittery, but she gathered enough strength to sit up from Jesse's wrapped arms.

In the cabin, Tom had continued attempting to throttle the vessel back to the island, but to no avail. Smoke billowed from the engine, and finally, the vessel died. Cursing every word in the book, he reached into a large cabinet under the radio and pulled out a large inflatable raft. The yellow rubber was wrapped around a rigid object. Tom stepped out of the cabin and yanked a red cord, which automatically unfolded and inflated the lifeboat. As it unfolded, the rigid object became visible. A motor! The vast majority of inflatable rafts did not include a motor, but this one was way different; it was custom made. Leave it to Ray Dillard to throw a couple thousand dollars away on a special motorized raft he likely would never use. Rebecca jumped to her feet. She grabbed the frantic Jesse by the arms and lifted her to a stand.

"That thing won't last ten seconds!" Jesse sobbed.

"We have no choice!" Tom nearly yelled. "The boat's sinking and the engine's dead!" Just as he finished speaking, the *Babe Magnet* quaked as the creature rammed its pincer into the side of the vessel with a hard thrusting motion. Wood exploded upward like magma from an erupting volcano. The two women didn't argue with Tom. They dropped the inflated raft over the side. Jesse jumped in after it, followed immediately by Rebecca. After splashing into the water, they both climbed aboard. As they secured themselves in the rubbery haven, they looked up at Tom, who was about to jump in after them. He jumped as if he was competing in the Olympics, over the edge of the vessel aiming just left of the raft. He was in mid air, looking down at the water, and quickly realized the tightening around his waist, and the fact that he appeared to be floating above the ocean. The barbs had just begun piercing his abdomen as he realized one of the creature's rubbery tentacles had gotten a hold of him, holding him in mid-air. His eyes bulged from their sockets and the tentacle pulled him into the water, underneath the sinking vessel, into the jaws of the monster. Jesse put her hands over her eyes and screamed non-stop. As she panicked and rendered herself helpless, Rebecca forced herself to focus. With a yank of the cord, the motor kicked to life and immediately pushed the little raft forward. Rebecca monitored the creature's position. It was still with the sinking *Babe Magnet*, which was now crushed into a V-shape, with the stern and bow pointing upward and the middle section bent into an arrowhead-shape. It wasn't long before it too was swallowed by the ocean, leaving behind a floating trace of rubble in the midst of thrashing tentacles. Twenty feet, thirty feet, forty feet, fifty feet. Just as Rebecca was ready to feel secure, she noticed the center mass of the creature turn in their direction. She knew it could sense their presence, and that gut feeling was confirmed when she watched it kick up water in pursuit.

"Damn it!" she cursed. She looked ahead and immediately saw red-blue flashing lights on a white vessel heading her way. It was closing the distance fast, so she turned off the motor and immediately threw her hands in the air, flagging the police cruiser.

****

"There!" Deputy Burg pointed to the small yellow raft just thirty meters ahead of them. Jones slowed his vessel to a stop, bringing it alongside the raft. Burg held a rope in his hand and tossed it over the port side out to the women on the raft. Jones quickly stood along-side him.

"Are any of you hurt?" He called down to them.

"We're okay, but we need to go now! It's coming back!" Rebecca responded, grabbing the rope. Jones and Burg both looked to each other in confusion as they pulled the raft up around the stern of the cruiser, where they could climb aboard. Jesse, hearing Rebecca's words, began to panic once again, after just beginning to enhance her calm.

"Oh no!" She sobbed. "It's coming back! It's gonna kill us!"

"Wait!" Jones said. "What the hell happened out there? What's coming? Were you on the fishing boat that sank?"

"There's something in the water, and it's coming this way!" The approach of a large vessel grabbed Jones' attention. Looking out past the stern, he could see the *Catcher* approaching. *Excellent!* He thought. *Napier, you're timing couldn't be better.* He grabbed his radio.

"*Forty-nine-eight* to *Catcher*. Can you hear me, Rick?"

"*Loud and clear,*" Napier's voice answered through the radio.

"Listen, I've got two women here in a raft that need to get picked up. Could you give them a lift please? Something weird's going on over here." The line that Burg was holding suddenly went weightless. Both Deputies looked to the water and saw that Rebecca had started the motor and sped the raft away.

"What the hell," Burg said.

"*Forty-nine-eight* to *Catcher*," Jones continued. "Looks like they're heading in your direction. Let us know when you pick them up--" Both deputies suddenly fell to the deck as the vessel's bow literally exploded as if struck by a freight train. Bits of vessel blasted out in nearly every possible direction, and the engine briefly erupted into flames before the ocean water rushed into the gaping hole where the bow used to be. Jones felt his teeth puncture the roof of his tongue at he fell forward to the deck, cracking his chin on the wood floor.

"Sweet love of--" Burg cursed as he sat up from the deck, holding a hand over a bleeding gash on his forehead which resulted from him hitting the starboard edge.

"Get on your feet!" Jones shouted as pushed himself up to his feet and rushed to the radio.

"What in the hell was that?!" Burg yelled. Jones ignored him as he was focused on getting someone to help their situation. As he grabbed the radio, Burg looked out to the bow, or at least where the bow used to be. All that remained was a massive hole, outlined by splintering bits of vessel, fogged by steam.

"*Forty-nine-eight* to command! Our cruiser is sinking fast. We've been hit by something large and unknown." He paused for a minute, and realized the radio was dead, possibly due to short-circuit from the impact. "Fuck!" He yelled as he threw it to the deck.

"Holy shit! What in the hell is that?!" Burg yelled as he pointed to the water. Jones directed his attention, and his hand instinctively went for his holstered Glock 40 caliber as soon as his eyes captured the sight of the enormous entity thrashing about in the water in front of the vessel. The hairs on his neck stood on end and his heart rate greatly increased. He wasn't sure whether he was in shock or disbelief as he watched the rigid, goblin-like shape emerge at the vessel's former-bow. On all sides of the creature, the water thrashed as the tentacles squirmed around it, as if they had minds of their own.

"I'm not waiting for this thing to kill us!" Burg panicked and aimed his Glock at the monstrous creature, firing all ten rounds in under five seconds. Each full-medal-jacket bullet was crushed against the thick exoskeleton. The creature's eight enormous tentacles thrashed more rapidly in irregular formations. Within seconds, they lashed viciously into the air like the heads of a hydra as they began assaulting what remained of the sinking vessel.

****

"What in the hell is going on?" Napier said, after witnessing the front of the police cruiser burst into pieces. He got on the radio to Police Headquarters. "Chief Bondy, this is Rick Napier from the *Catcher*. It looks like *Forty-nine-eight* just suffered some damage, although I'm too far away to see what caused it. I'm about to pick up the two women on the life raft, as a matter of fact I'm ten-twenty-three on that issue." He slowed the *Catcher* and aligned it to allow the women to come up the stern ladder. Thompson was already on the lower deck with a line in hand, ready to toss it to the raft. She could hear the whimpers coming from the women on the inflatable.

Rebecca turned off the motor to prevent going past the *Catcher,* allowing the raft to drift with considerable momentum. With her hands, she paddled the water to steer towards the vessel's stern. She saw Thompson standing at the edge, holding a rope line in hand. Rebecca held out her hands, and the Lieutenant tossed it with all of her might. Her aim was spot on. The line landed precisely in Rebecca's grasp. She held on tight as Thompson began pulling the raft in.

Lisa Thompson grunted with each tug on the line. The raft was still several yards out, and bringing it in proved tedious. The sounds of footsteps signaled to her that Napier was on his way down, and within a few seconds, he was there at the stern to take the line from her.

"Get ready to pull them aboard," he said as he tugged on the line. His arms flexed with each motion, bringing out the display in his muscles. After a tense minute, the raft was against the edge of the stern. Thompson looked down the ladder, but quickly moved out of the way as the younger girl sprang up onto the deck like a person possessed.

"Oh God! Oh God! It's gonna kill us!"

"Wait. Wait, please calm down," Thompson said. "Tell us what happened."

"It's killed a bunch of people. It's trying to kill us!"

"Slow down," Napier said as he pulled up the line. "What's killing people?"

"I don't know what it is!" she screamed. Thompson placed a blanket over Jesse's shoulders.

"Relax, relax," she said. Rebecca then made her way onto the deck, still dripping wet.

"Can we please get out of here?!" she quickly said.

"You're welcome," Napier said with an ice cold glare. Rebecca paused for a minute, realizing that her saviors were not quite aware of the…nightmare.

"I'm sorry; I'm not trying to be difficult. But there's something enormous in the water! It just sank my boat, as well as this girl's vessel."

"What the hell is it?!" Napier nearly yelled. His temper was beginning to send the girl into another panic spasm.

"I don't know! I haven't seen anything like it!" Rebecca said.

"What the hell are you talking about?" Napier felt like he was in the Twilight Zone. His nerves were flaming, as a result of a combination of confusion, frustration, and a slight sense of fear. "You mean some animal or something sank both your boats? What did it look like? A shark?"

"I just said, I don't know!" Rebecca almost yelled. Jesse hyperventilated, rocking back and forth with severe anxiety. With tears spewing from her eyes, she stood to her feet and screamed.

"It has tentacles like a squid! But it has a shell like a crab! A CRABSQUID! A behemoth nightmare!" There was a long, silent pause, save for the sobs of the panicking girl. Napier and Thompson looked to each other, finding nothing in the other's eyes except a greater sense of confusion… and a growing, tingling fear. Napier quickly rushed to climb into the cabin, while Thompson stayed on deck with Rebecca and Jesse. In moments, the *Catcher* pressed forward, intent on catching up with Jones.

****

Jones threw his arms over his face and ducked down as the flailing tentacles assaulted the crumbling police cruiser. Bits of wood, plastic, and metal were tossed in every possible direction like sparks in a welding factory. The deck beneath the deputies' feet began to splinter and the edges of the vessel cracked. The bow, or what little remained of the bow, sank underneath the thrashing surface of the water, allowing water to leak into the cabin, which weighed the vessel down further. Deputy Burg crouched as he fought against gravity and the slippery slope, while struggling to get a fresh magazine into his Glock. The tentacles did not grab ahold of anything. Instead, they slapped the boat repeatedly, causing the breaking of boards, railing, and pipes. They assaulted relentlessly from the sides, as well as the top.

Burg cursed as he finally slapped the loaded magazine into the handle of the Glock, and yanked back on the already locked slide to chamber the first round. Balancing carefully on his feet, despite the overwhelming terror and mindless destruction of his police vessel, he stood up from his crouching position. With both hands clutching the handle, he extended the weapon toward the demonic enemy, and squeezed the trigger. Despite the chaos surrounding him, he could almost hear the 40. Caliber rounds stopping cold against the beast's solid exterior.

Down on the wood deck, unable to maintain his balance, Jones looked up to see his partner attempt to fight back. He was a few feet behind Burg, and he could easily tell that the bullets were having no effect on the thing. Suddenly his eyes went to the right as another tentacle rose from the water. Unlike the creature's main body, the tentacle was clearly flexible, slimy, several feet thick, and well over a hundred feet long. It drew back, like a baseball bat, and suddenly sliced through the air towards its target. Jones' realized something critical in that moment: the tentacle's aim was not simply towards the side of the crumbling boat.

"Burg! Look out!" Jones' urgent warning came too late to make a difference. Burg didn't feel a thing as the swinging tentacle swiped just above his shoulders, taking his head clean off his neck like a golf ball from its tee. Burg's headless body quivered for a moment before collapsing to the deck, with blood gushing from the stump. At that moment, what focus and sanity Deputy Jones had managed to maintain had disappeared. Screaming like a madman, he stood up, ankle deep in water, and he drew his sidearm. He immediately fired mindlessly at the beast while his boat crumbled apart and sank beneath him. Within seconds, his gun was empty, with the slide locked back after expelling the final round. In a state of panic, he continued pulling the trigger repeatedly, seemingly unaware of the empty clip. Also unbeknownst to him was the tentacle that had slithered its way towards him. Jones finally managed to eject the empty clip and had grabbed a hold of a fresh one. Suddenly, within a single moment, he felt intense pressure around his ribcage, and the jerking motion of his body being lifted into the air like a kite. The gun and magazine were flung from his hands, leaving him to flail his arms helplessly in the air.

"NO!" he yelled with what air remained in his lungs. He begged to the Savior that he was only in some horrible dream, from which he'd wake up; that what was happening couldn't possibly be real. Those hopes were quickly crushed, along with his ribs and spine as the tentacle squeezed mercilessly. The pressure also caused blood to burst from several vessels in his body, leaving them with nowhere to go except out his ears, nose, and mouth.

****

Napier had been throttling the *Catcher* toward Deputy Jones' vessel, after failing to get a response from him over the radio. In the cabin with him was Thompson, who had been previously busy trying to calm down their new passengers. The radio was filled with police chatter, particularly from Chief Bondy as he barked instructions to his other police units, as well as get in contact with Deputies Jones and Burg. It didn't take the *Catcher* long to reach the location of the police vessel, or what was left of it. However, there was something else where it was. Something huge. Alive.

"What in the name of--" Napier couldn't manage to finish his exclamation. His eyes widened, and Thompson was equally as shocked. The tentacles thrashed around the bulging, sixty-foot long rigid mass, like natives worshiping a deity.

"Oh my God," Thompson whispered. It was as if she had re-encountered a demon from her worst nightmares. Napier understood the tone in her voice. It wasn't just shock, it was recollection.

"Jesus, Mary, and Joseph," he exclaimed as his voice instinctively elevated to a shout. "What the hell is that thing?!" Before Thompson could respond, one of the tentacles grabbed their attention further. Rather, what was gripped within the tentacle. The blue uniform trousers were unmistakable. "Oh shit! Jones!"

"Rick, turn the boat around and let's get out of here!" Thompson shouted, just as she would bark orders to personnel in the Coast Guard. Napier felt the urge to argue for Jones' life, but he forced himself to think rationally. There was no chance for saving the deputy, assuming he was even still alive in the grasp of the monster. Still, Thompson had no patience. "NOW!" The engine roared as Napier steered the vessel portside, turning it to the island. He pushed the *Catcher* to its maximum speed and quickly grabbed the radio.

"*Catcher* to Chief, please acknowledge," he spoke into the device.

"*This is Chief Bondy. Napier, is that you?*" Bondy's voice came over the receptor.

"That's affirmative."

"*What is it? I'm unbelievably busy right now.*"

"Chief! You need to make an emergency announcement. Tell everyone to get out of the water right now! I repeat: Tell everyone to come back to the island. Swimmers; boaters; deputies; EVERYONE!"

"*Rick, what the hell are you talking-*"

"Damn it, Chief! Jones and Burg are dead! There's something huge in the water out there, and it's killed over a half-dozen people just now!" For a few moments, there was silence over the radio traffic. Napier and Thompson both knew that the Chief was trying to wrap his mind around what he was just told.

"*Rick, you've better report to me ASAP! And you've better not be screwing around with me! I'm making the emergency announcement! And when you get here, you'd better explain this to me in greater detail! Over and OUT!*" This was one of the extremely rare times Bondy would actually treat Napier like one of his deputies, rather than a friend. And Napier wasn't complaining. Getting out of the water was the *first* thing on his mind.

****

It welcomed the replenishment of energy resulting from consuming its most recent meal. However, its sensory nerves flared once more upon picking up signals from another mass in the water, quickly moving away from it. It was no longer about hunger, but about territory. It released the grip from its massive pincers from the inedible creature which it had just defeated, allowing it to break into more pieces. It filled its numerous sacks with seawater and propelled itself after its new enemy, thirsty to kill more and more.

****

On Palm Beach, Chief Bondy fumbled through his giant supply bag for his microphone to call in the swimmers. He had been so focused on organizing his patrol unit's the entire day; he hadn't properly organized his materials. As he dug through the bag, his mind pondered over what to tell his men. Rick Napier was definitely not someone who would over exaggerate, leading Bondy to understand that whatever he was talking about over the radio was true. But the chief was still confused. Perhaps it was learning the knowledge that two of his deputies were dead, and he would have to explain this reality to their families. But what was that reality other than simply death? He forced his mind to push that issue to the side after he located his large red microphone. Before doing anything with it, he quickly grabbed his police radio to communicate with his other deputies.

"Attention all units, this is Chief Bondy. We appear to have a major emergency in progress right now. I need all boating units to sweep the island perimeter and make sure every fishing vessel comes back to port! When finished with your side of the island, immediately make your way to East Port, where you'll receive further instructions from me." The police units acknowledged their instructions over the radio, which Bondy didn't pay too much attention to, as he picked up his microphone and quickly made his way from his post to the sandy beach. Briefly before making his announcement, he scanned the water to see how many swimmers were in the water. There were too many to count, with some swimming over a hundred yards out. In addition, the area stretched for nearly a quarter of a mile. And Bondy was alone to see that everyone got out safe. *Just my damn luck!*

"Attention!" He called out through the microphone, which carried his voice out into the distance. "Attention please. I need everyone to...calmly, and carefully," he put strong emphasis on those two words, "come in from the water immediately. Do not panic. Please be calm and careful. But I need everyone to please come in from the water." His announcement earned him stunned looks and glares from every direction. It was as if the 'deer-in-the-headlights' response had gone viral. Bondy had initially feared that the large mass of people would come swarming out of the ocean, crawling over one another, creating a panic all by themselves, as well as several injuries and further confusion. What happened was the opposite. Hardly anyone moved. Some people in the distance even continued swimming; they probably couldn't hear the message. Without holding the microphone to his lips, he simply flung both arms into the air and called out.

"Come on!" It was as if his natural voice spoke louder than with the microphone. The people were moving slow, but they were finally beginning to come in. Slow was good. However, as Bondy scanned, it appeared that several swimmers were still far out, either swimming or on floating devices. All he could do was hope that they begin coming to shore quickly.

****

"Oh God," Thompson said. She was on the upper deck, looking out to the aft of the *Catcher*. Napier glanced back through the open cabin doorway, but quickly redirected his attention to the bow to focus on steering his vessel.

"What is it?" he called back to her. His voice barely carried over the roar of the boat's engine and the strong wind. Thompson turned back to face him, and although he couldn't see her, his senses could detect the worried expression on her face.

"Rick! I think that thing is after us!" Napier, with his hand still on the throttle, took a prolonged look back. He focused his vision out to the distance behind his vessel. He could see the bulging and splashing in the water nearly a few hundred feet back.

"Oh shit! Shit! Shit!" he called. He already had his vessel at the maximum speed. Thompson quickly joined him in the cabin.

"Can't you go any faster?!" she worriedly asked.

"I'm already pushing her as far as I can. If I go any harder, the engine will blow, and I don't know about you, but I don't see how that would be helpful in getting away from that thing." Thompson simply nodded, indicating that she understood and looked back to monitor the distance between themselves and the 'thing'. As Napier got himself to calm down mentally, he recalled noticing Thompson's initial reaction when they first saw the beast taking down the vessel. While she was somewhat shocked and puzzled, there was something else in that expression as well. There was a sense of reminiscence and recognition. Then he remembered the circumstances of them meeting. Her incident at Mako's Edge…

"Lisa?" he spoke. "Is that the thing you saw when that diver was killed?" There was a few moments of silence.

"It is," she answered softly.

"Well," Napier said, "at least we know you're not insane." Despite everything going on around them, all of the terrible things that have just occurred, and may yet occur, Lisa managed to crack a smile. It was a little smile, and it by no means signaled that she was in a good mood, especially being on the run from an enormous unknown creature that appeared to be on a killing spree. But she was relieved that she didn't hallucinate, or mistake something for another while diving down there. However, that enlightening feeling was extremely brief, and her mind snapped back to reality. She looked back once again to try and monitor the distance between them and their pursuer. "How far is it?" Napier asked.

"I don't see it," Thompson said.

"Huh?"

"I think it gave up!" she exclaimed. Napier took an extended look over his shoulder. There was no splashing in the water. No clear indication of any mass anywhere near the *Catcher.* "I think we're in the clear."

"Fine with me!" Napier remarked. "Now to get back home to Razortooth Cove."

"You're not heading into East Port?" Thompson asked.

"No," Napier answered. "Bondy's instructing all of the boaters to come in. East Port will be jammed packed within twenty minutes. It'll be easier to head back to my place, and then we'll use my truck to drive the girls to the beach area. Bondy will probably take a statement from them." The two remained silent for a few minutes, both feeling relief that they had escaped the near grasp of the deadly ocean predator. In addition to the relief, Napier also felt Lisa's hand on his shoulder, and the affection they were unknowingly sharing.

****

Several electric impulses seemed to hit the creature's sensory receptors at once. The vibrations were so strong and distinct, that its instinct instructed it to cease the pursuit of the larger, inedible creature. Its small brain analyzed the signals, concluding them to be originating from more of the small, edible life forms which it had been gorging on. Except in this case, there were several of them to feed upon. Abandoning the chase of the large inorganic species, which had retreated from its expanded territory, the beast moved in toward the land, where these organic creatures flourished in shallower waters.

****

"Please move in from the water! This is the Chief of Police speaking. I need everyone to come out now in an orderly fashion!" Bondy moved up and down the beach, struggling to get the swimmers to come in. While the beach was beginning to flood with compliant tourists, there were still several people out in the water. Some of them were even still swimming, much to the chief's frustration. He overheard some static over his handheld radio, which was clipped to his belt. He clutched the device and held it to his mouth.

"Was there traffic for Command?" he asked.

"*This is Forty-nine-nine. We've made contact with all vessels in our area, and they're complying with our instructions. We'll be heading into East Port.*" Forty-nine-nine unit was comprised of two reserve deputies; Deputy Nick Piatt, and Deputy Kyle Tindall. Both men served in the Florida Department of Corrections before becoming emergency medical technicians in Mako's Center, and had served the local police department since moving to the island five years earlier.

"Before you come in to port, I want you to come to Palm Beach. I've got several people swimming far out and I can't get them to come in. Not sure if they're unable to hear me, or if they're just fucking stupid. Pardon my radio etiquette. Either way, I'm gonna need help getting some of these individuals to cooperate."

"*Ten-four. Forty-nine-nine in route.*"

****

Approximately seventy yards from the beach was a twenty-seven year old man, Terry Willis. He had been swimming for hours, without taking a break. He extremely enjoyed the sport of swimming, being a swim instructor for the University of California swim team. He had just surfaced from a deep dive, finding himself next to a couple of other enthusiastic swimmers, who happened to be an engaged couple. As he took a deep breath to fill his lungs with fresh oxygen, he noticed the swimming couple looking toward the beach.

"I think the police want us to come in from the water," he heard the man say. His girlfriend let out a drawn out sigh. She obviously wanted to stay in, and did not appear to have too much concern for the law.

"Why?" She said. "There doesn't appear to be anything wrong." Her tone expressed her frustration.

"Well, honey, we're a little far out to know that for sure," her man said. After listening to this conversation, Terry could finally hear the echoes of Bondy's microphone. *Don't care about these people. I'm heading in,* he thought to himself.

****

The sensory impulses grew stronger, originating from multiple sources. The creature was nearing its many targets, which were occupying shallow waters. But this did not present a problem for it, as it was plenty capable of coming on land for short periods of time.

Its bulb-shaped eyes locked their vision onto many of the smaller prey. With the targets in range, the creature unleashed its multiple tentacles, intent on capturing as many victims as possible.

****

Two. Three. Four strokes. Terry did not complete the fifth when the petrifying sounds of screams from behind him stopped him cold. He looked over his shoulder, only to see the man and woman elevated over the water's surface, held there by two slithery tentacles, wrapped around their waists and torsos in a corkscrew shape. He could see blood oozing from their bodies, and heard the sound of their screams transform into an airless gurgle as their skeletons were crushed by the constricting tentacles. Finally, after a horrific five seconds which felt like several long minutes, Terry witnessed both people get pulled into the depths of the sea. The swimming instructor was left in a bewildered state of shock, although he was able to gather his thoughts together enough to begin swimming to shore as fast as he possibly could. Six. Seven. Eight. Nine strokes. He completed the tenth, and then the eleventh. Then the twelfth. However, he realized he did not appear to be moving forward, despite completing several more strokes. His heart raced and he frantically lashed out at the water to pull himself to the shore, which felt as if it was forever away. It took several more seconds for his mind and body to finally recognize the crushing sensation in his waist, right before being dragged under the water. The safety of the shore was now truly forever away.

****

Chief Bondy continued monitoring the beach area, as several more compliant swimmers were coming in, crowding the beach. Realizing the overcrowding situation, he took his eyes off the several remaining swimmers to address the crowds.

"Ladies and gentlemen, if you please, I'd like you to please move back and make space. We're starting to overcrowd the beach, and we have more people coming in." Almost immediately, several individuals in the crowd had begun raising their voices. Bondy expected a horde of questions, such as 'why can't we swim?' or 'what's going on?' However, the crowd appeared to be quickly collapsing into a state of panic, with several people pointing out toward the water and screaming.

"Oh my God!"

"What in the hell…?"

"What the hell is that?!"

"Let's get out of here!

"Did you see that?!"

Chief Bondy turned around, and his eyes beheld the horror that the terrified horde was witnessing. The air filled with panicked screams from all over the beach and from the water, as the chief helplessly observed an enormous mass surfacing a little over a hundred feet from the shore. The bulk of the bizarre life form was a sixty-foot shell, with four long tentacles protruding from both of its sides. The front of the enormous 'thing' reared up, revealing its two thick, shelled arms and pincers - like those of a crab. He could see the creature's face, including the expressionless eyes held up like antenna's, and the flapping mandibles surrounding a gigantic bird-like beak, which also opened and clamped shut like the pincers did.

"Jesus, Mary, and Joseph…" Bondy exclaimed, hopelessly watching the flexible, slithery tentacles wildly flailed into the ocean for the numerous tourists who were frantically swimming to safety. In single swift motions, one swimmer was snatched from the water and fed into the creature's chomping bird-like beak, which was quickly turning red with blood. Bondy grabbed his silver Smith & Wesson Model 66 revolver and aimed it at the beast, but held fire due to several people in the line of fire. He then used his other hand to lift his radio to his mouth.

"Attention all units! There's an enormous creature at Palm Beach. I'm gonna need any unit with a high powered rifle here ASAP! Police dispatch, if you're copying this, I need you to alert the Coast Guard immediately!" He could only hope the other units could understand his instructions despite the deafening screams filling the air around him. He didn't wait to find out, rather he ran toward the beach to assist people out of the water. "Let's go! Come on out! Run!"

The creature appeared to be in a massive frenzy. It was as if there were so many victims in the water and on the beach, it almost didn't know what to do with them all. While many of its tentacles were frantically scooping up one hapless swimmer after another to feed into the eagle-like beak, some of the other slithery arms acted more sinister. One male swimmer in blue swim trunks kicked against the water, only forty feet from the sand. But those forty feet may as well have been forty miles once he felt that intense pressure around his waist, followed by several raw piercing sensations. However, the tentacle did not stop squeezing. The swimmer's mouth, nose, and eyes pooled with blood as his internal organs ruptured from the pressure overload. The squeezing continued, and the barbs dug deeper, as if trying to meet the ones on the opposite side of the body. Finally, the swimmer's belly skin met back tissue, which itself quickly tore, and the man simply fell from the tentacle's grip... in two pieces.

One tentacle had been successfully grabbing up one person after another, then dropping each one into the chomping beak as if it were trying to make a quota. After feeding its previous victim to the mouth, it whipped viciously into the water to target another swimmer. Its speed was too fast for its own good. Instead of getting a grab on the person, it simply whipped his body in two pieces, in a nearly perfect diagonal cut, from his right shoulder down to his left side mid-ribcage, causing anything on top to simply peel off.

Another tentacle had also been moving too fast for itself. A female swimmer took one stroke after another towards the shore, getting into very shallow water. She was beginning to feel the sand and pebbles at the bottom of her feet. But the next feeling wasn't so pleasant, which was a much more slimy, tightening sensation on her left arm. In an action which was as quick as each of her individual heartbeats, the tentacle yanked with so much force, it didn't even succeed in lifting the swimmer off the beach. Just her whole left arm.

Throughout the midst of panic, confusion and hysteria, Chief Bondy did manage to hear the radio traffic:

"*This is Forty-nine-nine! We're ten-twenty-three!*"

****

Deputy Nick Piatt, a slightly chubby man in his early thirties, grabbed the fully loaded M-16 rifle from its wall casing, as the skinnier Kyle Tindall took the wheel. They approached the shallow waters, coming up from behind the enormous creature.

"Shit! Don't get too close! This thing is bigger than our freaking boat!" Piatt demanded. The creature was several yards away, seemingly unaware of their presence. The tentacles were thrashing through both the air and the water, as if the beast was intentionally in a murderous rage. He witnessed one swimmer after another get scooped from the water and fed into the razor sharp beak, where they met their end. Within minutes, the beach water was becoming a sea of blood. Piatt did not allow the intensity or the shock of the situation to distract him from his duty. "Be prepared to get us out of here in a hurry!" he said to his partner and good friend.

"Don't have to tell me twice!" Tindall said. Piatt gripped the weapon appropriately, pressing the butt of the rifle against his right shoulder, and balancing the barrel with his left hand. Taking aim was the easiest part, as the creature was nearly impossible to miss due to its incredibly enormous size. He squeezed the trigger, absorbing the kick of the recoil. The rifle was semi-automatic, and he quickly fired one round after another.

"Die, you bastard!" he yelled. There did not appear to be any reaction from the creature whatsoever, leaving Piatt uncertain whether the bullets had any effect. It was clear that the creature had a thick shell, and it was highly likely that it was too thick for the bullets to penetrate. He continued firing until he emptied the thirty-round clip. He quickly dropped the empty clip and grabbed a second one which he had tucked in his waist. After chambering the first round of the fresh clip, he realized that the creature was suddenly submerging. Within a single moment, it had disappeared under the water.

"Did you kill it?!" Tindall asked from the cabin.

"I'm not sure," Piatt said. His voice expressed his uncertainty. "Tindall, I think we should move…" His warning was too late, cut off by the sudden rearing up of the thirty foot police vessel. Piatt hit the deck, losing his grip on the M-16 which fell over the guardrail, into the thrashing water. More horrifying than that was the sight of what appeared to be all eight tentacles, rising upward from the water on all sides of the vessel. Piatt looked up to the sky as he grabbed for his Glock. Each tentacle then reached across the vessel from its relative position, clasping together as if making an enormous fist. Both Piatt and Tindall let out a terrified scream before they, along with the vessel, were crushed by the constricting power of the combined efforts of the tentacles as they pressed their enemy against the submerged shelled body of the monster. After the cruiser disappeared beneath the surface, all that remained was a floating graveyard full of broken up metal, wood, flesh, and bone.

****

It had slaughtered countless enemies, and expanded its territory. At the moment, there were no enemies within reach, as the rest of the smaller creatures had retreated further inland, leaving no more in the water. But the creature had fed and was momentarily satisfied. Instinct took command, instructing it to return to the safety of the cave. Soon, it would forget the events of the day, aside from the memory, itself serving as instinct, that its rightful territory had been greatly expanded, and any life form lurking in those waters would have to be eliminated.

It filled its jelly-like sacks and propelled itself away from the island, leaving behind a beach full of debris, despair, and blood.

CHAPTER 12

The sun was slowly beginning its descent from its position in the sky as the late afternoon transitioned into early evening. Rick Napier hated this time of the day, because the sun always shined into his rear view mirrors, which in turn redirected the light into his eyes as he drove his truck into town. After arriving back home, he and Thompson immediately took the girls they had rescued to the Main Hospital, and stayed long enough to make sure they would be alright. After nearly a half hour at the hospital, they witnessed the main lobby suddenly overflow as over a hundred injured tourists flooded into the building like a rampaging tsunami. Within a few minutes, the whole hospital was in chaos, with several injured and dying people seeking medical attention, and the hospital only having limited doctors, staff, and resources to immediately care for everybody. Realizing the doctors and nurses had more important concerns, Napier and Thompson both knew their services were no longer required and they let themselves out of the building. Now they were on their way to the police station, knowing that Chief Bondy was probably in need of assistance following the events of earlier. He didn't know the half of it.

He steered his vehicle to their destination, but had to pull off to the side of the road several dozen yards from the police building, due to the several hundred angry people grouped outside. To Thompson and Napier, it appeared to be a protest of some sort. They could see the front of the building, where a couple of reserve deputy sheriffs whom he did not personally know were trying to calm the crowd. He could tell, by the exhausted expressions on their faces, that they were not anticipating pulling such a long and agonizing shift.

"What the hell is this?" Thompson exclaimed.

"Whatever's going on, it clearly has something to do with what happened earlier," Napier said. He eyeballed the crowd, checking for any signs of hostility. He was confident they would be able to get through to the building. "Come on, let's go on in. They'll probably know who I am, and hopefully let me in." They moved in, squeezing their way through the crowd. "Excuse me! Pardon me. Let me pass, please."

"U.S. Coast Guard member! Let us through, please!" Napier had to hide his astonishment when he heard Thompson play the officer card, despite being on suspension. Not only did that not work, it completely backfired, as now every single individual had expressed interest in them now. Almost instantly they were bombarded with question after question, all asked hurriedly, with everyone talking over each other.

"U.S. Coast Guard? What's going on?"

"Are you here to help us?"

"What are you waiting for?! Go out there and kill that thing!"

"What good are you doing 'Coast Guarding' here inland? Aren't you supposed to be looking for that thing?!"

"When can we go back into the water?"

"How long will fishing be suspended?"

"I hear nobody is allowed to leave the island? What about my rights?!"

"HEY!" Bondy's frustrated voice called out via microphone from the front porch. The crowd, most of them at least, turned their attention to the chief. "Let those individuals pass!" They crowd complied, only because they were more interested in directing their countless questions to the chief. Napier and Thompson squeezed passed person after person. Finally, they managed to get to the safety of the officers who created a protective barrier between the police quarters and the horde. Bondy stood there like a military general watching over his troops. "Hurry up and get inside," he said to Napier and Thompson. He then looked to his reserve deputies. "Keep those people back!" He then followed his guests inside.

Once the door shut, the chattering of the crowd was somewhat muffled, although it could still be heard. Napier and Thompson followed Bondy through a little door which allowed passage around the service counter. Deputy Drake was in the corner of the large office pod, sitting alone in a cubical in an attempt to temporarily escape the stress of the current events. There were two other reserve deputies in the building, both sitting at desks as they frantically coordinated with other agencies via phones.

"Good Lord!" Napier exclaimed. "Chief! What the hell is going on?! At the hospital, there was a flood of people who rushed in as we were finishing dropping off the girls we picked up. And this crowd outside? What did we miss?!" Bondy slammed his microphone on the desk next to him, out of anger of the situation.

"You tell me!" he said. "You're the oceanographer guru. What the hell was that thing?"

"I... I don't know. There has never been anything documented of a sea creature of that size and description. I know nothing about it."

"It had chased us for a distance, and it appeared to have given up," Thompson said. "Did it attack other vessels?"

"That... 'thing'... actually came to shore! To the beach! And it killed several people, including two more of my deputies. Volunteer deputies! And then Deputy Jones..." he looked over to Drake, whom Jones was best friends with. "We're a little overwhelmed." He looked Thompson in the eye and pointed a finger at her. "Lisa. When you alleged you saw a creature off of Mako's Edge, I'm guessing our visitor was the one you saw." Thompson simply nodded her head. "Well, I suppose myself and a lot of people owe you an apology. But I hope you don't mind if I save it for later. My mind's fucked up right now." He took a seat, and breathed deeply. "It's been several years since I've had to inform a deputy's family member that their child or spouse had been killed in the line of duty. Today I had to do that four times. Needless to say, it sucks."

"I'm sorry," Napier said.

"I'm sorry too," Thompson followed. There was a few moments of silence. "Were you able to get in touch with the Coast Guard?"

"That's the other screwed-up thing about today," Bondy said. "We can't seem to get any transmissions out of the island. Not by phone, or radio. It's almost as if there is something wrong with the radio towers. Land lines are only good for use inland. Cell phones aren't getting any signals either. Check yours out." Napier pulled his Verizon cell phone from his pocket. *Searching for Service,* it read on the front screen.

"As if this day hasn't gotten weird enough," Napier said.

"If only I could contact the Coast Guard," Bondy ranted angrily. "The Coast Guard Cutter *Ryback* is only just a few miles out. Commander Tracy has been ordered to remain on standby. It would not take long for them to get here." As if triggered by Bondy's statements, a light bulb lit up in Napier's mind. Although somewhat inconvenient, he thought of a way he could get in touch with the Cutter.

"I've got a proposal," he said. Bondy and Thompson turned their attention to him. There was another brief silence, as Napier struggled to gather his thoughts, although the idea was rather simple. "Well… all we need to do is fuel up the *Catcher*, and if the *Ryback* is that damn close, then why the hell don't we just head out to them?"

"Approaching a 360 foot long, armored Coast Guard Cutter this late at night with no radio transmission? A cutter armed with a navel gun capable of firing seventy-caliber shells that would sink a rival ship? That's asking for trouble!" Bondy said.

"Wait!" Thompson cut in. "It can work. The *Catcher* has a spotlight, which we can use to make ourselves visible. When we get close enough, if the boat's radio won't work, we'll be able to use the microphone to get the attention of any Guards on board."

"We can leave tonight, but it has to be now," Napier said.

"Hold on!" Bondy said, holding out his hand as if about to bark an order. He exhaled sharply, anticipating what he was about to say. "I'm gonna have to go with you."

"But Chief, what about everything going on here?" Napier questioned.

"I understand, but right now, the Lieutenant here is still suspended, despite the fact that the three of us know the truth: that she saw what she saw and didn't cause the death of her diver. But unfortunately, the rest of the military may not know that, and may not necessarily take you seriously when you continue telling them about a creature under the water. They might listen better to me. I'll put Drake in charge until we get back, but this is only happening if I go with you." There was another brief pause, and Napier didn't have time to stop and think.

"I recommend you get into more comfortable 'seaman' type clothes. We've got ourselves a trip. And better pray to God we don't run into that thing out there."

CHAPTER 13

"How's the Mayor handling the situation?" Napier asked the Chief, who was seated in the back seat of his pickup truck. Thompson sat in the passenger seat as her high school sweetheart drove them to his house, of which they were not far from, to conduct their mission to take the *Catcher* to the Coast Guard Cutter *Ryback*. The chief had changed into a pair of light blue jeans, and replaced his work shirt with an older, brown police shirt with a badge clipped to the left breast, resembling a shirt worn by a town sheriff.

"He's going apeshit with everything that's going on. And he's pissed that I'm leaving the island," he answered. "I don't know what he expects me to do."

"This is the best option," Thompson said. "Even if they won't believe us about the sea creature, they'll have to send units to the island. The important thing is to get medical transports here to get people to bigger hospitals on the mainland. If the Mayor can't see that, then he's a moron."

"Not a tough one to figure out," Bondy said. "He's not too thrilled about when this hits the media. He's more worried how this will affect the touring industry. Rather, there's an election coming, and he's more concerned about how that'll affect his campaign."

"Well, none of that matters right now," Napier cut in. "I'm more concerned about that thing leaving. If it doesn't, someone's gonna have to kill it, which does not appear to be an easy task."

****

The sun was very low in the horizon when Napier steered the truck into his driveway. He put the vehicle in park and turned off the engine, and the three of them piled out. Bondy, in addition to his Smith & Wesson .357 Model 66, held a Remington 12 gauge shotgun. He wasn't going out into the open ocean unprepared. Rick Napier, a gun owner himself, planned on bringing his semi-automatic Ruger SC9 hidden in his closet.

"Alright," he said. "I need to get some stuff from my house. And I need to talk to Jane to let her know what's going on." Thompson and Bondy followed him to the front entrance, when he suddenly stopped at the door. He looked at the window, and then looked at his watch. His companions noticed that he appeared confused.

"Everything alright, Rick," Thompson asked.

"Yeah..." he said, still appearing confused. "It's just that, it's only eight-thirty, and the lights are off. Jane's usually home by now, and she doesn't go to sleep until... much later than I do." Thompson and Bondy both observed through the window that the inside of the house was dark.

"Perhaps she's not home," Bondy said. Suddenly, he finally realized his friend's concern. Napier was afraid his daughter was at the beach earlier. "Let's just go in and check," he said, quickly but calmly. Napier twisted the handle and pushed the door open, quickly stepping into the dark of his home, followed by Thompson and Bondy.

"Jane!" He called out. There was no answer, prompting him to call again. "Jane!" Again, there was no answer. "Shit!" He mumbled to himself as he fumbled for the light switch. Even in his own home, it was tough to locate simple things in the dark. Bondy and Thompson were about to start calling for her when he finally located the switch near the doorframe, flicking it on.

"Oh hell...Rick!" Thompson called out, drawing Napier's and Bondy's attention to the kitchen table. On two chairs sat Jane, and her boyfriend Greg Piper next to her. Both looked at the three adults with wide terrified eyes. Each of them had duct tape over their mouths, and their hands were bound behind them around the back of the chairs. Jane's face was clearly pained and red from hours of shedding fearful tears.

"Oh, jeez!" Napier called out. He quickly rushed to his daughter's aide. Bondy, reaching for his revolver with his right hand, attempted to get his attention.

"Rick, wait!" he called out. He was ignored.

"Jane, baby," Napier said as he pulled off the tape. He then identified her companion. "Greg? What the hell happened?" Jane was still crying and terrified, barely able to get any words out.

"D-Dad!" She sobbed. "They-- they…"

"Who?" He tried to calm her down, while moving behind her chair to work at her binds. "Who the hell did this?" By this time, Thompson was attempting to free Greg. Napier looked toward the living room area to speak with the Chief. "Chief! We need to…" He froze in place after seeing the Chief still, with both hands placed behind his head. Behind him was a sinister man, dressed in black tactical gear, holding a Noveske Rifleworks Diplomat assault rifle to the law officer's head. This individual, while a bit shorter than Napier, clearly was not one to mess with. His face had several jagged scars, including one long one that ran straight down the left side of his face. He had brownish-red hair, and in addition to his rifle he was armed with a Smith & Wesson M&P .40 Caliber semi-automatic on his right leg, and a deadly combat knife on his left hip.

"I'll complete your unfinished sentence with 'don't move'," he said, revealing a sinister smile. Napier and Thompson slowly lifted their hands above their shoulders, remaining completely still after. They each even made sure they breathed slowly. Another armed man, equally equipped, approached the Chief from behind and removed his revolver. He opened the cylinder and let the bullets drop to the floor. "Take it away," the first man instructed. Napier could already tell he was the leader. The other man was just as tall, more of an Asian descent. Possibly Thailand. He sported long dreadlocks, as if he was a wannabe football star. He moved out of sight to discard the seized weapon in an undisclosed location.

"What is this," Napier spoke up. "Who are you people?" Both he and Thompson shuddered when they sensed another man's presence revealing itself behind them.

"I do apologize that we had to barge in on your home like this," the man said. He sounded older, and rather formal. "Oh, and yes, you can turn and look at me. My friends won't shoot you. As long as that's all you do." Very slowly, Napier and Thompson turned around. The man was not like the others. He was a skinny individual; elderly, in his late fifties at least, and dressed in black cargo pants with a black long-sleeve shirt tucked in. Napier could hear the door open, followed by the sounds of two more men entering his home. They were definitely as geared as the other intruders, and they spoke with the scarred leader. Napier didn't focus on their conversation, rather he was intent on getting answers from this unarmed, older man.

"I figured the other guy in my living room, the one who's pointing his gun at the chief, was the leader. But I'm guessing you actually are," he broke his silence.

"You wouldn't have been entirely wrong," the man said. "Allow me to introduce myself. My name is Dr. Isaac Wallack. I'm requiring your cooperation in order to achieve a very important goal. Under normal circumstances I would've simply asked you for your time and efforts, but unfortunately this is a time sensitive matter."

"A time sensitive matter?" Thompson said, in a somewhat cold tone.

"Cool it, lady!" The scarred face intruder snapped. He had secured Bondy's hands behind his back with zip ties, and after landing a swift blow to the gut with his right fist, he forced the law officer to take a seat on the living room chair with his wind knocked out.

"Please forgive my friend over there," Dr. Wallack said. "That is the leader of this mercenary group here, Redford Gibson. We simply call him Red."

"Blood Red," the mercenary leader added. His voice was raspy and chilling. "What do you want done with the cop?" He said to the scientist. "Want me to kill him? Dump the body in the water? Perhaps use it for bait?" Both Napier and Thompson felt their bodies tense up as if jolted with electricity, which was nothing compared to what Bondy was feeling in that moment. Dr. Wallack maintained his professional, indifferent attitude.

"We'll take him with us," he answered. His response somewhat calmed the nerves of the three adult hostages. Only somewhat.

"What the hell do you guys want with me? Why do you have

my daughter and…" Napier looked at Greg, "and this young man like this?"

"As I've said, Mr. Napier," Dr. Wallack began to answer.

"Wait!" Napier cut him off. "You know my name?"

"Yes," Wallack said. "I know who you are. I know about Jane and her boyfriend Greg here." Napier's mouth nearly dropped open. This day was not failing to get more and more interesting. He did his best to hide his surprised expressions, including his fresh feelings of disapproval, due to more important matters clearly being at hand. He wasn't doing such a good job, and Wallack could see this. "I see there are even some things I know about your family that you didn't."

"I-- I, uh…," Napier stuttered. "I… What the hell is this about? And again, how do you know me?"

"I have very good resources," Wallack said. "However, I'm on a very limited budget and schedule. I need you because I need a good-sized boat. You've got the largest one within a good distance of this island. The *Catcher* is a little bit smaller than what I need, but it'll have to do."

"What do you want his vessel for?" Thompson said, while taking a look behind her. From her limited view of the living room, there appeared to be four mercenaries altogether, led by the clearly bloodthirsty man called Red. There was the Thai individual with dreadlocks, who had returned after discarding Bondy's firearm. The two other men were Caucasian individuals, armed with a different type of assault rifle; possibly M4A1 Carbines. One of these men was much taller, standing at a height of approximately six-foot-two, with an extremely muscular build, short black hair, and a rock hard jaw. His chin almost literally appeared to have a solid square shape. The fourth mercenary was just a couple inches taller than his deadly leader, sporting a bald head and a Fu Manchu. The look really didn't work for this man, Thompson thought. She had been listening in on the chit chat between the men, and she was able to get the names, or rather the nicknames of these hired killers. The tall man was Goliath, the Asian man was called Roketto, and the fourth man with the Fu Manchu was referred as Morgan. Thompson redirected her focus to the scientist as he answered her question.

"Well, I understand the civilians and the tourists of this island have had some rather rough encounters with *Architeuthis Brachyura,*" he said. "We're here to capture the beast, and return it to my laboratory."

"*Architeuthis Brachyura?*" Napier exclaimed.

"What in the hell is that?" Thompson asked.

"Well… nothing like it has ever been documented," Napier said. "But judging by the name, it's a… well… *Architeuthis* is the name for a giant squid, and *Brachyura* is the common scientific word for… a crab."

"Hey Doc!" Red called out. "Sounds like you have yourself a new buddy! Since he actually understands your lingo, unlike the rest of civilization." He stepped out of the living room into the kitchen area, pointing his rifle to the floor.

"Well, it makes sense, since our helper has an advanced degree in Oceanography," Wallack said.

"You plan on using my boat to capture that thing?!" Napier refrained from yelling. "Are you even aware that that thing is almost bigger than my boat?! And that's not even including those damn tentacles."

"We're aware, but we have a plan," the scientist said. "I'll explain it better when we're boarded. But your vessel is the best we've got, and besides, you've got something good out of this. We replaced your air winch for you. Well, mainly for our own benefit, because the plan involves netting *Architeuthis Brachyura*. But we'll let you keep the upgrades we made to the *Catcher*."

"And don't waste our time," Red cut in. "This is supposed to be a quick job. Basically, if you want your baby girl and her boyfriend in one piece… and able to continue going out boating together, you will cooperate." He pulled out his knife and placed the straight double edged blade to Jane's throat. She closed her eyes and began whimpering. Napier felt his blood boil in his body, and all he wanted was to take that knife and castrate that mercenary with it. But unfortunately, he was at a major disadvantage and knew that the only way to keep his daughter alive was to cooperate.

"When do we leave?" he said. His tone was expressionless.

"Now," Red answered. He withdrew the blade and sheathed it.

It had left a thin red mark on his daughter's neck, infuriating her father further. He looked at Red directly in the eyes, and in the darkest depths of his mind, he hoped that the enormous beast out there would claim itself at least one more victim before it was eventually stopped.

"Fine," Napier said, nearly spitting on the mercenary. The veins in his head were bulging, and his face was growing more and more tense with anger. "Whatever you want, 'Red'." The merc smiled, and leaned in closer to his captive.

"Blood Red."

CHAPTER 14

It was only several minutes later when the crew had begun boarding the *Catcher.* Napier, Thompson, Bondy, and the kids stood at the deck, guarded by the big brute mercenary properly nicknamed Goliath, while the other guns-for-hire aided Dr. Wallack in loading the equipment on the vessel. Chief Bondy still had his hands tied behind his back, as did the teenagers and Thompson. The only one left not bound in any way was Napier, due to the fact that his 'job' was to operate the vessel. The five hostages stood in the dark, watching their captors load all sorts of special equipment, most of which was packed in large black bags. Dr. Wallack barked orders like a drill instructor at the contractors, which visibly irritated their leader, Red.

Watching his vessel being overtaken was unbelievably difficult for Napier to stomach. It brought forth a terrible feeling of violation. But what infuriated him even more was seeing his daughter tied down. Her face was still red from crying earlier, and her shaky expressions demonstrated the intense fear she was experiencing. Standing beside her was a very ill-looking Greg. Napier was certain that the young man had probably vomited at some point earlier in the day. Somewhere in the back of his mind, he wondered why Jane never told him about having a relationship with Greg, although he actually knew the answer: he wouldn't have approved. When teaching at the high school, he did not care for the spoiled teenager who was very uncooperative and disruptive in class. And Greg was without a doubt the first person to express his joy when Napier was laid off from the school. However, these were just lingering thoughts at the back of his mind, and right now he was smart enough to focus on the much more serious matter at hand. The daughter dating situation could wait for another day, as long as they came out of this scenario alive…

...Which prompted Napier to think on his main concern. The body alone on that creature out there was at least equal to the size of the *Catcher*, if not larger. And then there was the added length provided by the pincer arms and the eight huge tentacles. While the *Catcher* was a bigger, more durable vessel than most in the local area, it was still clear that the beast could easily tear it to shreds. What was worse was the fact that the doctor's objective was to capture it, and he didn't provide a plan. Killing it would be hard enough, but Napier couldn't fathom a method possible for securing an animal of that size and strength. The sound of metal clanging on the main deck snapped him back to reality, and he watched the two subordinate mercenaries, Morgan and Roketto fumbling to load the supplies.

"Hey! Careful with that! That's expensive equipment that you're screwing up!" Wallack yelled from the upper deck. Roketto mimicked a half-assed salute, basically sending the message 'fuck you, boss'. Red climbed the ladder to the upper deck, and supervised along with his employer. From down on the dock, Napier could hear the conversation.

"We've got most of the gear stocked down below," he briefed. "That's where I plan on storing the kids, the woman, and the cop during this trip as well. I know you want the fisherman to drive the boat."

"That's fine," Wallack said. "As a matter of fact, bring them aboard now. We're almost set to go anyway." Red looked over the port side of the deck at Goliath, who stood at the back of the single-file line of hostages. He looked up at his boss, who simply signaled him with a high-pitch whistle and a nod of his head. The brute understood the message.

"Get on board!" he spoke in a deep, emotionless voice. Led by Napier, the group climbed aboard the main deck of the vessel, now accompanied by the other two mercenaries. There were several black duffle bags near the front end of the deck, and a huge black net properly rolled. Even in its condensed condition, the net was still considerably large, almost resembling a thick black tree trunk. Napier looked up to Wallack, who stood almost proud at the upper deck, looking back down at him.

"I'm still quite confused over several things," he said.

"And you can stay confused," Red spoke down to him. "You can just drive the damn boat, and as long as you do that, Mr. Biology Teacher, you won't have to grade my men's attempt at a dissection on your daughter." Once again, Napier felt his body tense and his blood pressure increase. He wanted nothing more than to feed this evil excuse of a man to that monster out there.

"Let's not be too hasty," Dr. Wallack said. "After all, this is Rick Napier's vessel, and we are quite grateful to be using it, despite his inconvenience." After giving the doctor a glare, Red stepped back. "What is it that you would like explained?"

"Well, there are many things," Napier said. "First, how the hell do you plan on capturing that thing? I see the net, but I don't know how you plan on actually getting your pet entangled in it."

"We're putting your storage containers to good use," Wallack explained. "We're using bait to lure *Architeuthis Brachyura* out of its claimed habitat over in Mako's Edge. Particularly dead shark."

"I'm not sure you're going to need bait to tempt that thing," Thompson cut into the conversation. Her voice expressed her disdain for the mad kidnapping scientist. "Judging by the events earlier, if that thing detects this boat, it'll be more than happy to come after it."

"We're not just intending for it to lure it out, but drug it," the doctor explained. "We're loading the dead shark carcasses with a tranquilizer, enough to bring down a creature twice its size."

"Oh really?" Thompson scoffed. "You know this from experience? You tranq a lot of sixty-foot mutations?" Dr. Wallack ignored her remarks.

"We also have another delivery system for the tranquilizer. Mr.... Goliath?" The brute looked up in acknowledgement. "Please show them the harpoons." In compliance, the enormous mercenary reached into one of the thick duffle bags, pulling out a large steel three-foot-long harpoon. The four-inch arrow at the end of the rod was not barbed, rather it was more of a cone shape, and a few inches behind it was a large cylinder tube.

"What's the idea?" Napier asked.

"The harpoon has a drill on the tip, to help penetrate the specimen's shell," Dr. Wallack said. "We launch them from a high powered gun, which will be enough to get the tip in at least one or two inches, upon which the harpoon will automatically start drilling and embed itself even deeper. Once the harpoon has drilled for several seconds, it begins to inject the tranquilizer."

"You don't think that thing won't shake it off before it finishes the injection?" Napier responded.

"Our canisters inject the fluid at a very fast rate. In addition, we have several harpoons loaded with tranquilizer. Once the specimen is sedated, these men here," Wallack points his finger to the mercenaries, "will dive into the water and hook up the net, which will be hooked up to the vessel. Afterwards, we will drag *Architeuthis Brachyura* out of Mako's Edge, to a new destination."

"Whoa, wait," Napier interrupted. "What the hell are we doing?!"

"Your engine has enough power to carry the creature's weight," Wallack assured him.

"No," Napier continued. "I mean, where the hell are we going after that?"

"Not your concern at this moment," Red snarled. "Just know we brought plenty of fuel for the ride."

"It's a secondary facility," Wallack said. "I'll let you know where when we've secured the specimen." He paused for a few moments. "Any other questions?"

"I have one," Bondy spoke up.

"Ah, the Sheriff speaks," Red remarks. Bondy ignored the sarcastic hired killer.

"Do you have a tracking device on that thing out there?"

"It escaped before we could successfully install one," Wallack answered. "Why do you ask?"

"I'm curious as to how you were able to figure out the creature was here," Bondy clarified. "The reports of today's sightings haven't been released yet, due to a strange failure in communications on the island. How did you know your 'baby' was over here?"

"I'll answer that, and I'll answer something else," Wallack said. "You mentioned the failure in communications. We're responsible for that."

"How the hell did you manage that? And why?" Thompson

almost yelled. "We need more medical assistance in Mako's Center, thanks to the carnage that thing out there is responsible for."

"Because I didn't want the world knowing about the existence of my creation until I had recaptured it. At least then, once I've secured the creature and have it once again hidden, the story of the attack on the beach will be discredited as an unexplained disaster, and any remarks of a 'sea monster' will be disregarded as conspiracy theories. These men I have working for me, well, they have access to special advanced equipment. Some of which are designed to block signals on a wide scale, including those originating from phones and radios."

"Explains why we couldn't call out," Bondy said, more to Napier than anyone else.

"And that leads me to your main question: how I knew the creature was here. Well, of course there was the story of the diver that you got killed," he said, pointing to Thompson, "and how the Coast Guard wasn't so pleased of the story of a sea monster. But it wasn't just the sea monster part that intrigued me, rather it was the location. Mako's Edge."

"What the hell is so special about Mako's Edge? Other than the fact that you believe the damn thing is making a home there right now?" Napier asked.

"Because, years ago, that was our original base of operations," Wallack admitted, much to the shock of his captives.

"You were based in Mako's Edge?" Bondy exclaimed.

"I'm sure you're aware of the recent discovery of the cave. The initial discovery wasn't so recent. That tunnel travels throughout the island, which allowed us to house a laboratory inside. The creature was bred there, and I believe it has a natural instinct that led it back there. Back home, where we believe it remains when it's not feeding. Hiding in the cave is likely why the Coast Guard was unable to locate it during their radar operation." He said with a sinister smile. "Of course there was further cvidence that came to me that convinced me further. Such as, since my investigators are so good at their jobs, they were able to hack police records in Mako's Center with their advanced electronic equipment. Those records indicated the finding of a piece of metal, which just so happened to be discovered by you, Mr. Napier."

"What significance does that have?"

"That metal came from the laboratory that *Architeuthis Brachyura* escaped from. Probably got snagged on a splinter in its shell or something. Does the word *Warren* sound familiar?"

"The word engraved on that piece of metal," Napier answered.

"Good memory," Wallack said.

"So you think you're going to be able to contain that beast again?" Thompson asked, though it sounded more like an accusation to the doctor.

"I'm positive," Wallack said. He then clapped his hands together and turned to Red. "Now, I think I've done enough explaining. I want Napier up here at the helm, and I want the rest of them down below."

"You're not thinking of putting me down there!" Thompson barked. Roketto and Morgan began to approach, and they did not appear to have good intentions.

"Lisa, don't," Bondy whispered. "They're just looking for a reason to…" he looked into the eyes of the mercenaries, letting his voice trail off. While he knew what he was telling her was true, accusing these men would probably not lead to good things for him. Or her. Thompson knew what he was implying, and agreed to shut up.

"Fine," Wallack said. "The lieutenant can keep the oceanographer company. The rest go below! Now let's get moving please!" His voice was getting more aggravated and impatient. Goliath untied the bounds on Thompson's hands, and she then followed Napier up the ladder. She looked down and watched the mercenaries open up a lid in the front right corner of the deck, which led to the storage area below. One by one, the teenagers and Chief were herded like cattle into the dark abyss of the vessel. Napier stepped up onto the upper deck and stood eye to eye with Wallack.

"I'm sure you wish you finished your doctorate degree now," Wallack smirked. "You'd probably be doing better things than fishing."

Napier, keeping his cool, simply returned a smirk of his own. "At least I can afford my own boat." Wallack, rather than taking offense, simply laughed.

CHAPTER 15

Napier stood at the wheel, silent as the night as he carefully maneuvered the *Catcher* around the minefield of rocks surrounding the island of Mako's Edge. Standing to his right was Lisa Thompson, who was equally silent. She kept a hand on his shoulder, which was the best she could do to offer support for a father concerned for the safety of his daughter. The *Catcher* had been trailing off the coast of the rocky island exterior for over two hours, with the mercenaries Roketto and Morgan shoving the shark corpses, loaded with tranquilizer, into the water. Spotlights installed on the bow illuminated the pathway for Napier to steer the sixty-foot vessel. However, there was no sign of the creature. The sharks had been injected with oil, in addition to being hooked to a buoy, allowing them to float so they could be monitored by the crew. Not one shark had been touched. Standing outside the cabin on the upper deck was Dr. Wallack, and the lead mercenary Red. Napier and Thompson listened to their conversation, which was all they really could do. Red had already demanded they not speak to each other, going as far as to threaten to put his boot so far up their asses, he'd need to put polish down their throats to shine it.

"You do realize you're asking my men to actually get in the water with that thing?" Red said to the doctor.

"I don't realize, because I'm not 'asking'!" the doctor chastised. "I won't say it again; I want your men to suit up and locate that thing."

"Forgive me, but I'm not so keen on telling my boys to play marco-polo with a freaking oversized piece of calamari!" Red shot back. As dark as his ugly soul was, there was still the loyalty to his comrades, whom he had undoubtedly served many missions with. "I thought you said you were an expert on this thing! You said it would take the bait; that it was used to being fed!" Dr. Wallack remained silent for a moment to process a thought while looking in to the rocky water. He wouldn't admit it, but he was beginning to experience legitimate concern over the possibility for success in this plan.

"Perhaps the specimen is not in the area," he said. He tried not to make it sound like a guess. Red wasn't fooled.

"Hold on, doc!" he was beginning to lose his normally short temper. "You said this thing made a habitat of this place. You said it actually remembers living here."

"That's not true," Wallack corrected him. "It doesn't remember things, like you and I can, for instance. Us, we're able to actually think back, play recordings of thoughts and events in our minds. *Architeuthis Brachyura* does not do that. It has instincts however. Instincts serve as memory. It doesn't actually look at this place and think 'ahhh, home sweet home!' It's more automatic. It knows it is supposed to be here. And it works that way with everything else concerning it, such as feeding."

"So why isn't it here?" Red asked again.

"I don't think that's the question," Wallack said. "I think the better question is: why isn't it taking the bait?"

"Perhaps it just isn't hungry, so you want my boys to dive in and send it a little invite to our party?" Red snarled.

"I have an explanation," Napier said from inside the cabin. Both men stopped talking and looked at him. Red's violent sadistic facial expression grew more intense as he made eye contact with the fisherman, whose back was facing them because of operating the boat.

"Listen, 'Captain Morgan'! Speak one more time, I'll stuff sweet Jane with tranquilizer and throw her over the bow for bait!"

"Knock it off, Red," Wallack ordered. Red shot him a look of disdain, but quickly withdrew it. "Forgive the rudeness, Mr. Napier. What is your take on the situation?" Napier knew how he truly wanted to answer that:

Well, let's see. Four armed men, led by a crazy ass scientist, kidnap myself, my high school sweetheart, along with the Island Chief of Police and my daughter and her boyfriend. The take would be a felony abduction, with aggravated assault added to that jerk off Red. What I would like to see of this situation would be you assholes off my boat, stranded out here in that raft that was left here by that Rebecca person we saved.

His mind suddenly illuminated as if a switch had been flicked on. He stopped the vessel and turned to the deck. He needed to walk to the edge and look down to the main deck. *It must still be there. Rebecca's raft. It must!* And Wallack had given him the perfect excuse to check.

"Why'd you stop the boat?" Red asked in his cold raspy voice.

"I don't want to be distracted while driving," he remarked while stepping out of the cabin. "That's how accidents happen."

"That's fine," Wallack said. "I want to hear the input from the oceanographer."

"He dropped out," Red complained.

"Didn't I tell you to shut up?!" Wallack raised his voice. He exhaled sharply, cooling his nerves. "Again, I apologize. What's your advice?"

"I think it may still be here, most likely in the cave," Napier began. He walked to the edge of the deck, and casually looked down as if admiring everything going on down there. There were lights illuminating the whole deck area, allowing the mercenaries to be able to see what they were doing. Tools and equipment were scatted all over the place. Goliath stood in the middle of the deck, with a large duffle bag placed down near his left foot. That bag likely contained the scuba supplies. Morgan and Roketto tirelessly continued to throw bloody chum over the stern of the vessel. The stink of the fish guts radiated throughout the entire boat, including the upper deck. And in the back corner, starboard side, was the deflated raft, which Rebecca had conveniently brought along when she got rescued by Napier and Thompson. Beside it was the motor, which had been detached, but could easily be reinstalled once the raft got inflated. The raft would be too small for all of them. Hopefully he would be able to get Bondy and Thompson on it at least, and have them flee to the Coast Guard Cutter *Ryback* and get in touch with Commander Tracy.

"You have anything original to offer?" Wallack said. Napier's mind refocused on the current task: BS-ing the mad scientist. However, he actually did have some reasonable thoughts for the scientist.

"I think the reason your baby isn't taking the bait is because it has evolved instinctively regarding its diet. It used to carry the dietary patterns of a scavenger, particularly when your lab fed it on a regular basis. Since it came here, it had to track down prey. Kill food on its own to live. Now that it has a taste for blood, that's the new instinctive memory." Napier looked at Red. "I think it's actually waiting for something to come down there. Or someone." Red cracked a crooked smile.

"Oh, you'd like that, wouldn't you," he growled.

"What he says makes sense," Wallack said. "Now, tell your men to get suited up. They're going into the cave." Red looked the doctor in the eye. He hated being given instructions, at least by non-military individuals. However, he resisted the nearly irresistible urge to argue with the doctor.

"Fine! We'll go test out your handyman harpoons for you. Hopefully your drugs will actually put *Arthetu*-Blah-blah to sleep."

"*Architeuthis Brachyura,*" Dr. Wallack corrected him.

"Christ," Red exclaimed. "Why can't you just call the damn thing a crabsquid?! Instead, you lab-coats have to use these unpronounceable words."

"I'd explain it to you, but it's a moot point for somebody who cannot appreciate science," Wallack said.

"I appreciate it just fine," Red said. "I just appreciate the English language a lot more." He stepped over the rim of the deck and climbed down the ladder to speak to his men.

Napier ignored their conversation. Instead, his attention had gone to the rumbling to the south, which had been growing steadily louder. Streaks of light began briefly illuminating the starless night sky, providing view of the massive storm clouds that resembled huge mountains tumbling toward them.

"Looks like we're gonna get a little wet," the doctor said. "Now get us to the south side of the island. We're gonna give our friend some company." He tapped his hand to Napier's shoulder.

After tightening his fists and playing out his mental fantasy of punching out the doctor and his mercenary accomplices, he complied with his command by going back into the cabin to steer the boat. In the cabin was Thompson, whose concern for him was growing by the minute. She looked at him, wanting to say something. Anything. Particularly one thing: that she cared for him, and she wanted to be there for him. Napier put his hands on the wheel and begun steering the *Catcher* to the right. He looked over to Lisa, and held his gaze. It was affectionate. He opened his mouth, trying to find the words to convey his message. Thompson waited patiently, her heart skipping a few beats.

"I have a plan," he said in a whisper. Thompson didn't say a word. It wasn't what she expected, although she herself wasn't sure what she expected him to say. After a moment she nodded along.

"Okay."

"I need you to listen very carefully."

CHAPTER 16

Thunder rumbled high in the black moonless sky above, while lightning flashed from one horizon to the other. The ocean surrounding Mako's Edge sizzled as a torrential downpour spilled down to earth. Water vapor that developed from the bombardment of warm water was scattered in the air by the wind before it could thicken into fog. The water splashed between the numerous rocky structures and the *Catcher,* which was stationed as close to the cave as possible.

Rick Napier had no choice but to anchor the large vessel, which naturally tended to drift with the current. He had put the vessel in the most open area possible in order to avoid crashing on any rock formations. And he felt tense. This was no area for any fishing vessel to be, especially one as large as the *Catcher.* He stood on the main deck with Thompson, who shared his concern. His thoughts were also on the creature, and what it would do to his vessel. It wasn't his property that he was worried for, rather it was his friends and his child.

Rain pummeled down on them from above, soaking Napier's jeans and t-shirt. He had given Thompson his one raincoat from the cabin, which she reluctantly accepted after briefly debating that he be the one to wear it. The temperature around them had dropped a few degrees, yet there was a heaviness in the air in the form of humidity. On the wet deck were the three mercenaries, Goliath, Roketto, and Morgan, all geared up in their black wetsuits. Each of them had a tactical belt around their waists, which held all sorts of gear, including a side-arm, flares, and large canister-shaped objects. They each wore headsets along with their goggles and mouth pieces, in order to hear instructions from Red by radio. Goliath's goggles also contained a small tube-shaped camera that protruded from the frame like a straw. The camera would transmit images to a computer Red had stored in the cabin, which Wallack would monitor as the team infiltrated the cave. The doctor was still up at the upper deck, waiting for the team to make their jump so he could begin monitoring the screen. Red stood at the portside stern, holding a large loaded harpoon gun pointed down like a soldier on guard duty. He would provide any cover fire if the team needed to get out of the water in a hurry. And considering what they were dealing with, that was a large possibility. He also had a small video monitor, which he had screwed into the rim, under the guardrail. Most of the spotlights had been turned off per Wallack's instructions, believing that the intense light could be playing a factor in keeping the creature away. The only lights were a few lanterns on the deck, which allowed the men to be able to see what they were doing.

Napier watched the men collect their harpoons. The canisters attached near the drill tips were filled with a yellow-green liquid. Rain continued to beat down on them, and the thunder rolled as if an avalanche was taking place up in the clouds. Thompson was growing anxious watching them gear up. She recalled what she had experienced, trying to locate Steve Hogan's sunken fishing vessel. Even with a light, it was very difficult to see down there. And she had even had a little bit of daylight remaining. She noticed that the mercenaries' goggles appeared completely dark, like sunglasses.

"You guys sure you'll be able to see down there?!" She shouted over the intense rainfall. The Thai mercenary with braided quarterback hair looked at her with lustful eyes.

"We've been to darker caves," he remarked, spawning laughter from the other men, prompting Thompson to realize it was a sick perverted remark.

"They have night vision goggles," Red spoke up. "They'll be able to see just fine." He turned to look at Napier. "While we have a few minutes, I suppose you'll want to say 'hi' to your kid and your cop buddy." Napier was somewhat shocked. This was probably the first time the mercenary leader had spoken to him without directly insulting him and without threats. He figured he'd take advantage of that.

"I would appreciate that," he said. Red nodded his head to the lever door near the front of the deck on the starboard side and clicked his tongue, basically telling him to go ahead without supervision. The weapons had already been moved out of the storage area, so there was nothing Napier could do that had Red concerned at this point. Rick and Thompson opened the hatch and climbed the small five foot ladder into the storage area below. The light was on down there, giving a clear view of the room. It was actually quite spacious down below. The ceiling was high enough to allow an average height person to stand up straight. The room was about fifteen feet long and twelve feet wide. There was a door on the starboard side leading to a small bathroom, with a pump system that allowed the user to flush the waste into the ocean. On both sides of the room were two long seating benches, where the hostages were seated. Bondy was on the portside, while the kids were on the opposite bench.

"Nice to see you, Captain," Bondy remarked. His hands were still bound behind his back.

"You guys alright?" Napier asked. He rushed to his daughter, while Thompson worked on the duct tape binding Bondy's wrists.

"Well, I suppose under the circumstances they aren't treating us too bad," he remarked. He glanced over his shoulders at Thompson, who was working to free his hands. "You sure you want to do that? Might piss off the sheep herders up there."

"At this point, I'm not concerned at whatever they may do," she said. "They're gearing up to dive in the water and harpoon the creature."

"Well, shit then," Bondy remarked. "Wish they let you come down five minutes ago. I tell ya, it's not easy using the bathroom with your hands tied behind your back." Thompson chuckled along with him. Across the room, Napier successfully freed the wrists of Greg and his daughter. First things first; he embraced Jane with a tight hug.

"You alright, baby?" he questioned.

"Yeah, I'm doing good Dad," she said. She flexed her fingers, working blood back into her hands.

"You sure? Did they hit you? Anything like that?" he asked insistently.

"No, no," Jane answered. "They threatened to, but they didn't.

We were on Greg's boat when they came across us earlier. The police told us to go ashore because of the attacks, so we found the nearest place to beach, which happened to be near his place. And that's when they found us." She paused for a minute and looked to her boyfriend, and back to her father. "Dad, I was going to tell you about me seeing Greg. I was just afraid of how you'd react."

"Honey, don't worry," Napier said. He turned his attention to Greg. "Hey bud. You doing alright?" The young man appeared almost as terrified as his girlfriend.

"Y-yes. Yes sir," he spoke up. Napier put his right hand on the boy's shoulder.

"Listen," he spoke very carefully, "I'm going to need your help. You need to help me protect my daughter. We're gonna get out of here, but in the meantime, your mission is to keep Jane safe. Can you do that for me?"

"Absolutely, sir," the former disobedient student answered.

"If you can do that, then you don't have to worry about my approval," Napier said.

"What's the plan?" Bondy asked, massaging his wrists. Napier took a seat next to Jane, putting his right arm around her shoulder.

"When we responded to the attacks earlier during the day, we rescued some survivors on a ripcord inflatable raft. The good news is that we still have the raft. The cool thing about this is that it's a custom brand that comes with a small motor. All you have to do is pull on the ripcord and the thing just sucks in air, inflating it automatically, and then you hook up the motor afterwards. When we have the chance, I'm hoping to get you and Lisa on that raft, and have you guys high-tail it over to the *Ryback* and get the Coast Guard over here.

"You don't want us to take the kids?" Bondy asked, sounding surprised.

"I want that more than anything right now," Napier said. "However, the raft can only hold a couple people, and I think the people who'll convince them the most of this situation are the two of you. So, right now, the mercenaries are about to make their dive to harpoon the creature."

"Okay," Bondy said. "So that's when we'll make our move."

"No," Napier corrected him. "I don't want you guys out there until we're sure that thing is put under. At that point, the mercenaries will be busy trying to hook up the net. That's when we get you off this boat."

"You think all four of them will be distracted?" Thompson asked. Napier shook his head.

"That guy Red will undoubtedly still be on deck," he said. "I'll have to distract him while you guys make a run for it."

"Distract him? How?" Bondy asked. His eyes were wide open. He wasn't very comfortable with what he believed Napier had in mind. Red was a trained killer, and only God knew how much vicious action he had partaken in over his years. The idea of going toe-to-toe with him was not sitting well in the chief's gut. Granted, he had actually been punched in the gut by the merc, and it wasn't pleasant.

"Let me worry about that," Napier crossed his arms. The conversation was interrupted by the clunking noises from above, indicating footsteps. Quickly after, Red's raspy voice called down from the hatch.

"Hope I'm not interrupting the lovely reunion! It's time for you two to come up!" Napier gave Jane one more hug before standing up.

"We're coming!" he called out. He let Thompson climb the small ladder ahead of him, following her closely. The thunder was still rolling, and the rain was still coming down, though not as hard. The other three henchmen were all geared up and ready to dive. In addition to the tactical belts and swimming gear, each of them wore a simple harness over their suits with a metal ring in the center of the torso.

"Napier, we'll need you at the winch," Red said.

"What's the plan?" Napier asked while following his capture's instructions.

"There should be enough cable to extend to the mouth of the cave. We've attached three simple clips to the end of the cable, themselves attached to three foot long lines, which also have a clip. If we need to get those guys out in a hurry, they'll swim to the cable, hook the clips to their harnesses, and we pull them in at full power."

"And hope they don't smack into a rock during their ride

back," Napier said.

"It's that or be eaten," Red said. "First we'll need you to put slack in the cable." He looked up at Wallack. "You ready, Dr. Frankenstein?"

"Whenever you are," the scientist called back down. Thompson and Napier's eyes met once more. She was about to climb up to the cabin.

"Please be careful," she said to him.

"You too," he said.

"Oh for crying out loud," Red barked. "It's not like you guys are going swimming with it." Thompson ignored him and began climbing the ladder, and Napier stood on standby with the winch lever.

CHAPTER 17

The three mercenaries took a simultaneous splash into the dark water. Goliath swam around the portside of the vessel, taking a hold of the heavy cable. His harpoon gun was strapped to his back, allowing him to use much of his strength to tug the long cable to the cave. Napier pulled the lever for the air winch, releasing slack at a slow steady rate. He didn't want to release too much too fast, or the weight of the overall cable would sink to the bottom, likely becoming too much even for the Olympian sized gun-for-hire to drag it along. Morgan and Roketto led the way, aiming their harpoons in every direction they turned. With night vision goggles, they did not require flashlights to see where they were going.

Red stood at his post at the portside stern, keeping a grasp on the harpoon gun he wielded. He kept it pointed at the sky, while watching his small video monitor. He continuously had to wipe the rainwater off the screen, which caused him to curse the weather. Dr. Wallack took a seat in the cabin as he observed his own monitor, which had a larger screen and had a better signal receiver than Red's. Thompson watched beside him, forced to stand due to the fact that Wallack was occupying the only folding chair. The screen showed everything lit in green night vision. The detail was incredibly clear. Thompson could see Morgan and Roketto swimming in front of the camera that was installed on Goliath's headset. Other underwater details were very well defined in the night vision, such as the underwater view of the huge rocky structures which appeared to form a deserted underwater city. Shredded seaweed floated across the screen, with every loose strand rippling like a flag in wind.

The thunder rumbled above the *Catcher*, and occasionally a bolt of lightning would streak across the night sky. Down on the main deck, Napier continued slowly releasing slack on the winch. While he could see the lit screen of Red's monitor, it was too small and he was standing too far away to see any detail. His shirt and jeans were drenched in water and sweat at this point, but his concern was still focused on his family and friends. He hoped this mission would prove successful, as he would not dare risk an escape with the possibility of that monster lurking in the depths around them. He certainly did not envy the mercenaries, who fearlessly dove in to challenge it.

"I hope those guys will manage to make it out of the cave in time to hook themselves to the cable," Napier said.

"They're good swimmers," Red simply said, only half listening to the fisherman.

"I don't doubt that," Napier said. "However, I question the ability to outswim a sixty-foot predator that actually lives in the water, with tentacles that extend further than its own body length."

"Didn't I warn you earlier about talking?" Red commented back with a brief glare. "I'd suggest you stop. Because otherwise, I could call my men back to collect some bait to entice it out of the cave. And who wouldn't be enticed by young Jane?"

"You son of a--" Napier stopped himself, both from cursing out and making a rush at the sadistic trained killer. His inner voice spoke to him, helping to keep his adrenaline from stirring him crazy. *Just keep your cool and cooperate…for now.* He took a few deep breaths through his nose, and exhaling through his mouth.

****

It took several minutes for the divers to reach the mouth of the cave, particularly because dragging that heavy cable was no easy task for Goliath. Once they had reached the destination, he removed a bolt gun from the back of his duty belt and aimed it towards the bottom floor. The bolt gun was like those used by rock climbers. At point blank range, he pulled the trigger, firing a bolt into the rocky sea floor. An explosion of bubbles erupted from the gun toward the surface, seemingly unveiling the bolt which was now posted firmly. Goliath clipped the cable to it, allowing the three hookups to dangle freely.

"Proceed inside," the voice of Red instructed the mercenaries through the radio. Without the weight of the cable, Goliath felt light as a bird. He holstered the bolt gun and then unstrapped the loaded harpoon from around his back. The other two mercs waited for him, and once he was set they entered the huge circular mouth of the cave. The night vision made the dark tunnel as clear as day. Every speck was made visible. Every grain of sand, every stray piece of seaweed, each spike-shaped rock formation that pointed from the roof of the cave. Each of them kept their harpoon guns aimed into the deep throat of the tunnel, aware that a giant surprise could turn up at any moment.

****

"How fast should that tranquilizer take effect on the thing?" Thompson asked, while admiring the view of the tunnel through the video monitor.

"Once the harpoons are drilled in, and the liquid is injected, the desired effect should begin to take place within a few seconds," the doctor explained, never taking his eyes off the screen.

"And what if the shell is too thick?" Thompson asked. "Perhaps the harpoons may not dig in far enough."

"The shell is very thick," Wallack explained. "But there are blood vessels that run within the shell. Those are shallow enough for the harpoons to inject the tranquilizer. Perhaps the men can hit it in one of the softer tentacles, where the liquid will have easier access. Either way, it will work."

He continued watching the screen very intently, waiting for *Architeuthis Brachyura* to emerge from the darkness. He had not seen his fully matured creation out of captivity on its own, and was very curious to see any behavior patterns that it may have developed. In addition, he was very anxious for the operation to be successful, and hopefully have his prize back in time before the military had officially shut down his laboratory for good.

"What if they put the creature to sleep while it's still in the cave?" Thompson asked. "How will we get it out, since the cable's not long enough?"

"You're just full of questions today," Dr. Wallack remarked. Thompson scoffed.

"Well, I figured it wouldn't be much of an inconvenience since you did kidnap us," she remarked back at him. Dr. Wallack smiled, still not taking his eyes off the screen.

"I suppose you have a point," he said. "In response to your question, I'm hoping it'll chase the men out of the cave before the canisters take effect. If not, we'll have to move the boat closer to the cave in order to get the cable and net strung up to it, and winch it in."

"You'd sink the boat! There's no way we can get close enough!"

"We'll cross that bridge when we come to it," the doctor said. He finally took his eyes off the screen and looked at her. "You're a Coast Guard lieutenant. I saw your record, which is actually quite impressive, minus the recent portion of getting a diver killed and reporting a sea monster to the world, ruining your reputation, and possible discharge from the military."

"Actually, it's your monster, meaning YOU got Denning killed," she corrected him. "And I'm not too worried about my reputation, especially when the truth comes out."

"Well I was hoping you'd accept a job working for me," he said, leaning back in his seat. "There are many open positions in my lab. I need divers, particularly people with experience. If you'd just let things be, and accept the discharge from the military, as well as help me keep this 'monster story' under wraps from the public, I assure you the money will be well worth it."

"That's an insult to me, the people you've hurt, and my country," she said. Dr. Wallack smiled again.

"I take that as a 'no'."

"Damn right."

Wallack redirected his eyes to the screen. The view, while incredible, was more of the same. Rocky formations; muck; darkness, illuminated by the night vision. The men were over a hundred feet in. He watched and waited. One meter after another, the men proceeded inside. After several more yards, the bottom of the cave began to change. There were more rocks built up in multiple weird formations. Wallack examined the screen closely.

He had a radio, which was on the same frequency as the divers.

"Halt," he instructed. "Get a closer view of the cave floor."

Down on the main deck, Napier could hear Red's radio. Wallack's voice sounded intrigued, enough to make Napier interested. He knew that they had not yet located the creature, meaning there was something else that interested the scientist. Shamelessly, Napier marched to Red's monitor, not caring if the mercenary would threaten him for the tenth time. Surprisingly, he didn't seem to care. Napier looked at the green lit screen, observing the multiple rocky formations. The funny thing was that these rocks did not appear to be connected to the cave floor. These were smaller rocks, broken into pieces and laid out throughout this particular area of the cave.

"What the hell are those," Red said, talking more to himself than Napier. He wasn't referring to the rocks, but other objects mixed into the mess. Napier leaned in closer, getting as good of a look through the small screen as he could. These other objects were flatter, and came in more miscellaneous forms and sizes. They didn't appear to be rock, rather…wood. Goliath had gotten closer into the mess, improving the view, which in turn confirmed what Napier was thinking. There were shredded pieces of debris spread throughout this vast area of the cave, mixed with small broken up pieces of rocks. The debris consisted mostly of wood, with bits of pipe and other metal pieces mixed in.

"Holy shit," Napier exclaimed. "That's Steve Hogan's vessel. What's left of it, that is." He turned, marched toward the ladder, and begun climbing.

"Hey! Where do you think you're going?" Red called after him. Napier ignored him. He stepped onto the upper deck and swung the cabin door open, quickly gathering Wallack's attention.

"Aren't you supposed to be at the winch?" The doctor said to him.

"You know what that is, don't you?" Napier spoke up, with accusation in his voice. "There's something here you haven't told us."

"I've informed you that *Architeuthis Brachyura* had made this cave his habitat," the doctor said. Napier shook his head, barely managing to contain himself.

"There's something you left out. What you're looking at down there are pieces of Steve Hogan's fishing vessel. Arguably the first victim from your experiment. When the police and I attempted to investigate the area, there was no sign of his vessel, minus some floating chunks of wood, which only amounted barely enough for a nice campfire. When Lisa," he pointed to Thompson, "and her team of divers investigated the area that night, they also found no trace of the vessel. Instead, they met your big friend out there."

"What are you saying, Rick?" Thompson asked.

"What we're looking at on the screen: that's a nest," Napier said. There were several moments of silence, during which he examined Wallack's body language. "Now I'm going to ask you this once. Is that creature capable of reproducing?" Wallack remained silent for a few moments before making eye contact with Napier.

"You really should finish that doctorate degree of yours," he remarked. "Then you wouldn't be pegged as a dumb fisherman so much. Yes, *Architeuthis Brachyura* is capable of spawning several fertilized eggs on its own. Long story short, the process of hybridization somehow rendered the specimen asexual, meaning it can reproduce without mating with another of its species."

"I know what it means," Napier said. "Like you said, I'm not just a dumb fisherman. Now tell me…do you believe that thing has reproduced already?"

"No," Wallack said. "That's why I had the men investigate the…'nest'. But there are no eggs as of yet. They'd be easy to spot. They'd be shaped like a normal egg, with a few scabby surface features, and they'd be around four feet high. Difficult to miss, even down there. So no, Mr. Napier, we can confirm that the specimen has not reproduced."

"Then we need to stop it before it does," Napier said.

"Stop it? You mean kill it?" Wallack dissected the fisherman's words. "Not a chance! This creature is a biological goldmine! It took several millions of dollars to successfully complete the hybridization process! Years of research and development!" He stood up from his seat. "We're continuing with the original plan. Tranquilize the specimen, net it, and take it to the facility, where we will provide a 'nursery' for it."

"You couldn't contain just one of those things! How can you expect to control several of them?!" Thompson cut in.

"I have more power and more technology and resources than you little people even knew existed!" The doctor raised his voice. He turned to Thompson. "You claimed you loved your country! The development of these creatures means wiping out our enemies! Can you imagine unleashing these things on the Iranian coasts? Or setting them loose near North Korea! The country that you love so much will have total dominance over the planet!" Now more than ever, he sounded like a true mad scientist.

"I believe in having an upper hand over our enemies," Thompson stated, "but these things are a bigger danger to us and countless other innocents than they are to the nation's enemies. You're in over your head. This one alone killed dozens of people in only a couple of days."

"Collateral damage," Wallack coldly stated. Napier and Thompson stood silent, looking at each other as if silently communicating their thoughts. They both knew that the beast must be killed, and that the doctor could not get away with his actions. And God only knew how many other experiments he had in store that could cause countless death and carnage to innocent populations.

****

The mercenaries felt weightless in the water. They remained in place, scanning the darkness with their advanced night vision goggles. They had not received any orders from Dr. Wallack or Red about moving in. Each of them was wishing they could speak on a radio to their commander regarding what to do. They were growing impatient from remaining stationary in their current position.

Goliath considered the thought of proceeding without instructions, but ultimately decided against it. He was practically standing on the bottom of the cave amongst the shipwreck remains, while Morgan and Roketto appeared to hover a few meters above him by flapping their flippers steadily. The brute was growing weary of being this deep in the cave. He knew if they were to find the creature the team would be forced to immediately retreat. And he knew there was not much hope of outrunning the beast. His nerves began to tingle. The water in the cave had been perfectly still, like a lake on a sunny day. But just now, he felt something different: a slight current. And it was as brief as it was slight, which caused the enormous mercenary to focus on the belly of the cave, where that 'current' had come from.

****

Due to the tremendous energy that had been spent from recent activity, *Architeuthis Brachyura* had fallen into another slumber. Having just fed on several smaller life forms, its body did not currently desire the ingestion of more nutrients. However, the electrical impulses raging through its sensory receptors drove the beast from its sleep. There was a new presence in its claimed territory. Multiple presences, each tiny in comparison to the creature. But regardless of size, they were intruders, and instinct dictated to the beast that it must defend its habitat. It was not hungry, but it was certainly bloodthirsty.

****

Another brief fluctuation occurred in the still water, drawing the attention of all three mercenaries. Goliath turned to the other teammates and motioned for them with his hand to move back. The three men backpedaled toward the mouth of the cave, keeping their eyes on the deep dark tunnel. There were other fluctuations occurring within the current, each one making the divers move a little bit faster. And finally, their night vision began to catch images in the dark tunnel. Tentacles rippled from coiled positions out towards both sides of the cave, originating from one enormous body. Even under the stress of trying to stay out of the creature's reach, the mercenaries maintained eye contact of their enormous target. To their advantage, the creature was too large to move very fluidly in the cave. Its gigantic shelled body dragged across the cave floor, pulled forward by the two razor sharp pincers that clawed at the floor. The mercenaries knew that this did not buy them too much time, as the walls widened closer to the mouth of the cave. These warriors had seen much action during their lives, and had encountered more than their fair share of experiences that seemed 'impossible'. But the sight of this monster nearly made their blood run cold. Suddenly, the radio in all three of their earpieces buzzed with static for a moment.

"*What the hell are you idiots waiting for? Fire the damn harpoons and haul ass!*" Red's voice commanded. The urgency of his voice snapped the mercs back to reality. While continuing to backpedal, all three of the men took aim with their high-powered harpoon guns. Goliath fired first, then Roketto, followed closely by Morgan. One harpoon impacted the shell just above the beast's left shoulder. Another struck its left arm near the elbow joint. The third harpoon did not hit anything, as it was swiped away from a writhing tentacle. The two successful harpoons immediately began drilling their way deeper into the shell, sending small bits of grit into the water around them. The mercenaries didn't pay close enough attention to see whether the harpoons struck or not. After firing, they turned toward the mouth of the cave and swam as if the devil was after them. In their minds, they believed it was something worse.

****

"Napier! Where the hell are you?!" Red called from his position. He kept his eye on the monitor, waiting for his men to clip themselves to the cable. He heard Napier and Thompson climbing down the ladder. He glanced to the former, who quickly took his position at the winch. "I'll let you know when to reel them in!"

"I'll be waiting," Napier said. Like Red, they weren't able to get a good look at the beast through the monitor, despite the high definition and advanced night vision. They had watched the mercenaries fire their harpoons at the beast, but there were no confirmed hits, although a target that size would be nearly impossible to miss. Thompson stood near Napier, watching the waters intently.

"Who would've thought it would take a sea monster to get us reacquainted," she remarked. Napier didn't say anything, but did crack a small smile.

****

The beast was feeling a strange sensation throughout its body, which its instincts did not recognize. While it was still moving forward with tremendous force, it felt a strange sudden lack of energy in its muscles. It did not have the intelligence to connect this event with the attack its intruders had just unleashed on it. The tunnel was steadily widening, allowing it more space to move toward the escaping enemies. They were out of reach for its eight tentacles, which helped to pull the creature through its tight habitat. It was too dark for its bulb-like eyes to see them, but it could still detect them due to the electrical impulses they created. Despite feeling suddenly weaker, *Architeuthis Brachyura's* instincts demanded it slaughter its challengers.

****

"Okay, they're at the mouth of the cave!" Red said, watching the monitor. Morgan had been instructed to motion to Goliath's camera with a thumbs up when all three men were clipped to the cable, an action the commanding merc was waiting for. Doctor Wallack stood outside the cabin, eagerly waiting to see if the creature would emerge after the divers. He certainly hoped for the hired guns to make it out alive. Otherwise, hooking up the net would certainly be difficult.

The images on the monitor were very shaky, due to Goliath's frantic motions. *Hopefully the bastard keeps it still so Morgan can let me know they're good to go*, Red thought as he watched the monitor. From what little he could clearly see, it appeared that the men had located the cable. At this moment, the camera's steadiness improved drastically, due to Goliath taking a foothold in order to clip his harness to his line. Red glanced to Napier.

"They're hooking up!" he updated the fisherman. The camera

panned over to the mouth of the cave, away from the other mercenaries. The tunnel opening was surprisingly clear at his angle, and the images showed large amounts of dust floating from the cave, as if a demolition charge had gone off in there. Suddenly, within the massive cloud of grit and dirt, a form began to take place. Rather, many forms, each one as slithery as the next. Each of these worm-like appendages rippled in the water, eventually slithering toward the camera. "Turn the camera back to Morgan, you idiot!" Red shouted into the radio. Immediately, Goliath panned the camera back, putting Morgan in the video monitor, giving a thumbs up. Red looked to Napier. "NOW! PULL THE LEVER NOW!!!"

Napier instantly complied. The air winch hummed a loud whirring sound, and the cylinder shape winch immediately began spinning back at a tremendous speed, reeling in the cable with its cargo. Red turned his eyes to the ocean, waiting for the men to pop up with the cable at any instant.

****

It continued to feel physically weaker, but the creature did not lose any determination. It had nearly closed the distance between itself and its enemies. It was even close enough to have them in its sight. Close enough it could snag them with its many tentacles. However, as it began to lunge for the retreating challengers, it was confused by the fact that they suddenly picked up an extraordinary burst of speed, 'swimming' way out of its grasp! Instinct demanded it pursue, in defense of its territory; to show dominance over any other organism that dare cross its path. As quickly as its sluggish body could move, the creature filled its sacks with water, propelling itself after its targets, smashing through rocky structures in the process.

****

"Okay! Slow it down!" Red said, after seeing the stirring in the water, indicating that the men were beginning to surface. Napier cranked the lever down a few notches, in order to avoid whipping the mercenaries over the edge of the boat. Like fish on a hook, the cable lifted the men from the surface of the water. Each of them tore their mouth pieces out, and had begun taking off their flippers and air tanks while still in mid air.

"Boss!" Goliath called out in his deep mammoth voice. "It's coming! It's on its way!"

"Yeah, yeah, I know!" Red said in a surprisingly calm voice. He raised his harpoon rifle to his shoulder like a hunter, scanning the surface of the water. The cable lifted the men over the edge of the boat, and Thompson helped to unclip the men from their lines.

"How close was it behind you?" she asked.

"Close enough," Morgan remarked while fumbling to get his gear off.

"Where are your harpoon rifles?" Red snarled, still scanning the water for the target. The men stood on the deck, dripping wet and breathing heavily.

"We had to ditch them," Goliath admitted. "That damn thing was coming at us too fast. We had to get rid of anything slowing us down."

"That leaves us with this one harpoon gun!" Red yelled. He gave an exaggerated sigh, gritting his teeth. "Get another harpoon ready! I'm gonna have to reload immediately after I shoot this one!" Morgan immediately opened one of the supply bags, pulling out a three foot harpoon with a canister installed on it.

****

The leviathan was able to detect each of its enemies, up until their impulses came to a dead stop. It was as if they had suddenly ceased to exist in the water. The creature propelled itself forward once more, detecting another presence in its territory just ahead of it. This presence was different than anything else it had encountered thus far. This particular creature in the water appeared to equal its size, making it a greater challenger than any other of the life forms it had slain. The creature continued to feel even more sluggish with each passing moment, but the determination to fight pressed it forward.

****

"There she is!" Doctor Wallack called out, pointing to the portside. All eyes watched as the water stirred, as if the area was a giant cauldron. Napier and Thompson, although terrified, could not help but watch as the huge mass slowly began to rise out of the ocean. Surrounded by its eight tentacles, the beast lifted its upper bulk over the surface of the water, pointing its antenna-like eyes and bird like pincers at its new enemy, as if deliberately meeting the crew of the *Catcher* face-to-face. Its two pincers snapped wildly in the water, while its tentacles flapped and wiggled around its body, like snakes dancing to a flute. The mandibles flapped open like the petals of a flower, revealing its enormous beak in full detail. The beak then opened as well, releasing a deafening scream, almost like that of an eagle, amplified several hundred times over. The mercenaries, along with Thompson and Napier, stood silent and still. Their fear had been replaced by a strange sense of fascination, mixed with a new feeling of terror.

"Oh my god," the Coast Guard lieutenant exclaimed. Each of them suddenly backed away toward the starboard side after the creature began writhing more viciously in the water, releasing another terrifying scream. The only one on the main deck who didn't move was Red. He stood patiently and waited. He had a clear shot of the beast, but he was waiting for the perfect moment the strike. And that moment was coming up as the creature reared up once again, about to attack the huge vessel. The mandibles peeled back and the beak opened to scream. It was at that time that Red squeezed the trigger. The harpoon rifle released the meter-long spear with a loud 'whoosh' sound, impacting the creature in the mouth. The sounds of the drill whizzing could be heard from the opposite side of the deck. Red turned to look at Morgan, who had fled to the starboard side.

"I could use that harpoon now!" he yelled. Morgan quickly tossed it to him. He clipped the fresh spear into place and took aim once again, this time not bothering to aim for the beak. He aimed left, pulling the trigger. Another whoosh sound followed and the harpoon hit the creature in one of the soft tentacles.

****

It felt a sensation it wasn't used to: pain. And following that pain was a stronger sense of sluggishness. The creature desired to attack, but it couldn't. The signals were not making it from the brain to its several appendages. Its vision ceased to function, and its senses stopped picking up signals from the challenger. Finally, its awareness of its environment seemed to slip away into a thick blackness.

****

Red watched as the enormous creature stopped writhing viciously in the water, and then sank into the depths of the sea. He turned to the rest of the crew, who were still backed away to the starboard side of the vessel, all still lost in a sense of amazement and disbelief.

"Hey guys," he said to his teammates, "don't take off those swimsuits. You're going back in. Time to hook this bastard up."

CHAPTER 18

Over the next several minutes, the three mercenaries had been getting looked over by Dr. Wallack and Red. The ascent from the cave to the *Catcher* was faster than what it should have been under normal circumstances. However, these were not normal circumstances, and the change in pressure had left the mercenaries feeling a bit nauseous and dizzy. However, their conditions were already improving, making Wallack believe that the pressure change did not take a drastic toll on them, possibly because they came in at a long angle instead of straight up.

Napier kept his post at the winch. The net had already been hooked to the cable, waiting to be dropped in the water once Red gave the go-ahead. Thompson stood at the port, looking down into the water where the creature had surfaced. She did not share Dr. Wallack's faith in the tranquilizer. She listened to him check over the mercenaries, giving them the OK to go. Even if the men weren't suited for duty, he probably would have forced them to dive back in anyway. There was no way he would leave his creation down in the depths like this, so close to recapturing it.

"Where's our gear?" Morgan asked after his checkup.

"You'll have your bolt guns, wire cutters, and spare cable to help secure the net," Wallack said. "There's no need for any weapons down there. The creature is sedated."

"You sure about that, doc?" Roketto questioned.

"Yes I'm sure!" Wallack retorted, insulted that these men whom he viewed 'lesser' than him tried to challenge his understanding of the beast. "Now that I deem you gentlemen fit for duty, I suggest you get into that water and secure that net. Afterwards, we will transport it to the new facility, which I will disclose once we leave the area.

Napier tried not to look at the inflatable raft too much, fearing the mercenaries, particularly Red, would take notice. But the time was nearing for Bondy and Thompson to make their escape. All they would need to do was inflate the raft and hook up the motor, which was almost fully fueled. Bondy knew the area fairly well, and knew the cutter's position, which was only a couple miles off. He wasn't sure if Wallack or the mercenaries were even aware of it. He certainly prayed they weren't aware of it. He was grateful they were in the dead of night. In broad daylight, they would possibly even be able to see the cutter way off in the distance. He would glance at Thompson occasionally. He could tell she was nervous for the task they were about to undertake. But it had to be done. All they needed to do was wait for the mercenaries to make their second dive, leaving the only true concern being Red.

Morgan, Roketto, and Goliath collected their gear and put on their flippers and air tanks. Each appeared somewhat woozy from the earlier events, but Wallack was confident they were capable of taking their time and hooking the net around the specimen. They tested their mouth pieces and their night vision goggles and then approached the ladder on the starboard side. One after another, they climbed down, settling in the water and swimming over to port to go down with the net.

"Alright guys," Red said, "don't take too long down there. I want to get the hell out of here as quick as possible." It was clear he wasn't too comfortable being in this location with the creature. The men each gave a salute from the water. Napier began lowering the net beneath the surface, watching the divers slowly descend along with it. It was difficult to determine how long it would take them to get the net properly secured. Wallack headed back up to the cabin to monitor the activity on the monitor. Goliath still had the camera device in his headset. Red also had his monitor still set up, and he stood near the edge of the deck to keep an eye on his men. In his hands was his Noveske Rifleworks Diplomat assault rifle, pointed downward. Napier took notice of this. *Well this isn't going to make our plan any easier, will it?* He thought to himself. He then saw Thompson walk away from the side of the deck toward the hatch. It was clear she was going to get Bondy ready.

"Hey," he whispered. Thompson barely heard him, and walked

up close to him.

"What?"

"It's important that you tell the Commander about this thing, despite how crazy it seems. It is so important that they kill this thing before it multiplies." He kept his words very silent, doing his best to keep Red from hearing anything.

"I know," Thompson whispered back. "Will you be okay?"

"I'm good. I'm gonna have to keep him from shooting you guys while you get off the boat. One way or another, these guys aren't leaving until they have that thing down there netted." Thompson remained silent for a few moments, failing to hide her fear from his eyes. It wasn't a fear for herself, or even Bondy's safety. It was a fear of what might happen to Rick while they escaped. Napier could see her looking uncomfortable. "Hey," he spoke up a little bit. "It's gonna be ok…." She pressed her lips into his, cutting him off. He instantly forgot what he was going to say. In this moment, he knew how important it was to get her off the boat safely. Thompson ended the kiss, giving him a small smile, before turning around and heading down the hatch. "Wow," Napier said out loud.

****

Bondy saw the lieutenant climb down the small ladder. He had been busy keeping the kids calm regarding the situation. They were afraid to be alone, but Bondy offered words of comfort, and specifically emphasized Napier's previous message to Greg, instructing him to take good care of Jane.

"That damn thing is not only huge, but it's damn loud!" he remarked regarding the creature's scream.

"It's that and more," Thompson said, with a small nervous grin. Finally her expression turned serious again. "You ready?"

"I suppose I'm as ready as I'll ever be, being cooped up in here hasn't helped matters," he said. He paused a moment. "I overheard the argument upstairs, in the cabin. Something about that thing reproducing soon?" Thompson simply nodded.

"It hasn't yet, but it will," she said. "When we get to the cutter, we need to make sure they help us kill it. Otherwise, God only knows how many of those things there'll be. And I'm not counting on the good doctor to contain them all."

"Agreed," Bondy said. He looked at the kids once more. "You guys are gonna have to be strong for your dad, alright?" They silently nodded. "We're going to be back real soon. And then we'll get you off this boat." He looked at Thompson and nodded, signaling he was ready to go. She turned and started to climb the ladder.

****

Napier had lowered the net all the way down, leaving a bit of extra slack for the mercenaries to maneuver it. He knew the winch was strong, but after seeing that creature up close he began to question whether the *Catcher* would even be able to lift it. That shell certainly had to carry a lot of weight on its own. He looked to the hatch and saw Thompson casually climbing out. She took a stance near the hatch, and Napier could see Bondy poised to get out.

It was then he got his bright idea. The mercenaries may be high-tech, experienced, and combat hardened. However, they were also sloppy when dealing with hostages. Near the front of the deck, Goliath had taken off some of his gear, leaving his sidearm. It was clearly unloaded, indicated by the slide being locked back and the magazine out and secured somewhere else. But he left something else unsecured: his flash grenades. Thompson followed his eyes, and realized what he was thinking of doing. She nodded, and looked down to Bondy, motioning to him to cover his eyes. Napier glanced once more at the scar-faced mercenary, whose body language suggested he was about to turn around from the monitor. Napier acted fast, leaning down to grab the cylinder shaped flash grenade. He had never seen these things in action, save for action movies, and who knows how accurate they are. But the object was self-explanatory. There was a pin to pull, and a tiny switch to flip. He yanked the pin, and flicked the switch with his finger. Immediately, he rolled it like a bowling ball toward Red's position before turning around and throwing his arms over his closed eyes.

He heard the metallic rolling of an object coming toward his feet, prompting him to turn his head to identify what it was. He was not immediately alert to the likeliness of it being a threat, which was a mistake on his part. The first thing he noticed was Napier and Thompson in a crouched position, facing away from him with their hands thrown over their heads. Then he saw it, the black canister object. His mind instantly identified what it was, and by then it was too late. The canister only made a small 'whoosh' sound, before unleashing a blinding white flash straight into the mercenary's vision. His eyes immediately felt as if on fire, his brain feeling like it was being electrocuted, while every muscle in his body tensed up rigid. "Son-of-a-BITCH!"

Bondy and Thompson immediately rushed to the inflatable raft. While in agony, and without any vision, Red could detect the sounds of their feet hitting the deck. He raised his rifle to his shoulder, pointing it to the direction of the sounds to blind fire in their direction.

Napier had uncovered his eyes, shocked that despite being turned around looking the other direction with his hands over his head, that the flash grenade even had a slight effect on him. But his vision was intact, and he was able to move fluidly. He saw the mercenary about to fire in the direction of his friends. His mind flared, and from his crouched position he sprinted at full speed towards the killer. Within a second he had closed the distance, throwing his body onto Red's, sending them both toward the back end of the deck at the guardrail. He grabbed the barrel of Red's rifle, shoving it down to the deck, right before the merc squeezed the trigger. An array of bullets riddled that portion of the deck, tearing up shards of wood like grass under a lawnmower. Pinning the stunned mercenary against the guardrail, he kept the gun pointed down with his left arm. He made a fist with his right hand, and like a heavyweight champion he swung a right hook into Red's left ribcage. In a flurry, Napier swung a second blow. Then a third. And a fourth. He then raised his right fist over his head, and in a hammer-like motion, he collapsed it down on top of the assault rifle, severing the disoriented opponent's grip on it. The gun fell to the deck, bouncing away from them.

During this intense action, Napier heard the raft inflate, and he then heard the splash it made as Thompson and Bondy threw it over the side of the boat. Two more splashes followed, caused from the two of them taking their own leap over the guardrail. They were successfully off the boat. Napier grabbed Red by the collar of his vest, and pulled his right arm back to make a large swing toward the scarred left side of his face. He swung with all of his might, only to have his fist stopped in midair, blocked by Red's left arm. Napier's eyes widened in surprise, realizing the merc had regained some of his vision. He felt Red's left hand grab a handful of hair on the back of his head, pulling him inward…connecting his face with the killer's right elbow. Napier saw his life flash before his eyes in an instant, and he stumbled back from the merc in a daze. This one blow had struck him between the eyes, nearly incapacitating him. His vision spun, causing him to collapse to one knee. Red took a couple steps to approach him. Napier began to stand up straight and hold up his fists. It didn't matter. With his right boot, Red thrust a heavy front kick straight into Napier's chest, sending him several feet back, landing him on his back.

"Oh shit!" he gagged. The wind had been knocked out of him. He coughed almost uncontrollably, spitting up saliva and a little bit of blood. His nose also began to bleed from the elbow to the face. At this moment, he didn't bother to try and get back up. He didn't have the energy, and besides, there was no purpose. He could hear the motor of the raft spinning as his friends made their escape. Red scooped up his assault rifle and rushed to the starboard side of the deck to fire upon them, but the effort was futile. The escaped hostages had already disappeared into the darkness. He threw the weapon to the floor in anger. His enraged, pained eyes turned back toward Napier, and he stomped back towards him.

"You think you're pretty clever don't you, you little piece of shit!" He snarled.

"Well we outsmarted you, didn't we? Huh, Red?" Napier wheezed. He continued to lie flat, catching his breath, unsure of what his fate would be. He looked to his foe, who stood at his feet.

"Blood Red!" The mercenary corrected him, pulling his Smith & Wesson M&P .40 from its holster on his right hip. Napier had never looked down the barrel of a gun before. He watched Red put his finger on the trigger, ready to squeeze. He closed his eyes and made his peace, praying for a good future for Jane and Lisa.

"What the hell happened?!" Wallack shouted from the upper deck, interrupting Red.

"This weasel's friends made a miraculous escape," Red said. His voice was a mixture of anger and sarcasm. He looked back down to Napier. "What's their bright idea? Go back to the island and bring reinforcements?"

Napier felt a great sense of relief that he did not mention the Coast Guard Cutter, proving that he was unaware of it.

"That's the idea," he lied.

"It doesn't matter!" Dr. Wallack called down. "By the time they manage to get anyone here, we'll be gone. Plus, most of the police force is voluntary, and Bondy will have to take time to get in touch with everybody since communications are still out on the island." He paused. "Mr. Napier, I can't really blame you for rescuing your friends. But if you try anything else, I'll personally feed your daughter to my experiments. Do you understand?"

"No more tricks," he replied in compliance. He watched Red hastily holster his weapon, bloodthirsty to use it. He sat up and listened to Red stomp back over to his monitor and speak on his radio.

"Hurry up, assholes! We haven't got all night!"

CHAPTER 19

Napier's chest still felt as if an anvil had been dropped on it. He stood at his assigned post at the winch, wanting nothing more than to go down the hatch and check on his daughter. He looked to the dark distance, hoping Thompson and Bondy were doing okay on their quest to reach the Coast Guard Cutter. It had been nearly an hour since they departed, and he was reasonably confident that the raft's little motor would have just enough fuel in it to get them there. He hoped they would get there in time, because the mercenaries were wrapping up their operation with the creature. Doctor Wallack had explained that they were injecting gas into its outer sacks, which would help it to float to the surface. It would certainly put less pressure on the winch.

"They're just about ready," Wallack said. He was on the main deck with Red and Napier. Red stood at his post, still appearing exasperated from the earlier incident. Wallack looked into the water on the port side, while Red watched the monitor. The spotlights had been turned back on, with one aimed into the portside water.

"Morgan's on his way up," the mercenary announced. "It appears that the other two are wrapping things up." After nearly a minute, air bubbles began popping up in the lit up section of water, followed shortly by Morgan himself. He spit out his mouth piece and yanked off his uncomfortable goggles, tossing them up to the boat.

"The other two about to come up anytime soon?" Red called down to him.

"They will in a minute," he said while swimming to the ladder. "They're just finishing up gassing up that thing's sacks, or whatever you call them. I don't know if it's gonna work."

"It'll work just fine," Wallack said. "Once we start pulling it up, the gas will be able to expand when there's less pressure on it, bringing it to the surface." As Morgan climbed back aboard the deck, Red looked up from the monitor toward the doctor.

"They're coming up now, as a matter of fact," he said. A few seconds later, as if on cue, both divers emerged in the same location as Morgan, performing the same actions by yanking off their gear. The brute carried a large empty tank, which was used for the injections.

"It's all done," Goliath said, trying not to inhale any water. "The net's hooked up, and the gas is injected. You can start the winch." Napier stood silent for a moment, until both Red and Wallack shot him a look.

"What are you waiting for?" Red said, giving him another deathly glare. Napier had gotten used to receiving his instructions from either him or the doctor, and hadn't realized that what Goliath said was actually an instruction. He took a deep breath, and prayed that the cable would stand the weight, as well as the equipment. He pressed the lever, pulling in the cable at full power. The circular winch rolled regularly while it took in the extra slack in the cable, but quickly after it creaked and whistled, indicating its struggle to lift the tremendous weight of the unconscious beast. Each whine of the unit caused Napier to tense up, fearing that it might snap away. Slowly but truly it turned, reeling in the cable and its heavy cargo. The vessel began to tilt slightly to port, worsening Napier's worries. The mercenaries even began to appear worried.

"Relax," Wallack said. "It'll hold. The specimen just needs to ascend a little more." His words were of little comfort. Even Red appeared slightly unnerved. The boat tilted a little bit more. But the winch kept cranking the cable upward, creaking all the way.

Finally, after several tense minutes, the creaking slowly began to cease, and the reeling speed steadily began to increase in more fluid motion. The gas was finally expanding, helping to lift the creature to the water's surface. The *Catcher* steadily began to level out from its tilt, calming the nerves of everyone on board, save for Napier's. Being anywhere near this creature was no picnic for him, and being stuck on a boat full of armed killers did not help the situation. The winch reeled in faster, and finally the water along the portside began to splash as it made way for the enormous mass taking its place. Appearing like a shelled atoll, the sedated creature emerged, coiled up in an enormous net that covered its entire body. Napier shut off the winch to avoid bringing the beast too close to the vessel.

"We finally have it!" Wallack exclaimed. "Now," he took a breath, "I'd say it's time for us to leave this godforsaken place. Napier!" He pointed to Rick, "Let's go upstairs! You're guiding us out of here!"

"Doctor," Napier said, struggling to search for words while staring at the net, which tightly constricted the objective. "Are you sure that this net is enough to hold it? What if the thing wakes up?"

"It won't," Wallack's voice trailed from excitement to frustration. "Now get up to the cabin and get us out of here." Napier paused briefly, looking to the beast. He grew more uncomfortable by the moment. Reluctantly, he followed his instructions and climbed the ladder behind the doctor. Once inside the cabin, he started the engine.

"Where to?" he asked.

"Once we clear the area we'll head northeast," Wallack said. Napier scanned the surrounding area. The rocks had the *Catcher* nearly boxed in.

"This is gonna take a while," he said.

"Just shut up and get us moving!" Napier ignored the doctor's impatience and panned the spotlights. To the starboard side appeared to be an area spacious enough for the vessel to squeeze through with the precious cargo, which should hopefully trail behind. He slowly throttled the vessel forward, spinning the wheel to the right. The propellers rotated, pushing the vessel steadily forward. Napier approached the open space, which appeared to be guarded by several rigid rocky structures on both sides. The vessel nearly stalled for a second when the slack of the cable had run out, adding extra weight for the engine to drag. However, the vessel was able to push forward steadily, slowly passing through the open space. Napier's nerves finally began to relax.

"See?" Wallack remarked. "Told you this would be easy." He barely finished that statement when the *Catcher* suddenly bumped upward, followed by a sharp grinding sound originating from the belly of the vessel.

"Oh shit!" Napier cursed, steering the vessel clear of the space before bringing it to another stop.

"What the hell was that?" Wallack asked. Napier switched off the engine and started out the cabin.

"We hit a rock!" he said.

"I didn't see any rock…"

"That's because it was just beneath the surface! That's why this area is a disaster zone for boats!" He climbed the ladder down, and the scientist followed him. Waiting for them on the main deck were the mercenaries, who were as stunned as Wallack.

"Now what's the problem?" Red asked, his tone sounding as frustrated as ever.

"According to the captain," Wallack pointed to Napier, "we have made a collision with a rock that was just under the water."

"A rock?" Red snapped. "You little bastard! This is another one of your tricks isn't it!"

"Yep, you're exactly right," Napier mockingly said, throwing his hands up into the air. "I happen to know the exact layout of this island, which is why I'm choosing to strand myself out here with a group of psychotics who want to capture an oversized squid/crab hybrid, which would love nothing more than to bring down this boat, which it could easily do, and have us for a midnight snack."

"We don't have time for this nonsense," Wallack yelled over the group. He looked at Goliath, who was getting ready to get out of his gear. "You!" he pointed at him. "Don't be in such a hurry! Get yourself a fresh tank and some tools. You get to assess the damage and make repairs." Goliath groaned in displeasure.

"Are you serious?"

"Get down there," Red said. His voice was softer, but still conveyed the message. He looked to the other mercenaries. "I'd suggest one of you guys go down after him. He'll probably need some sort of help."

"And hurry the hell up," Napier said. "Because, even though I can't get a visual, there's a good chance we're taking in water."

CHAPTER 20

Commander Tracy was in the abyss of a deep sleep in his quarters when the sudden knock on his door snapped him awake. It was times like these when he hated being a high ranking officer of the Coast Guard. Whenever any issue should arise, he had to be notified of it, no matter what time of day. He rolled to his right side and looked at his clock. *2:30 a.m.* it read.

"Come on in," the commander called out. His door opened and a uniformed young Coast Guard cadet stepped in, wearing his white fatigues and buttoned shirt. The light from the bright hallway illuminated the room, highlighting the Commander's sleepy features. His right eyelid was still nearly clenched shut, and his left eye drooped heavily. "What is it?"

"Sir," the young man said. "We're going to need you on deck."

"And…why?" Tracy said with little patience.

"We have two people on deck that approached the ship in a raft. They claim that there's a hostage situation nearby." This news helped the commander wake up completely. He stepped out of bed, wearing only a t-shirt and black shorts.

"Hostage situation? Where?"

"Mako's Edge, on board a large fishing vessel."

"Did you identify the people on deck? You have their names?"

"Yes sir," the cadet said. "There's Lt. Lisa Thompson and Steven Bondy, Chief of Mako's Center Police Department." The commander's senses grew alert.

"Give me a moment to get dressed and I'll be on my way down." The cadet left the room and closed the door. Tracy switched on the light and fumbled for his uniform. Although Thompson was in trouble due to her incident resulting in the death of Officer Denning, the commander knew she would not lie, or mistake rather, a hostage situation. And since Chief Bondy was with her, the odds were likely that there was a serious scenario that he would have to take care of. He just prayed that there would be no mention of any sea monster.

****

"Officer on deck!" one of the personnel called out when Tracy arrived from his cabin. The steel deck was well lit, allowing the Commander to see every face in the area. There were several Coast Guard personnel dressed in white and blue on the deck, forming a circle around the two guests that had arrived on board the *Ryback*. Bondy and Thompson were both dripping wet from diving off the *Catcher* into the water. The raft had been left in the water, secured by a line. An officer walked up to both of them, and wrapped them in a warm towel. The Coast Guard personnel opened a path for the commander, who walked in a beeline toward the Lieutenant and Police Chief.

"Okay, be to the point," Tracy said to them. "What's going on?"

"We've got a problem?" Thompson said. "There's a group of armed men occupying a fishing vessel, named the *Catcher*, over at Mako's Edge."

"How many men and how many hostages?"

"There are five suspects, four of which are armed mercenaries. The fifth is a scientist who had done some biological work for the government." Thompson answered.

"There are three hostages," Bondy added. "There's Rick Napier, who you met a couple days ago at East Port. And there are two seventeen year olds. They disarmed me of my sidearm and took us all aboard his boat to accomplish an objective over at Mako's Edge."

"Whoa," Tracy said. "Why didn't you radio anything in? We're you not able to?"

"They installed a device somewhere on Mako's Center that is currently blocking any frequency from leaving the island. Radios and phones won't work, and the mercenaries disabled the radio on the vessel."

"We need to act fast," Thompson said. "At any minute, they

will be leaving."

"What is it they want?" The Commander said. Thompson stood silent, hesitant to mention the creature in fear that Tracy wouldn't believe her.

"She wasn't wrong about there being something in the water," Bondy spoke for her. Tracy's gritted his teeth and looked down, putting his hands at his hips, clearly expressing his disbelief. "I know it sounds crazy but it attacked the island and killed several tourists, and a few of my deputies. Because of that damned device that the mercenaries installed on the island, we couldn't get in touch with you."

"The scientist's name is Doctor Isaac Wallack," Thompson said. "You can call Washington and ask about him, because he's acting rogue now. He's attempting to capture the creature, which he bred in some laboratory, and take it to some sort of facility." Tracy gave her and Bondy an intense glare.

"You two better not be pulling my leg," he said. "I have no patience for horseshit like this."

"Sir," Bondy said. "You think I don't have better things to do than to screw with you?" His tone was borderline angry. "Regardless of that huge thing out there, there's still the case that our friend is being held hostage over there, and will probably be killed if you don't help us intervene."

"Alright, you're right," Tracy said. He turned to another uniformed officer who stood beside him. "Send the order. Set course to Mako's Edge. It's close enough that we'll get there very soon. I want our helicopter pilot to get a visual and get any possible update on the situation. Get some men geared up and ready to board the *Catcher*." The officer saluted and immediately rushed off to the control room. Tracy looked back to Thompson. "So how big is this creature?"

"With its tentacles and pincers, nearly sixty feet," she said. "If you ready the naval gun, you'll be able to kill it."

"You guys realize, that even with the hostage situation, that by agreeing to go along with this monster theory, I'm risking my reputation, along with that of my men."

"Just call Washington," Bondy said. "This was government funded, and if they know this creature is on the loose, they'll want to know. Mention the doctor's name." Tracy breathed a heavy sigh.

"Okay," he complied.

CHAPTER 21

The rain had completely subsided and the wind was reduced to a light, occasional breeze. The night sky was still covered by a thick layer of clouds, and every few seconds a crackle of thunder would roll into the horizon. A light fog was beginning to build up around the shores of Mako's Edge, dimming any view of the rocky obstacles that guarded the island itself. On board the upper deck of the *Catcher*, Rick Napier watched this slowly thickening build up. The night sky already made his vision bad enough, but if they did not get moving soon, he wouldn't even be able to use the spotlights to light the way for him without the fog reflecting it right back. The *Catcher* was still at a halt, anchored just past the point where it had grazed the top of a rock just slightly submerged beneath the water's surface. Morgan and Goliath had geared up and dived once again to assess the damage. The decks remained quiet. Roketto and Red were clearly on edge, as well as Napier. He couldn't help but watch the unconscious body of the enormous beast they had defeated earlier in the night. All ten of its joints were curled up to its huge rigid, bulky body, giving it the appearance of a massive bowling ball. A bowling ball that everyone on board was afraid would spring out and crush them. Everyone except Doctor Wallack, who sat alone in the cabin. He continued to hold on to the belief that he could control his creation. A belief that Napier, and now even the mercenaries doubted.

Napier had grown tired of the overwhelming feeling of anticipation he was feeling from being on his own damaged vessel in the worst waters in Mako's Ridge, trapped with mercenaries who hated his guts and possibly had intentions of offing him at the earliest opportunity. Worse than that, his daughter was trapped in this same horror on the same boat, with an extremely aggressive creature in tow. With his daughter in mind, he climbed down the ladder from the upper deck down to the main, where he then went down the hatch. Red and Roketto stood silently on the deck, both armed with their automatic weapons, watching the creature carefully. Napier entered the storage room, where he saw only Jane sitting on the starboard side bench. She looked back at her dad and cracked a smile. While the situation hasn't gotten any better, it was comforting for Napier to see an increase in his daughter's spirits.

"Where's Greg?" He asked.

"He's in the bathroom," Jane answered, pointing to the door on the portside. "He's not used to being on boats. Which is funny, because before all this, he had gotten his own boat and was acting like some hotshot captain."

"Well seasickness is usually something everyone has to deal with when they're starting out," Napier said as he took a seat next to Jane. "So, how long have you guys been going out?"

"We're out here with a crazy scientist and a bunch of psychopaths, and you want to lecture me about my relationship?" Jane said, still maintaining a grin.

"No, no," Napier said. "It's an honest question. I'm not gonna lecture, I promise." He cracked a smile of his own.

"Three months," she answered. "Pretty much every time I said I was hanging out with Amanda, I was really…"

"Yeah, I figured that part," her dad said. "Well, after all this, hopefully I can get to know him better."

"You've had him in your class when you were a teacher," she commented.

"Yeah, well back then he was a little jerk," he said. "But I'd like to try again." Jane smiled and gave her father a tight hug, which he returned.

"I love you daddy," she said. Her voice wasn't tearful, it was genuinely happy, as if nothing was wrong in their world right now.

"I love you too, baby," he said. After several moments, they ended their hug when a pale faced Greg exited the bathroom. "You need your sea legs," he said.

"I guess so," Greg said, still looking green around the gills.

Napier got up from his seat on the bench. "I'm gonna have to go back up now. We're hopefully gonna be out of here soon." *Not too soon. The Coast Guard better hurry the hell up.* "Try to relax, and Greg…please don't puke on my daughter." The ill teenager managed a chuckle while Napier climbed back up the ladder and onto the main deck. As soon as he had stepped on the wooden surface, Morgan's head emerged from the water behind the stern of the vessel, alerting the attention of Red and Roketto, who quickly rushed to the edge of the vessel. Napier was quick to join them.

"What's the word?" Red was the first to speak.

"There's a big crack along the center of the belly," Morgan said, spitting up water as he tried to brief his superior. "There's a bit of an indent where the boat hit the rock, and that's where we're taking in a little water. Goliath has his underwater welder and is trying to fuse a piece of metal over it to cover it up."

"That's not a proper fix," Napier said.

"Well, what the hell do you want, Captain Nemo?" Red said to him, in his usual raspy voice. "We're trapped out in the middle of nowhere, with that thing in tow," he pointed to the creature, "it's the middle of the night, and we don't have the equipment for a 'proper fix'!" He looked back to Morgan. "How much longer?"

"Maybe ten minutes," Morgan answered.

"Make if five," Red demanded. "I want to get the hell out of here." Morgan gave a wave before inserting his mouth piece into his mouth and diving under the water. Napier was quick to distance himself from Red once the briefing was over to avoid any more name calling or threats of physical harm. As he walked away, he saw Doctor Wallack standing on the upper deck looking down upon them like a king.

"A word?" he said to Napier. Rick climbed the ladder to meet with him.

"What now?" he asked.

"I've been quite impressed with you during this trip. Your knowledge of the sea. Your ability to predict certain characteristics of my creation. Your dedication to the ones you love."

"Is there a point to this?" Napier didn't have much patience for the crazed scientist's monologues.

"I thought that when this mission is over, and *Architeuthis Brachyura* is secured in my facility, that perhaps I could offer you a job." Napier stood silent. Wallack made a small grin. "You may have never finished your doctorate, but you definitely possess knowledge and skills I could definitely use once I regain my funding from the government."

"What makes you so sure you'll get your funding?" Napier asked.

"The government has invested countless dollars into these experiments," he said. "Ultimately they won't want to see those dollars wasted."

"Well I'll contribute to that," Napier said. "I won't have them waste any on me." Wallack's grin transformed to a straight face.

"I figured a man in your financial situation would be fast to jump on such an opportunity. A high-paying opportunity."

"I get by," Napier said. "And I sleep well at night."

****

Goliath struggled to keep in place as he attempted to cheaply weld the sheet of metal over the damaged area of the *Catcher's* belly. Because of the flash of the waterproof welder, he was forced to use regular goggles instead of the night vision. It was very difficult to see in the pitch black water, nearly causing the unbalanced mercenary to burn himself. In addition, he was as impatient as the rest of his comrades to leave. Morgan had helped to keep the sheet in place while the brute fused it to the metal belly, but now it was holding on its own. At this point, Goliath was working on once more edge before getting back on board the vessel. It was a makeshift job, and that was all they needed.

****

Unknown to everything in existence, including the creature itself was that its metabolic rate had changed from having spent a massive increase in energy during the past few days. Its body was now quick to process any chemicals introduced into its system. Electrical impulses had been shooting through its body, starting with a tiny one every several minutes that would possibly lead to a twitch in the tip of a tentacle. Now the impulses were stronger, and more rapid.

Blood pulsed through its vessels, breathing life into its joints. Its vision slowly returned, unveiling like a bedside curtain. It had no memory of losing consciousness. Rather, all it remembered were the events leading up to its sudden slumber. The massive inedible enemy, the small creatures that crawled on it, with a few snapshot memories of the little creatures invading its habitat. It felt the constrictions of a binding object, also inedible, that had coiled around its body. The creature's brain went on alert, believing it was under attack, possibly to be ingested by the large life form floating nearby.

****

Morgan tapped on Goliath's shoulder to get his attention. He pointed to himself, and then pointed up to indicate he was getting back on deck. After a nod from the large merc, who was just finishing up his duties, Morgan swam up to the surface of the water, popping his head and shoulders clear. That's when he noticed a bizarre current stirring in the water. He looked to the sky and scanned the weather. There was hardly any wind, and the *Catcher* was anchored in place. But despite there seemingly being no cause, the water was beginning to rage all of a sudden. The phenomenon also drew the attention of the mercenaries on deck.

Morgan looked to the port side, and saw it. The enormous mass that had been trapped in a slumber was now moving. Viciously. Like a huge boulder on a steep hill, it rolled itself over and over, twisting the cables and the netting in the process.

"SHIT!" Morgan yelled out loud. Instinctively he swam for the ladder. Better to be on the boat than stuck in the water with that thing. His thoughts had briefly gone over the idea of going down to get Goliath, but the sudden intense burst of adrenaline caused his natural sense of self preservation to take over. And like a madman, he paddled through the water to the ladder. "RED!"

Red was standing on deck, and could hear the splashing of the water, which drew his and Roketto's attention to port. Once there, they beheld the sight that brought their worst fears to fruition. The creature that they had put into a slumber had suddenly woken from its anesthesia, and was clearly pissed!

"The hell with this!" Red yelled. He rushed to the second winch at the stern and pulled the lever, reeling in the anchor. At this time, Morgan had arrived on deck, running in his wetsuit to a bag to collect a weapon.

"Hey!" Wallack yelled from the upper deck. "What the hell are you doing?!"

"We're getting the hell out of here!" Red yelled back. "If you have a problem with that, well then you can stay here and go swimming for all I care!" His eyes turned to Napier. "Get on the throttle and be ready to haul ass!" For the first time, Red had barked an order that Napier was actually happy to comply with. He opened the door to enter the cabin, only to be blocked by Wallack who thrust his body in the way.

"We're not leaving yet!" he ordered. His eyes were wide open and his expression was flared like that of a madman.

"You've lost it," Napier yelled at him. Wallack ignored the comment.

"Red!" he yelled. "Just fire another harpoon and sedate it again!" His fiery expression suddenly showed a bit of surprise when he realized the mercenary leader had already begun loading the large weapon.

"I plan on it!" Red said. "But I'm also cutting it loose!" The activity in the water was getting worse, and the creature had begun to release several deafening screams into the air.

"No you will not!" Wallack commanded. Suddenly Red dropped the harpoon gun and drew his semi-automatic pistol with the speed of a John Wayne character, pointing it directly at Wallack's head. For one of the first times in his life, the scientist realized he was not in control. Seeing where the deadly weapon was aimed, Napier moved as far to the end of the deck as he could to be out of the way.

"Don't tempt me!" Red snarled. Wallack said nothing, which signaled his reluctant compliance. Red holstered his weapon.

Napier looked at the writhing activity in the water near his large vessel. Large waves were crashing into the side, as well as into the several surrounding rocks. His whole body tensed when he realized what the beast was now doing.

"Look!" He yelled to everyone. Their eyes turned to the creature and together they witnessed its two huge pincers clipping through the binds of the net like scissors to string. With each cut, the net pulled apart, uncovering the massive bulk. The tentacles expanded, peeling the cables off of its body. And without any hesitation, the tentacles lunged to the *Catcher* all at once.

Everyone fell to the deck as the large vessel suddenly tilted left from the weight of the creature, which had grabbed a hold of it and pulled itself closer for its attack. It did not have any intention of eating now. Just massacring.

****

Goliath heard the vibrations caused by the rising of the anchor, which caused him to wrap up. He noticed the strange currents in the water, but the darkness and disorientation made it difficult for him to realize what was happening. But just as he pulled away from the boat's underbelly he was suddenly knocked about by a force that was clearly rocking the *Catcher*. He dropped his gear and quickly swam to the surface. In seconds he broke the surface, and then he saw it. And it saw him!

Before he could do anything, he felt his ribs and waist constrict. Looking down, he saw the slimy tentacle twist around him just under his arms. Following instantly was pressure. Intense pressure! And lots of pain, all from the tightening of the tentacle, the cracking of his ribs and hipbones, and the piercing of the barbs that were inserted from the suckers. He let out a bloodcurdling scream as the tentacle lifted him from the water and high into the air.

Several tentacles slammed into the portside, tearing the guardrail away. Wood splintered from the deck while the snake-like arms slapped the vessel wildly and uncontrollably. Water splashed in waves so high the upper deck of the vessel was getting soaked and slippery, causing Wallack and Napier to fall to the floor. On the main deck, Red managed to keep his balance and grabbed for his harpoon gun. As he took aim, he saw his comrade, Goliath, held up high over their heads by one of the long tentacles, and was dumbfounded as he watched it sail him through the air like a kite guided by a string. The brute flailed his arms in a wild panic, screaming continuously. Red concentrated his attention and looked down the sight of his harpoon gun, lining his index finger over the trigger, and he squeezed.

At this moment, one of the beast's enormous pincers impacted the rear of the boat with a boxer-like punch. The tremendous impact sent a shockwave through the vessel and caused it to turn, facing Red away from his target. Just as he had pulled the trigger. The harpoon whizzed from the gun, flying high into the darkness, gone forever. Now the creature was along the bow, although its tentacles were still thrashing about on the port and starboard sides. In a crazed frenzy, the creature jabbed the jagged points of its pincers into the bow, rupturing the hull. Smoke and steam erupted from the wounds of the vessel.

On the starboard side, Morgan took a post with his assault rifle and begun firing wildly at the flailing tentacles. The overwhelming adrenaline shook his aim, making it even more difficult to hit any target. Being focused on the tentacles slamming into that side of the vessel, tearing up fragments of the *Catcher* in the process, he was unaware of one particular tentacle that had coiled just under the surface. It had winded up like a rattlesnake, and as if it had a mind of its own, it was focused on him. It finished winding, and with the speed of a 500 magnum bullet, it sprung directly at him.

Morgan never realized what hit him. All he felt was the shockwave throughout his body from the impact, after the tentacle speared right through his chest like a spear, coming out between his shoulder blades. It then rose up into the air, lifting its skewered prey off the deck like a shish kabob. The gun dropped from his hands and his arms and legs went limp as life slipped away from him.

Despite losing all air in his lungs, Goliath screamed while flailing his arms helplessly as he soared through the air crazily by the vicious tentacle. Blood begun oozing from his waist area, seeping between the tentacle's coils. The wind rushed through his hair, and he could feel the vapor from the thrashing water beneath him. He looked ahead of him and yelled one final terrified scream when he realized he was heading right for the bow. His arms flailed and his legs kicked, all before exploding from his body after the tentacle crashed him through the exterior of the hull. Upon impact, his head ruptured like a ripe melon, spilling the contents inside.

Napier struggled to get to his feet due to the constant battering of his vessel. As he lifted himself to his knees, he watched one of the huge pincers rip off the tip of the vessel, sending shards of metal spilling into the water. Looking down to the hatch on the main deck, he knew he needed to get to his daughter. He turned around, and instead of using the ladder, he jumped from the upper deck, landing on his feet down on the main deck.

"Shit!" he cried out from the painful impact. Before he could open the hatch, one of the slithery arms sliced through the air toward his head like a whip. He fell flat to his stomach, causing the leathery appendage to barely miss him. He got to his knees, driven back down by another massive impact to the portside. He looked up toward the shredded left side of the deck, seeing that one of the tentacles had breached the side completely.

****

"Oh my God!" Jane cried out. A portion of the portside wall had practically exploded as if a cannonball had burst through it. The force of the impact sent shards of debris across the room, also breaking apart the bench on that side of the room. From the massive hole in the wall slithered in a slimy tentacle.

"Oh shit!" Greg yelled from the floor, driven there by the force of the impact. The tentacle slid from the wall, reaching from left to right as if actually searching for them. Fragments of wall broke apart from the hole as it continued reaching in. Increasing speed, it headed straight for Jane. She backed all the way to the starboard side, pressing her back against the wall as the snake-like tentacle reached for her.

Suddenly Greg jumped in the way, holding a long piece of the broken bench in his hands. He drew it back like a baseball bat and repeatedly slapped it into the leathery smelly arm. Each impact made a large crackling sound, but did not appear to faze it. Greg drew back the piece of bench as far back as he could, and with all his might he swung it at the tentacle. The bench shattered, with bits of wood sent flying across the room. As if in retaliation, the tentacle snapped across the room in a whipping motion, striking Greg in the chest and knocking him to the floor, gagging and coughing.

"GREG!" Jane cried out, rushing to her boyfriend from behind. She put her hands beneath his arms and pulled him to his feet. Suddenly the hatch above flung open, and Jane looked up to see her father peering down on them.

"Get out of there!" he yelled. He didn't need to say it twice. They were climbing up the ladder as fast as squirrels up a tree.

****

Red and Roketto stood back to back at the center of the deck, firing their assault rifles in an attempt to fend off the onslaught. Red looked over the sights of his weapon, firing at two tentacles that wiggled over the port side toward him. The tips of the fibrous worm-like appendages erupted into pools of blood, creating a stench that even made Red want to hurl. He could see the creature itself. It was moving from the bow to the stern along the portside. Two more tentacles rose over his head, about to whip in his direction. He pointed his weapon and fired two short controlled bursts, one at each tentacle. Blood exploded from the center mass of each one, spraying onto the deck. Roketto looked over his shoulder, seeing the results of his superior's work.

"Nice shooting, boss," he said in his thick Asian accent, cracking a macho smile. Suddenly, his smile went away as he felt a sudden intense pain along his leg. He looked down, only to see that one of the tentacles had wrapped itself around his left ankle. He aimed his gun to fire, but before he could squeeze the trigger, the tentacle tugged away, pulling his foot out from under him. He fell to the deck on his back, losing his grip on his firearm in the process. Just as his brain began to register the pain from the impact, he suddenly felt weightless. The tentacle had lifted him into the air, holding him upside down by his foot.

"Oh fuck," Red said as he witnessed Roketto elevated twenty feet into the air. As quickly as it lifted him, the tentacle whipped down in a hammer-like motion, slamming the mercenary down to the deck. Blood blasted from his mouth like a fountain. He was alive just long enough to know that every internal organ had been ruptured in some way from the impact. His life ended just as the tentacle effortlessly dragged his sprung out body over the stern. Red gritted his teeth as he fired his gun madly at the creature's bulk. The bullets were crushed against the shell, having no effect, except to drive it into a deeper rage.

The kids crawled free of the hatch just in time to witness Roketto's gruesome death. The event had left them paralyzed with fear and shock.

"Climb!" Napier yelled at them, snapping them back to reality.

"Go first!" Jane yelled to Greg. His first instinct was to make her go first, but he quickly realized this was no time to argue. He began to make his way up the ladder.

At this time, Red's automatic rifle had run dry. Every word to come out of his mouth was a curse word, each louder than the previous. He drew his Smith&Wesson, blowing holes in three already wounded tentacles. The hollow point bullets created large exit wounds, tearing up muscles and tendons in the soft appendages.

The creature eyeballed him with its bulb-like antenna eyes, retracting all of its tentacles. Red looked into the face of the leviathan, watching the mandibles unfold and the birdlike beak shriek. He emptied his magazine, sending his last few rounds into the face of the beast, not sure if he was doing any damage. Red dropped the gun and drew his double-edged knife from its sheath.

"Come on!" he challenged the beast. As if in response, the creature suddenly raised its body out of the water in a jump-like action, revealing its underbelly. Its tremendous weight drew it back down, right onto the stern of the vessel. The vessel's bow reeled upward in a catapult like motion, shooting Red several feet up over the deck. He landed flat on his back, hitting the back of his head, sending him into a daze. His knife was flung from his hand, landing on the tip of its blade onto the deck several feet away from him, balancing perfectly in the wood.

The swift upward tipping of the vessel also threw Jane to the floor. She shrieked as she felt herself starting to slide toward the stern, where the creature waited. Napier clutched the bottom ladder bar with his right hand and lunged out toward her with his left, barely managing to clutch her wrist but stopping her descent.

After his vision cleared, Red looked down at the beast. Its two pincers were held in front of its face, snapping repeatedly in very fast motions, as if taunting him. And as he looked toward his impending doom, he felt gravity begin to do its work.

"No! NO!" he yelled as he helplessly slid down the slope of the deck. He rolled to his stomach and clawed his fingers into the wooden deck beneath him, hoping to grasp anything to cling on to. But he may as well have been sliding down a slab of ice. "Fuck you!" he cursed the creature as he slid down into the fatal butchery created by the huge pincers. Within a few quick moments, his body was diced into countless unrecognizable pieces. The creature slipped back down underneath the water, leaving nothing behind on the deck except a large pool of red.

Blood red.

The *Catcher* leveled out, relieved of the unbearable weight that the giant put on the stern. Jane got to her feet and quickly climbed the ladder up to the upper deck, followed closely by her father. As he climbed, Napier saw that the creature was now near the starboard side bow, almost appearing to be watching them. He stepped up onto the deck, which had suffered considerably less damage than the lower area. Standing near them was Doctor Wallack, who simply stared at the creature, appearing mesmerized by it.

"Get in the cabin!" Napier ordered everyone, including the doctor. The teenagers quickly followed the instructions, while Wallack simply stood motionless. He smiled while looking past his captive, fascinated by the destruction and brutality of *Architeuthis Brachyura*.

"It's amazing, isn't it!" he shouted over the loud splashing created by the monster.

"Are you insane?" Napier yelled. "Hurry up and get in there!"

The scientist just stood in place, watching his creation. Napier wondered if he was in a state of shock.

"It's more powerful than anything else on the planet! And I created it!" he shouted, as if to a large audience. Napier didn't have any more time to waste. He grabbed the doctor by the shoulders, attempting to force him into the cabin. However, the mad scientist struggled against him, resisting the fisherman's attempts to save his life. A slithery noise, followed by that of wood cracking caused Napier to look over his left shoulder. A bloody, fleshy tentacle, riddled with bullet holes had crept up the vessel and was poised behind him. Instantaneously he fell to the deck, just as the tentacle lashed out, passing just over him. However, it had another target. It twisted around Dr. Wallack, pinning his arms to his sides. Wallack inhaled sharply, and then shouted out in pain after his arms snapped at the elbows from the rapid tightening. The barbs were inserted into his chest, penetrating the flesh, breastbone, and one into his spine. It lifted him off of the deck and swung him over the starboard side. Gagging for every breath, he looked down at the enormous horror he had created, which was getting closer with every millisecond.

The last thing he saw: the mandibles unveiled, and the beak pry open. The last thing he felt: the crushing pressure of his insides being turned to mush after the beak chomped down on his body.

Napier closed his eyes after witnessing the doctor's gruesome death. He looked into the cabin at the two teenagers he was trying to protect. They were huddled on the floor, Jane in Greg's arms. She was shivering with fear. He was too, but spending most of his energy trying to hide it. The *Catcher* had sustained considerable, irreparable damage and was now taking in water. There was no lifeboat, and swimming would be a suicide decision. And staying was almost just as much of a suicide decision. He no longer felt fear, or the rush of adrenaline. What he was feeling right now was that of failure. He swore to protect these kids, and now he was right to believe he could not save them. *I'm going to die a failure to my daughter...*

Or maybe not...

From the dark night sky shined a light aimed right at him. He looked up, just as his ears processed the whirring sound of the helicopter. He held his hand over his eyes, looking at the white aircraft hovering down above him, lowering its altitude. The side door opened, and upon seeing who was behind it, Napier's feelings of failure were now replaced with sudden relief.

"Lisa!" he called up to her. She was in a blue jumpsuit with a helmet and headset on.

"Rick!" She called down. "Get on this ladder and climb up here!" She threw a suspended ladder out the door. It unrolled like a rug down a wedding aisle, stopping right at the upper deck. Napier grabbed a hold of it and looked to the kids.

"Come on!" he called to them. Greg and Jane rushed out of the cabin to the ladder held in place by Napier.

"You go first this time," Greg said to Jane. Instead of arguing, she grabbed the bars and begun climbing her way up to the safety of the Coast Guard helicopter.

"Go!" Napier ordered Greg as soon as Jane made space for him. He began climbing, staying a couple steps behind his girlfriend. Napier prepared to make his climb…just as a thick tentacle lunged for the ladder. Without regard for himself, he threw his body on the slithery limb, knocking it off course.

"Oh shit! Pull up!" Thompson ordered the pilot. The helicopter pulled away out of the creature's reach, allowing the teenagers to be able to climb aboard safely. She then held her ear to the microphone on her headset. "Commander! Do you have a visual?"

****

"Holy shit! Yes I do!" Commander Tracy said, standing in the command room of the Coast Guard Cutter *Ryback*, which was now drifting a quarter mile from the *Catcher*'s position. He held binoculars to his eyes, watching the fury of a beast he thought could only be real in the minds of fantasy writers. Standing beside him was Chief Bondy, who also watched through a pair of binoculars. Several crewmembers in the control room had to hide their astonishment upon seeing the enormous living thing.

"Position the Bofors 57 mm gun! One-point-zero-two degrees! Prepare to fire!" he demanded.

"*Wait!*" Thompson's voice called over the radio. "*Rick*

Napier's still on that boat! Let me get him off first!"

"Hurry up!" Tracy said.

****

Napier sprung to his feet after landing on his side, lucky not to end up coiled in the creature's grasp. *Architeuthis Brachyura* repositioned itself in front of the bow, crashing its pincers into the hull once more. Metal crunched as the monster ripped chunks from the engine, creating a heavy cloud of smoke. At this moment, Napier looked past the shelled beast, seeing a large rocky structure slightly smaller than the animal itself.

"You hungry?..." Napier taunted it as he hurried into the cabin, taking position at the wheel. "…Eat this!" He grabbed the throttle, shoving the *Catcher* into full speed. The vessel's engine grinded and protested, and smoke billowed heavily from the several holes made by the beast. The propellers spun to their maximum speed, rocketing the vessel forward. Napier braced himself, and felt his body ripple as the *Catcher* collided with the creature. It let out a massive screech as it absorbed the impact, which sandwiched it between the vessel, which was still propelling forward, and the large stationary rock. The creature was pinned. The bow was almost completely crushed, and the engine was making several grinding mechanical noises that definitely informed Napier that he needed to get to the chopper. He looked through the windshield, seeing the chopper starting to come back towards him. *Excellent, now I just need to get out of here and…LOOKOUT!* He ducked once again, just as a tentacle swung across the upper deck of the *Catcher*, tearing right through the cabin. Glass, wood, metal, and other debris exploded over the deck, some of which pricked Napier's arms and the back of his neck. He stood to his feet, the four walls of the cabin completely gone, along with the desk, throttle, and wheel. The creature hissed as it tried to wrestle the vessel away from it, but the propellers were still spinning at top speed, forcing the vessel into the beast.

"Hurry!" Thompson called down to him. The chopper lowered its altitude, dangling the ladder in front of Napier's face. And once again, another tentacle lunged for it, forcing the pilot to naturally draw the chopper up. Napier had no time. It was do or die…literally. He leapt over the side of the vessel after the ladder. He closed his fingers, grasping the bottom handle. Thompson and Jane looked down out the door, seeing him dangling by the bar, hovering above the flailing creature. "Tracy!" She called on her radio to the Commander. "You've got the go ahead!"

****

"Received!" Tracy replied on the radio. He looked to other personnel in the command post. "Is the Bofors in position?!"

"Yes sir!"

"FIRE!" The commander demanded.

A shockwave rippled through the vessel and the heavy gun began blasting away, creating a deafening sound that could nearly destroy a person's eardrums.

****

It unleashed its fury at the intruding beast, successfully killing most of the smaller intruders. And now, the large opponent seemed to be dying as well. It followed its instincts, which had led it to what it perceived to be victory over the enemy. It had learned to hunt for itself after years of being fed. It managed to establish a habitat, and its instincts developed so viciously that it was taking on invasive enemies. Now it had dominated a creature its own size. For the first time, the creature truly felt something outside of the basic need of rest, hunger, and territory. It felt pleasure. This was a new feeling for its small brain. Something it never felt before, and would never feel again.

****

Napier clung tightly to the handlebar, dangling freely in midair. Through the air he heard a light whistling sound, gradually getting louder and louder. He looked down at the beast beneath him. In that moment, it was proceeding to tear into his sinking vessel. And in the next moment, there was a fiery blast that illuminated the entire coast of Mako's Edge. A series of vociferous booms shook the air, creating a shockwave that even reduced some of the thick nearby rocks to granite. Thousands of gallons of water erupted into the air, spraying his dangling feet. In a instant the creature was suddenly reduced to several smoldering chunks of flesh and shell. Bits of rubbery tentacle splattered in every direction possible, while fragments of shell pelted the rocky structures nearby. The two main arms remained fully intact, each separated from the main body, which no longer existed as a whole. The blast also annihilated what was left of the *Catcher*. After raining throughout the air from the explosion, its many fragments proceeded to sink with the remains of *Architeuthis Brachyura*. After watching the intense event, Napier looked back up the ladder. He groaned as he reached for the next bar, only able to use his hands to pull until he could get a foot up. To assist, Thompson began reeling up the ladder, bringing him up into the doorway.

He fell to the floor, and Thompson quickly slid the door shut. Jane rushed to her father's side, giving him yet another tight hug.

"Are you alright, Dad?" She asked.

"I'll be a little sore," he joked. Lisa took a seat next to him, and he looked at her. "Interested in a seafood dinner?" The group laughed in unison. The radio buzzed, prompting Lisa to check her headset.

"Traffic for me, Commander?"

"Hey, it's Bondy. Just wanted to confirm you got my buddy on board," the Chief's voice sounded over the radio.

"Hey Bondy," Napier called, holding back a chuckle, "Since I've done you so many favors, I'd say it'd be time for you to do me one and get me a new boat!"

"Ha! Ha!" The Chief laughed. *"Even though I know you're kidding, I'm pretty sure I can work something out with our dumbass mayor! See you when you land!"* His voice faded out.

"Thanks, Chief," Napier said. He looked at Thompson, who tore her headset off. "So, since it's safe to assume you're not gonna get kicked out of the Coast Guard, you might not be sticking around long." Lisa smiled and stroked her hand through his hair.

"Actually, they owe me a favor," she said. "It's likely…very,

very likely, that I can remain posted in Mako's Ridge. But I'll need someone to show me around." She smiled at him, and he back at her.

"I know someone who can do that," he said, pressing his lips to hers, their kiss followed by a loving hug. On the most intense night of his life, Rick Napier felt more at peace than ever.

EPILOGUE

Dressed in a white buttoned shirt and grey dress pants, Jeb Keith stood in the main laboratory of the Atlantic Warren Laboratory. The government had ordered that the facility be cleared out, and all experiments destroyed due to a tragic event that took place on a nearby island chain. The laboratory would be recycled for other uses for the government, but genetic hybrid experimentation was confirmed to be a no-go subject for research. With a radio in one hand, Jeb Keith communicated with the underwater welding crews who were busy repairing the outside damage done during the escape of *Architeuthis Brachyura.*

"Gentlemen, we have nice weather today," he spoke into the radio. "I'm hoping you can have section five repaired by the end of today."

"*That's a large area,*" a voice commented through the radio. "*We'll do our best.*" Keith looked over the inventory list on his clipboard as several large crates passed by, each pulled by cart vehicles. With each passing crate, he checked a box on the clipboard indicating that the correct number of each 'species' was documented as leaving the facility.

"Hold up!" he called, stopping one line of vehicles, each containing a ten-by-twelve-foot crate. "These crates are for Isurus Palinuridae. There's supposed to be six." He counted the crates. "Why are there only five?" A driver, dressed in dirty jeans and flannel shirt, with a handlebar mustache shook his head and shrugged his shoulders.

"Hey man, we're just paid to collect these things," he said. "We're not told there's how many of what. There were only five of these things when we got here, and there's five leaving." He hit the accelerator of his vehicle and pulled away, followed by the other vehicles towing crates, taking them to a freighter that would transport these creatures to an undisclosed location.

Jeb looked at his inventory notes, hoping that there was a mistake in the paperwork about the number of specimens. But it was confirmed, there were supposed to be six. It was thought that *Architeuthis Brachyura* was the only hybrid to have escaped.

"Oh, God," Jeb said to himself. "This is Jeb Keith to welding units! Cancel your current assignments and come back in!" He paused, waiting for a response. "Keith to welding units, come in please." He waited another moment. Still no answer. "Welding units, this is Jeb Keith! Somebody respond, damn it!" His heart thumped heavily and his hand begun to quiver as he looked over his notes for the missing creature: *Isurus Palinuridae.* Lobster-Shark.